DATE			

THE WATCHMAN

A Selection of Recent Titles by Adrian Magson

The Marc Portman Thrillers

THE WATCHMAN *

The Harry Tate Thrillers

RED STATION *
TRACERS *
DECEPTION *
RETRIBUTION *
EXECUTION *

The Riley Gavin and Frank Palmer Series

NO PEACE FOR THE WICKED
NO HELP FOR THE DYING
NO SLEEP FOR THE DEAD
NO TEARS FOR THE LOST
NO KISS FOR THE DEVIL

* *available from Severn House*

THE WATCHMAN

A Marc Portman Thriller

Adrian Magson

severn
House

This first world edition published 2014
in Great Britain and the USA by
SEVERN HOUSE PUBLISHERS LTD of
19 Cedar Road, Sutton, Surrey, England, SM2 5DA.

British Library Cataloguing in Publication Data

Magson, Adrian author.
  The watchman. – (A Mark Portman thriller ; 1)
  1. Great Britain. MI6–Fiction. 2. Hostages–Somalia–
  Fiction. 3. Spy stories.
  I. Title II. Series
  823.9'2-dc23

ISBN-13: 978-0-7278-8370-4 (cased)

All Severn House titles are printed on acid-free paper.

Severn House Publishers support the Forest Stewardship Council™ [FSC™],
the leading international forest certification organization. All our titles that
are printed on FSC certified paper carry the FSC logo.

Typeset by Palimpsest Book Production Ltd.,
Falkirk, Stirlingshire, Scotland.
Printed and bound in Great Britain by
TJ International, Padstow, Cornwall.

As always, this is for Ann, with cosmic gratitude and love; my alpha reader, fan, supporter and spotter of the patently bleedin' obvious.

ACKNOWLEDGEMENTS

With grateful thanks to Geoff Weighell, pilot and CEO of the British Microlight Aircraft Association (BMAA), for his patience and clarity. Without it, Portman's role in this book would have been short, sharp and painful.

One

I know the sound of a semi-automatic weapon being cocked. Some might mistake it for a briefcase lock mechanism or a workman slapping a power unit into a high-speed drill. It's similar but not the same.

And I'd just heard it in the corridor outside my hotel room.

I stepped over to the door and listened, heard the brush of footsteps on the carpet, a hushed cough and heavy, nasal breathing. The movement stopped outside the next door along and I was guessing it wasn't the room maid.

Wary of getting my eyeball blown out, I took a quick look through the peephole.

Three guys, heads in close like they were having a team talk. Their features were blown out of shape by the fish-eye lens, but I made out dark, unshaven faces and the standard Colombian attire of crumpled jackets and pants.

And guns.

Two of the men were holding semi-automatics with big macho can suppressors, while the third, who was gesturing a lot and therefore the leader, was holding a machine pistol. It looked like a Steyr TMP, a nasty weapon capable of spitting out 900 rounds a minute. Lucky you can't get a magazine that big. The men looked jumpy, turning to watch both ends of the corridor, like they had no business being there.

Definitely not cops.

FARC, at a guess. That's *Fuerzas Armadas Revolucionarias de Colombia* – the national guerrilla group with a brutal reputation for high-profile kidnappings and killings. If not them, it would be one of the drugs cartels in town looking for an easy ransom. Whoever they were, I was thinking the man next door had been selected as their next source of income.

It was none of my business.

I'd heard my neighbour in the bar the previous evening. He was an American mining engineer, middle-aged and well dressed, head of a minerals company. He'd been friendly and chatty and everyone within earshot knew he was in the country talking business with the government. Careless of him. What the two guys he'd hired as security clearly hadn't told him was that here in Colombia, you don't go round pushing that kind of detail about yourself. It's asking for trouble.

Worse, he'd dismissed his two minders saying he'd got some shopping to do before heading home and could handle that all by himself.

I watched the man with the Steyr lean across and knock on the door. He called out in accented English, 'Sir? Room service.'

Like I say, it was none of my business. I could wait right here and let it blow on by; let it be somebody else's bad-hair day. No point inviting trouble.

I picked up my overnight bag, opened the door and stepped out into the corridor.

For a second nobody moved. The nearest gunman, short, heavy in the gut and sporting a large moustache, rolled his eyes at me in surprise. The other two were busy waiting for my neighbour's door to open. None of them were expecting any interference from the hotel staff or guests.

Moustache was the first to move. He made an 'O' of his mouth and began to haul his gun round at me.

I threw my bag at the other two to distract them, then stepped forward and kicked Moustache into the opposite wall. He bounced back with an *ooff* and dropped his semi-automatic right into my hand. I smacked him across the head with it and turned to face the others.

The man with the Steyr was already looking up in surprise from the bag at his feet, and his colleague was only marginally slower. There was no time for niceties; if the Steyr began firing, I'd be mincemeat. I shot them both, Steyr first, then his friend, the suppressed shots sounding flat in the confines of the corridor, a round each to the head to reduce the chance of a reflex firing.

'Hey! What the—?' The engineer was standing in the doorway, a bag in one hand, briefcase in the other, white around the eyes as he saw the blood and bodies lying right where he usually picked up his *Herald Tribune*.

I reached forward and grabbed his collar, dragging him out into the corridor, then picked up my bag. 'Express check out,' I said, and hustled him towards the emergency stairs. We had to get out of here *now*.

Not that he came easily. 'What the hell is this – *who are you*?' he demanded, trying to break free. He was pretty strong and wasn't making it easy to save his skin.

'Those men were here to snatch you,' I told him. I kneed the emergency door open and pushed him towards the stairs. 'If you'd argued or fought back, they'd have cut their losses and killed you where you stood. They'll have friends who still might. The choice is yours: you haul your ass and come with me and do exactly as I say . . . or you stay here and die.'

He complied but I had to nudge him all the way down the stairs and out through a narrow door close to the kitchens. I was hoping we didn't bump into hotel security along the way. They'd just be doing their job, but I didn't want to take a chance that they were in on the set-up and have to start taking them out.

I opened the door and we stepped outside into a blanket of warm, spicy air and the rasp and clatter of city traffic in downtown Bogotá.

And more trouble.

Two

A large black 4x4 with blacked-out windows was waiting outside, engine ticking over and adding to the polluted atmosphere. The driver was doing his bit, too, blowing smoke through a narrow gap at the top of the window and nodding his head to a *currulao* beat of drums, marimba and some sort of shaker instrument whose name I'd forgotten. He was trying to be the cool, bad dude, but his eyes were too freaky, constantly flicking to the mirrors then back along the street on the look out for cops.

When he saw us appear, his jaw dropped. Then he did the wrong thing: he tossed the cigarette aside and tried to get out of the car.

I waited until the door was half open, then kicked it hard, slamming him back inside the vehicle. He tried to get out again, this time reaching for a semi-automatic in his waistband, so I opened the door and dropped him with a chop to the throat. He fell out and rolled choking into the gutter with the other debris.

'Get in,' I said.

The American looked shocked. 'Where are we going?'

'The airport. You're leaving the country, aren't you?'

'Yes, but how did you know?'

'I heard you discussing it in the bar last night. My guess is, so did these men, which is why they marked you down for a ransom.'

He gestured back at the hotel. 'But I haven't paid the bill . . . and we should call the police, tell them what happened.'

'Nothing happened. Remember that.' I pulled out my cell phone as he placed his bags in the back and slid into the passenger seat. 'What's your name?' I threw my bag in and got behind the wheel, stuffing the semi-automatic from the man upstairs under my thigh, where I could get at it. I threw the one dropped by the driver under the seat.

'Nate Sweetman. Why?'

I ignored him and dialled the hotel reception. I could hear shouting from inside the building and guessed the man I'd disabled upstairs had come round and was back in the game.

Time to go.

I checked the street for obstructions. All clear. Fifty metres to the main drag, then left towards the airport. Hit the gas.

As we reached the end of the street, a voice answered. I said, 'This is Challenor in three-oh-two. I've paid and checked out, but meant to ask for Mr Sweetman's bill in three-oh-four to be added to mine. Can you take care of that?'

The receptionist was unfazed. 'Of course, Mr Challenor. No problem. I trust everything was satisfactory during your stay?' In the background I could hear shouting echoing around the reception area.

'Almost perfect,' I replied neutrally.

'In that case, have a good trip and thank you for staying. We hope to see you again soon.'

Unlikely, but nice of him to say so. I snapped the phone shut and took us out on to the main street heading north east.

'Listen good,' I said to Sweetman. 'If we have to leave the car for any reason – any reason at all – you do exactly as I say, when I say it. Do you understand?'

Sweetman just stared at me. He was in shock.

'Say it.' I slapped his shoulder to focus his mind.

'Yes. Yes, I understand.'

For good measure I added, 'They were probably planning on lifting you for ransom on your way out of the country.'

'What?' He didn't understand.

'It's what they do to gain time. Nobody would have been any the wiser until you failed to show up at your destination. During that time they'd have had you tucked away out of reach and ready to make their demands.'

'But why? What value could I have to them?'

'You're a mining engineer, right?'

'How do you know that?'

'You told everybody. I know you've had meetings with the new Mines and Energy minister and his officials; Colombia's high up on the world's exporters of coal, and you're here to advise them on that and about the Canadians who are seeking licences for gold and silver projects. That makes you valuable.'

His mouth dropped open. 'But I've been very careful about my itinerary.'

'No, you haven't.' I'd found out all that by being in the bar – and I'd only been here a couple of days. 'It doesn't take much; once they had that and got your name and somebody on the hotel staff to fill in the details, you became a high-value target.'

Sweetman shook his head. He didn't buy it yet and looked lost. 'I can't believe this is happening.'

'Believe it. It happens all the time.' I steered past a broken-down delivery truck and a bunch of guys arguing about what to do. 'You got lucky; some people don't.'

I ran through the only available plan in my head. We had a

small window to get clear of the city and head for the airport. Dead bodies in the corridors of a hotel – even dead bodies of armed FARC kidnappers – meant the cops would be shutting down the streets as fast as they could, the net moving inexorably outwards. Only at the airport would we be relatively safe.

But we had to get there first.

'Why not call the police?' he repeated.

'Because we'd get tied up for hours, maybe days, while they figured out what to charge us with. Do you want that?'

'No. I guess not.' He shook his head and went silent for a few moments. Then he said, 'You've done this before.' He was coming out of the first phase of shock and looking at me carefully, like a scientist might study a lab rat, part fascination, part revulsion.

'A few times,' I replied. More than a few, as it happened.

'So it's your job, your work?' He was looking at my suit, white shirt and tie, like he doubted I was entirely sane. He was probably right.

'It's what I do, yes.' I checked the mirrors. No signs of pursuit so far, which was good. The local cops like to do things noisily, with lots of lights and sirens. It gives everyone fair warning to clear the streets. Living in a drugs capital, where the car right next to them might be full of men with guns and bad nerves and no conscience tends to make them like that.

'So you were here on an assignment?' Now he was intrigued, which was a nuisance, but better than him freaking out on me.

'Yes.'

'You sound American. What are you – Delta? SEAL? One of those black-ops units fighting the cartels? It's OK – I was in the Marine Corps, so I know.'

'Do you mind not asking so many questions? I'd like to get us out of here in one piece.'

He wasn't accustomed to being told to shut up, and bristled. 'What the hell – you think I should be happy seeing you kill two men in the blink of an eye? I should be grateful and shut the fuck up, is that it?'

'It would help. Or I could always leave you here to face the cops – and their friends in the cartels or FARC.'

He didn't like that idea so much. 'No. I guess not.' He shook his head. 'Sorry . . . what just happened threw me, you know? I'm guessing you aren't a desk man, not with what you did back there. You're a security guy, right? Close Protection.'

I didn't say anything and let him jump to his own conclusions. There are two kinds of Close Protection: one is, as it says, up close, a visible barrier to a would-be attacker, designed to dissuade as much as shelter. The other is an outer shield – a shadow – deliberately out of sight, but with a wider view of the area around the protectee or principal. The shadow bit is what I do, unseen and often unknown by high-value assets whose people want protection without the high visibility of a gorilla in a suit.

This time I'd been in Colombia shadowing an A-list French tenor with a kidnap phobia. He was in town at the express invitation of the president's wife, to put on a show at her birthday bash. It had gone smoothly enough and the Frenchman was already halfway home by now, relieved he hadn't got himself kidnapped, shot or otherwise compromised so far from home, but unaware that I was with him right up to the departure desk. It had been an easy job for me, and I was now otherwise unemployed until the next one came along.

'If you want to do something useful,' I suggested, 'keep your eyes on the wing mirror. Any vehicle stays behind us too long, tell me.'

He nodded and leaned forward, eyes on the mirror. It wouldn't be much help, but it might keep him buttoned up for a while until we got clear of this mess.

I concentrated on my front, trying to keep to a reasonable speed yet constantly on the move between sticking points in the traffic. We had about ten kilometres to go to the airport of El Dorado, and I wanted to get there without delay.

The whole point about staying out of trouble in hostile territory is to avoid attracting attention and keep moving; once you stop you're at a disadvantage. There was also the local law enforcement angle to watch out for. Being picked up by a nosy or bored traffic cop would be awkward, especially as I still had the kidnapper's semi-automatic in my pocket and another gun under the seat. I was counting, however, on the car's tinted windows to get us through any potential trouble. Traffic cops don't like upsetting people who might just shoot them for the hell of it.

'There's another car like this one,' Sweetman muttered. 'It jumped the last set of lights to stay with us.'

He was sharper than I thought. I'd spotted the car and it was coming up too fast to be casual. When it slotted in behind us on a relatively clear stretch of road, matching our speed, I began to worry.

'Buckle up,' I said.

'Wha . . .? Oh.' He tugged at the strap and sat back, then gave a nervous chuckle. 'It's like that scene in *Bullitt*.' When I looked at him, he added, 'You know – with Steve McQueen. It's a classic.'

'So?'

'The bit where the bad guys do up their seat belts . . . you know things are going to get hairy.'

Jesus, a film nut on adrenalin. 'It's nothing like that. Believe me.'

I checked the mirror and got a whole load of black 4x4 and tinted windows in return. Whoever they were, they must have recognized the car and were sticking close to figure out where we were going. My guess is, they were nervous of stopping us and busy calling whoever was the usual driver of this particular vehicle.

I took a chance and lowered my window a few inches, then gave the hazard warning lights a single flash, followed by a brief flick of my hand out of the window. The air felt hot and sticky and my mouth felt dry.

A few seconds went by as the 4x4 stayed on our tail. Then it dropped back with a flash of its lights before turning off down a side street and disappearing.

I breathed more easily. For now, we were OK.

Sweetman noticed the move and looked at me like he was impressed. 'What did you just do? What happened?'

'Not sure,' I said. 'I'm hoping it was kidnapper-speak for "I'm good, thanks, so back the fuck off".'

As we arrived at the airport, I said, 'One thing you need to remember.'

'What's that?' He was looking a bit calmer, but it was probably short term.

'Make it two things. First is, have a strong drink as soon as you can. Make it *aguardiente*, the local brandy – it'll paralyse your vocal chords and settle your nerves. Second thing is, you know *nothing* about what happened. You saw nothing, you heard nothing, you left your room and went home. And you never come back here. Ever. Understood?'

He nodded. 'I get it. Reprisals. What about you?'

'Me? I was never here in the first place.'

Three

S ecret Intelligence Service Officer Thomas Vale stared at the message on his monitor in the MI6 headquarters at Vauxhall Cross in London, and wondered what the hell was going on. It had just arrived on the internal Secure-X system, yet was timed over an hour ago.

From: C. Moresby (Operations Director 4)
To: List A
Subject: Extraordinary meeting of sub-committee AL/213/4(JIC)

On matters relating to Somali hostage negotiations and in accordance with guidelines laid down by ISC (Intelligence and Security Committee), this matter requires the presence of all List A personnel or their nominated delegates from Cabinet Office, Foreign & Commonwealth Office, MI5, GCHQ and MOD, and includes a special invitation to London head of CIA or his nominated deputy.

SIS personnel:
Operations Director 4
Controller Africa
Controller Middle East
Controller Europe
Chair: Operations Director 4
Time start: 10.30a.m. – room 2/15

Vale checked his watch. It was already 10.30. He'd be late, which he hated. He called immediately for a duty driver in the services section to meet him downstairs. Getting round to the Cabinet Office, room 2/15, where these cross-departmental meetings often took place, was going to take a few minutes.

'Have you seen Mr Moresby, Joe?' he asked the driver.

'About twenty minutes ago, Mr Vale, on his way out of the building.' Joe eyed him in the mirror with a raised eyebrow. They had known each other for four years now and got on well. 'I didn't think you were included.' Joe always seemed to know a lot more than he should for his pay grade. Typical ex-army driver.

The devious little shit, Vale thought angrily, the thought aimed at Colin Moresby, Operations Director 4 and chair of the meeting. One of the new brand of directors appointed in the recent re-shuffles of the security community, Moresby had hit the ground running and seemed unconcerned by the need to make allies in the corridors of SIS unless they could further his career. He had a love of meetings, which he used as weapons to denigrate his enemies and as forums to suck up to those more important than himself. Sleek and confident, he was too fond of marketing-speak for Vale's liking, which the older man saw as a means of obfuscation.

He thought about the note again, trying to decide whether the delay in receiving it and the lack of any earlier notification was carelessness or a deliberate move to freeze him out. A senior field officer for many years, he was approaching retirement. But with a shortage of skilled personnel undergoing training, he'd been offered a consultancy post within the organization and asked to stay on for the foreseeable future. His role was no longer in the field, but more of an oversight function on operations. As such, Moresby was obliged to include him in all aspects of field officers' and agents' work abroad. It was, Vale knew, little more than a box-ticking exercise to meet new monitoring standards, but still an essential footbrake function for those with less field experience.

People like Moresby.

The car eased to a stop near the Cabinet Office. He hopped out and told Joe he would walk back; he had a feeling he might need the fresh air. Passing through security, he made his way up to the second floor, room 15. He could hear the buzz of conversation from inside, and felt unaccountably like a pupil arriving late for a lesson.

The talking stopped as he opened the door, and a number of familiar faces turned towards him.

'My apologies,' he said easily, addressing nobody in particular. He noted Moresby, sitting at the head of the table. He looked as if he had swallowed a bug. 'I didn't get the note until a few minutes ago.'

'Really?' Moresby grunted. 'You'd better take it up with IT. Probably a systems glitch.'

There were no gaps at the table, Vale noted. Significant or accidental? He grabbed a chair from against the wall beneath a dubious portrait of Gladstone, and dragged it to a spot between Bill Cousins, Controller Africa, and Peter Wilby, Controller Middle East. The two men shuffled sideways to let him in.

He nodded and sat down, noting that each person present had a folder on the table in front of them. There were no spares.

Bill Cousins moved his folder so that Vale could share.

'As I was saying,' Moresby resumed, his face stiff with disapproval, 'this is an all-hands notification that we will be running a contact mission within the next two weeks, possibly sooner. The location is in east Africa, on the Somali/Kenyan border near the coast, and the precise timing is as yet unconfirmed, but will be reactive, depending on outside bodies.' He glanced around the table, hovering just a moment on a man Vale knew as James Scheider, the deputy chief, CIA London station. He was an up-and-coming figure to watchers inside SIS, and Vale instantly recognized Moresby's tactics: make powerful friends before they reach the top and they are likely to boost one's own rise to prominence.

Moresby referred to the folders on the table and continued, 'Two weeks ago our Nairobi liaison officer was approached by a known middleman named Ashkir Xasan. Xasan is thought to be of mixed Somali/Kenyan parentage, and has acted as a mediator several times over the past two years in the release of tourists and other hostages in the region, taken mostly by pirates but also other non-aligned groups. He secured the release of two cargo vessels taken by pirates further north, one in the Gulf of Aden, the other off the coast of Oman. Both vessels, one the Madras-flagged *Oonyong*, the other the *Belladventure* from Rotterdam, had been held for three months near Hobyo, Somalia. Their crews were released unharmed.'

Vale breathed easily and scanned the briefing notes passed to him by Bill Cousins. So far so mundane. He wondered where this was going. Moresby was perfectly entitled to run operations wherever his brief allowed, especially where there were intelligence implications. But Vale had the strongest feeling that his own name had been left off the list deliberately and he wasn't sure why. But it couldn't be good news. Moresby was making a power play of some kind and signalling that old-timers like Vale were no longer needed, oversight roles or not.

'As a backgrounder,' Moresby continued, 'several weeks ago a group of aid workers was taken hostage by pirates off Djibouti. They were on a combined fact-finding mission to visit refugee camps set up by three aid agencies.' He paused for effect, scanning the faces. 'Unknown to the kidnappers, two of the people taken were advisors to the United Nations; one British, one Dutch.'

A sigh whispered through the room as they each considered the implications. Aid workers were an easy target for extremists, although often left alone by kidnap groups because they usually had little real ransom value. But serving UN personnel were like gold dust, with an appropriate value to anyone negotiating for their sale.

'What the hell were they doing there?' queried Ruth Dresden, the Cabinet Office representative. 'And why go in by sea? Don't they like flying?'

Moresby gave a hint of a shrug. 'Regretful, I know. My understanding is that they were going in by the back door to avoid being picked up on the airport radar by the Somalis.'

'Why? We're on friendly terms with them at the moment.'

'True. But they wanted to gain an insight to the problems on the ground without being shadowed by government minders every step of the way.'

'Well, that worked a treat, didn't it?' muttered a gaunt individual from the Ministry of Defence. 'I suppose they now want us to drag them out of there?'

'Actually, no.' Moresby looked around the room. 'In fact, we'd had no contact with them or their kidnappers until Xasan came forward.'

'Is he one of the gang?'

'Not as far as I'm aware. But he claims to know the group holding them and says he can secure their release unharmed if we're prepared to talk. There was no mention of the sum involved, but there was a condition attached.'

Was, Vale noted. Past tense. So the build-up to this has already taken place without being broadcast. 'What kind of condition?'

'They want to enter formal negotiations, but we have to supply a representative on the ground at a location to be advised once we give the nod.'

'Why?' Bill Cousins shifted in his seat. 'What do they think this is – an agreement on extended trade credits?'

By his tone, Vale wondered if he wasn't the only one who might have been left out of the loop. Cousins clearly hadn't been fully briefed, either.

Moresby nodded. 'According to Xasan's latest communication, which came in yesterday afternoon, the group holding the hostages is led by a clan chief – that's Xasan's description, not ours – named Musa Yusuf Musa.'

'Clan chief my arse,' Peter Wilby, the Controller Middle East muttered in disgust. 'He's a terrorist; al-Shabaab down to his toenails. And right now they control a large part of the country around Mogadishu – whatever the African Union Forces say. How come we didn't hear about this?' Like Cousins, he looked irritated, but sounded more cautious.

'Because I didn't want to make it known more widely until I had formulated a plan.' Moresby seemed unconcerned by any shortcomings in approved procedure, and stared hard at both controllers, who said nothing. He gestured at the folders, which contained a map showing the distribution of forces in the country, including government, Kenyan and other African troops . . . and the huge Islamist-controlled region in the centre around the capital.

'But you're correct. The Islamists do have a serious foothold. However, they don't control every clan. The plan – my plan – is simple: we will send an officer to meet with Xasan and Musa at a time and place of their choosing. They will state their demands and we will negotiate the release of these hostages. They have also indicated that there are other groups known by Musa looking to do similar deals for hostages and boats held along the Somali coast.'

'Seriously?' Ruth Dresden again. 'How do we know we can trust them?'

Moresby tapped the folder in front of him. 'Because we must. This is, lady and gentlemen, the opening I believe we've long been waiting for: the chance to secure the release of hostages and shipping on a scale nobody has managed before.' He smiled suddenly as if warmed by his own brilliance, and looked round as if for approval. 'Anyone care for coffee?'

Four

'Interesting idea,' said the CIA's deputy chief of station, James Scheider, who was staring at the briefing paper with a faint frown. 'I'm not sure why it involves us, though, and not the Dutch. It's their man and yours. According to our sources in the region, none of the captive aid workers is an American citizen.'

'I invited you as a courtesy, first of all,' Moresby replied easily. 'But in acknowledging your agency's considerable knowledge of the region, any advice would be gratefully received. We will, of course, be bringing in the Dutch at the appropriate time.'

Scheider shrugged. 'Of course. Glad to help.'

'What support will this officer have?' Vale queried. He was referring to hard protection and assistance. In areas such as the Middle East and eastern Africa, where tensions were high and dangers unpredictable, the general convention was to plan for trouble, which was why high-risk ventures usually involved armed escorts.

'Minimal.' Moresby's response was almost dismissive. 'Too

much accompanying traffic is likely to attract attention. There will, of course, be the standard operational rules and systems in place, and we'll be keeping a close eye on the personnel involved throughout the transition.'

'How close?' Vale insisted. He was growing increasingly worried by Moresby's almost cavalier attitude, and neither Cousins nor Wilby had shown signs of concern beyond their initial comments. What the hell was going on? This was their back yard, but they were letting Moresby run the show. *Operational rules and systems*? He made it sound like a Health and Safety assessment. Didn't he know how dangerous the world was out there?

'Communications traffic will be monitored throughout by GCHQ's feeder stations in the region, and I hope our friends in the CIA and National Security Agency will offer whatever assistance they can.' He looked at Scheider with raised eyebrows, adding, 'It would be nice to have coverage via any drones you might have in the region.'

Scheider nodded, as Vale knew he would. The CIA man was in a difficult position; saying an immediate no to the availability of unmanned camera drones or UAVs, used so effectively to track down insurgents in Iraq, Pakistan and Afghanistan, would not go down well; even a *maybe* would question his ability to make on-the-spot decisions without running back to his superiors.

Vale had to intervene. As superb as they were at monitoring signals intelligence and comms networks around the world, GCHQ, the Government Communications Headquarters in Cheltenham, couldn't perform miracles. 'Satellites and drones are not the same as boots on the ground. There's no protection if anything goes wrong, and camera footage merely gives us lots of nice grainy photos for the archives. These people need a support team.'

Moresby turned to him with a faint huff of impatience. 'I disagree. The risk to any personnel has been judged extremely unlikely, in view of Xasan's assurances and his record so far. In any case, they will be on the ground for a brief period only – a couple of days at most.' He waved a hand to emphasise his point and turned away.

But Vale wasn't finished. 'They? So there's more than one.'

'Yes. The officer will have an escort – a specialist. We demanded that and Xasan agreed.'

'And if anything does go wrong?' Vale pressed him harder, if only for the record.

'Why should it? As I said, the risks are minimal. The other side has nothing to gain by putting our people in harm's way. This is a straightforward opening negotiation where each side stands to gain in the long run and nobody loses.'

'I'm glad you see it that way,' Vale countered. 'Sending officers or assets into regions such as this is never without risk. And you're talking about an area known to be under the influence of terrorist groups including al-Qaeda. Risk is only minimal if you never leave the office.'

A sharp intake of breath from a Ministry of Defence representative along the table was the only indication that Vale's comment was seen as a personal dig. Moresby had served time as a field officer, but it had been brief and, by most standards, uneventful. As Vale was well aware, the younger man's meteoric rise through the ranks had been seen by some as too far, too fast, with no real hands-on experience of the kind that had tested many others.

'I think that's pushing it, Tom,' Wilby murmured, and Vale sensed him shrinking away as if not wanting to be associated with any dissent.

'Really?' Vale looked at him. 'Are you saying A-Q *aren't* involved in the region? If so, where have they gone?'

'Easy, Tom,' Cousins murmured softly on his other side, as Wilby flushed and stared down at his folder. 'Nobody's saying you haven't got reason to be concerned. But it's being covered, don't you think?'

Nobody spoke, although Vale saw Scheider give a faint lift of his eyebrows. The CIA man's weathered face showed little emotion, and he was rumoured to have been a world-class poker player in college, funding his education and his later years prior to recruitment by the intelligence agency.

'Quite right, Bill. Thank you,' Moresby said smoothly. 'I'm sure the personnel involved are more than adequate to the task.' He looked around the table, adding, 'At least, I hope so.'

'You hope?' Ruth Dresden, who seemed blithely unaware of any undercurrent in the room and more concerned with statements of fact, stopped making a note and looked up sharply.

Moresby's eyes rested on Vale with a faint smile. 'Well, the officer concerned was recruited by one of us. By Tom Vale, in fact. Weren't you also her mentor, Tom?'

Vale hesitated. 'I recruited and mentored several officers. Which one are you talking about?' He had seen no mention of the names involved so far.

Bill Cousins slipped his folder sideways and flipped it open so that Vale could read it. A name leapt off the page.

Angela Pryce.

Vale felt the blood drain from his face. Every mentor in SIS had a favourite, and Angela Pryce had been his. Highly intelligent and steady under pressure, she was incisive and wore a toughened veneer around her that occasionally dropped to reveal a genuinely likeable personality. They had got on well, and he'd envisaged her heading for greater things. But this assignment was too soon. Angela had completed the full training programme required for active field officers, and had accumulated a number of missions in tandem with other more experienced staff. But none had been as intensive or demanding – or simply as dangerous – as laid out in Moresby's plan.

In spite of that, he doubted Angela would approve of his interference on her behalf.

'Of course,' Moresby murmured silkily, thrusting his point home, 'if you believe Pryce is not up to it, then you should say so now. We can always find an alternative.'

Vale shook his head, hardly able to believe what he was hearing. Suggesting Angela Pryce wasn't capable would put a serious dent in her career. He couldn't do that to her. But allowing her – or any other officer he could think of – on this kind of assignment without objection would be madness. Moresby was playing with people's lives, whether serving officers or local assets on the ground. Missions that went bad were never confined or selective; there were ripples which spread outward like a malevolent echo, picking up others in the process and bowling them over.

'Well?'

'No. I'm not saying that. I think we should proceed with greater caution, that's all.'

'Point noted.' Moresby nodded and moved on, and Vale sat waiting for the meeting to end. Now was not the time or place to have a stand-up fight with the man; Moresby had friends and mentors of his own who would support him and his new energetic approach to field operations. Vale, by comparison, would be seen as old school and over-cautious.

He'd been out-manoeuvred. But he wasn't done with this. Not by a long way.

Five

S ome of the jobs I take on have a surreal inter-connection. After Bogotá I got home to New York to find a message requesting an escort assignment across the border from the US to Tijuana, Mexico. Just like Bogotá, among its other delights Tijuana is known as a centre for drugs activity. Some things you just can't get away from.

I kicked my heels for a couple of days, using the down time to catch up on a few personal and business-related matters, like gun practice in a local indoor range, intensive workouts at the gym and checking out a couple of security-related websites I use. Then I packed an overnight bag and flew down to San Diego.

I was to meet with a man named James Beckwith from the Drugs Enforcement Agency. His bio included responsibility for Intelligence Research, which gave me a small insight to the job he might want me to do, but without specifics. He said he'd been given my name by a mutual contact in the Department of Justice.

Beckwith's office was located in a large building situated along a meandering road in the sandstone- and scrub-covered hills in the north-eastern sector of the city. But he didn't want to meet me there. Instead he'd suggested the Sheraton out near the airport, a busy but anonymous block of brick and glass where business meetings were common and therefore unnoticed.

Middle management types in the spooks business no longer meet in back alleys or smoky beer joints; they do so in smart hotels or business suites. It's called hiding in plain sight. For the most part it works like a dream, since most of them look, walk and talk like corporate drones, complete with tablets, smartphones and briefcases.

Special Agent Beckwith was true to type. I spotted him waiting in the foyer when I arrived. He was stocky and neatly dressed in a dark-blue suit, although he had the tightly-knit build of a man who works out a lot. He had a light tan, pretty standard for anyone in southern California, and the buzz-cut of a former marine. And a smartphone which he was studying carefully.

He apologised for the subterfuge. 'I figured the further you stayed away from the office, the better. I need a clean face for this assignment.' He didn't explain and looked a little tight around the eyes. I wondered if it was because I was an outsider he'd been forced to bring in. He hustled me into a sports bar where we grabbed a corner table away from the constant foot traffic of travellers, luggage carts and uniformed staff.

'This is your brief,' he said, placing a folder on the table in front of me. 'I'd prefer it if you read the details right here and gave it back.' He caught the eye of a waiter cleaning tables. 'You want to eat?'

I shook my head. I'd eaten lunch earlier and didn't feel like prolonging this meeting. It's often the same with briefings, wherever they occur; there's a lot of preliminary talk, like dogs sniffing out the opposition, none of which actually accomplishes anything. I'd rather get to the basics and get on with the task.

He looked relieved and stood up, straightening his already immaculate jacket. 'I'm going to call the person you'll be escorting. He should be here within thirty minutes.' With that he turned and walked away, leaving the waiter standing there looking hopeful. I ordered coffee and opened the folder.

It was a simple enough job – on paper: escort an agent named Oscar Parillas to a hotel in Tijuana, where he had a meeting with unnamed persons. All I had to do was watch his back, then return him safely to San Diego. The folder included a map of the area, details of the route in and out, and a number to call if we needed assistance.

When Beckwith returned I asked him, 'What's the threat level?'

It was a straightforward enough question with a town like Tijuana; drugs and guns live side by side down there, and tensions between rival gangs and distributors are always high. Throw in a dubious police force and the Mexican government's own anti-drugs units, and death was commonplace, often with collateral damage to innocent bystanders.

'You've never been there, right?'

'That's right.'

'On the surface it's a nice enough place. Leave out the areas you shouldn't go – and there are plenty – and you could be anywhere on the gulf coast. But the law doesn't control Tijuana, the cartels do. It makes the threat level real and unpredictable. We've lost good men down there; men who happened to be in the wrong place at the wrong time. I don't want to lose any more.'

'It sounds hot.'

'It is. Once on the other side, you will be issued with personal weapons by a local contact. Make no mistake, using them will draw the attention of the cartels *and* the law. And we have no agreement with the Mexican government that allows us to send armed personnel into the country unless under special circumstances.'

'Sounds like this doesn't qualify.'

'It doesn't. They don't even know you're coming. Going through official channels over there means risking too many leaks – and this assignment's too important to us to lose the initiative. So use your weapons only as a last resort. In the event of trouble we will make every attempt to extract you.'

Extract. I was accustomed to that word in all its meanings. Not rescue, but extract. If extraction was so simple, why weren't they taking this Oscar Parillas into Tijuana themselves? They certainly had the resources and networks.

He read my mind. 'I decided to bring you in for the same reasons of security. Too many of our San Diego and local personnel have been blown recently by the cartels. We suspect they've been building up an extensive database of employee files with information stolen from our own servers. Three of our agents and two confidential informants have been targeted in the past two weeks, and another two CIs have disappeared.' He didn't explain what that meant, but the look on his face told me it wasn't good.

'You think it was an inside job?'

I expected him to reject the suggestion out of hand, but he surprised me. 'Possibly. We're currently undergoing a complete overhaul of our systems trying to find a leak. But we know they've improved their hacking capabilities. The Tijuanas especially have invested heavily in IT and the personnel to run it, including setting up a programme to put IT-literate kids through school.'

'That's ambitious.'

He pulled a wry face. 'Blame the cult of the MBA. Suddenly even the drugs gangs have seen the sense in their people having a business degree. Their operations have spread south to Latin America, where they source the drugs, and they've increased other operations in arms smuggling and people trafficking going north. It's a multi-billion dollar operation and they don't want to lose it. But they've also recognized that they have to use the money pouring in, which means employing legitimate channels to invest it and spread it out – mostly overseas to Europe and the Far East.' He sighed and added, 'It's on a huge scale; they've actually got more cash than we do and no legal restraints to worry about.'

'A losing battle?'

'I'm not admitting that. But if we can find a way to disrupt even a small corner of their operations, it could have significant long-term benefits.'

He made it sound like he was discussing an investment opportunity, and I guess he was. 'I take it this guy Parillas isn't known to them either?'

'Correct. He's been shipped in from one of our other divisions, but he's been working on it remotely for a while, so he knows all the details.'

'So we're both clean skins.'

'You got it.' He hesitated, then said, 'When we began to look at this assignment, we were given your name by a reliable source. We know you've done this sort of work before, so you know the risks, right?'

'I do.'

'Good. Do you mind if I ask what your background is?'

I ignored the question. I like to stay private as much as I can, and he was already probing for more information. 'Which reliable source was that?'

'An arm of the administration. That's all I can say.'

We could dance like this all day and I didn't press him. He probably meant CIA but didn't want to sully his mouth by voicing it. There's a degree of dissent between the two organizations, both of which have been fighting the drugs lords for years. It must have taken desperate measures for him to approach them looking for someone like me.

'The situation down there at present is very fluid,' he continued, getting back on track. 'There's some intense negotiating going on between the Tijuana Cartel and their rivals, the Sinaloas, and it's throwing up a lot of distrust by long-term members on both sides who see themselves losing out if any agreements are signed.'

'Seriously?'

He shrugged. 'Same with corporate takeovers; you don't need two sets of middle-managers, so someone has to go. Don't forget, these people are in a high-risk, paranoid environment; suspicion and betrayal comes with the territory and they'd all like to retire old and rich. We've had approaches by people affiliated to both camps offering information which we believe signals a way for us to break them up – or at least disrupt their activities. One contact is especially promising. He's a long-time middle-ranking member of the Tijuana Cartel and claims to know the whereabouts of two of the Felix brothers, both on our Most Wanted list. The Felix family runs the Tijuanas.'

I'd heard of them. They had a reputation for dealing harshly with people they suspected of crossing them. 'He's taking a big risk, isn't he?'

'The way he explained it, it's all or nothing. His opposite number in the Sinaloas is younger, smarter and married into the clan, so he's feeling threatened. If this assignment works, and we bring them in, we'll put a severe dent in their organization for some time to come.'

He knew a lot more about it than I did, but I figured he was being optimistic; take out one figurehead and another will rise up quickly in their place. Like he'd said earlier, the amount of money the drugs cartels generated day to day made sure they all wanted to hold on to it and keep it running smoothly.

Just then a slim man in his forties with slick black hair appeared at the entrance and looked around. He caught Beckwith's eye and started across the room like he was treading on glass.

'This is Parillas,' Beckwith said quietly. 'I'll introduce you, then leave you to it. He's your lead on this operation. Is there anything you need on the other side apart from a sidearm?'

I thought about it and mentioned two items.

He promised to have them delivered. 'Any questions?'

I closed the folder, which told me as much as I needed to know, and slid it back across the table at him. 'Just one: when do we go in?'

Six

Tom Vale made his way back down to the street with a heavy heart. His misgivings about what Moresby was planning were instinctive, formed by many years operating in hostile environments and sending out men and women to uncertain fates. That was a good thing; it engendered caution and a respect for the other side. But there was something in the new Operations Director's approach which worried him. It smacked of recklessness inspired by ambition, and a cavalier attitude to the dangers out in the field that were not his own.

As he approached the exit, he heard the clatter of footsteps behind him.

'Tom?'

It was James Scheider. The CIA man was shadowed closely

by a smartly dressed man in his early thirties who looked as if he'd been drawn from the Marine Corps store, muscles, buzz-cut hairstyle and all. As Vale stopped, the minder cruised past him and went to the door, eyeing the street.

'How's Cavell doing?' Vale asked. Scheider's boss and CIA station chief, Wilton Cavell, was off sick with suspected cancer. It had thrown his deputy in at the deep end, but he seemed to be handling it well.

'Not good. He's going to be replaced – but you didn't hear that from me.' He glanced back up the stairs, then said, 'You got a minute?'

'Of course. Here?'

'It will do. This, uh, business.' He lifted his chin upwards. 'Anything I should know about? Only, I got the feeling you weren't keen.'

'A little.' Vale knew he had made it obvious, so there was no point denying it. 'I'm uneasy about certain aspects. Why do you ask?' He'd only known Scheider a short while, and was cautious about revealing his feelings to the American too readily.

Scheider surprised him. 'Because I share your doubts. Not that it has anything to do with me directly, but it sounds like it could be a dirty business if things go wrong. Your people are going to be very exposed with no backup.'

'That's what worries me.'

'Can you do anything to stop it?'

'Short of taking out a hit on Moresby, no.' Vale smiled to show he was joking, and added, 'I need to think about it. But I'd be interested to hear what you think.'

Scheider studied his fingernails, which were immaculate. 'The plan's adventurous, no denying that. Hellish risky, too. On the other hand, like it or not, engaging with these people might be a way to resolve the problem. It's worked with other organizations.'

'But?'

'We can't interfere.'

'We?'

'The US.'

'That sounds official. Are you saying this has been aired already?'

'Briefly, yes. Moresby floated the approach made by Xasan when it first came in. I think he was testing the water to see how we might react.'

Vale should have known. Moresby had by-passed procedure, probably under the banner of inter-agency co-operation to see if an idea would float in theory. It explained why Cousins and Wilby had been a little off guard, yet supportive. 'And?'

'It's a clear-cut issue as far as the administration is concerned: we don't have any assets in the immediate area, save for some aid workers. But they're not our concern until and unless they fall into real danger. We're limited, therefore, in being able to commit any hard facilities. Drones for camera coverage, yes; signals intelligence via NSA, no problem. Anything more solid would be too . . . direct.'

It echoed what Moresby had said. Even Vale could see the sense in it. There were some operations where an overload of assets became a distinct disadvantage. The other side was likely to be tuned in to the presence of outsiders on their turf, and any sudden show of force in the region would signal an operation in progress. But he wasn't about to give up.

'Forgive me saying so, James, but you're sounding a little oblique.'

Scheider smiled, showing perfect white teeth. 'Oblique. That's a good word, Tom. I guess oblique is what it is.' He hesitated before adding carefully, 'What I mean is, if you decide to add any . . . additional material of your own, shall we say, I might be able to help. But in a strictly advisory capacity.'

'I think we have all the advisory we need, thank you.' Vale had to rein in a touch of impatience. Scheider sounded as if he was offering some kind of help, without saying precisely what it might be. He was going to have to tease it out of him. 'Could you be a little more explicit?'

'Well, as I said, we can't commit any hard facilities.'

'You mean boots on the ground. I understand that.'

'Exactly. And by the sounds of what was said upstairs, Mr Moresby isn't about to call on more than one of your resident tough guys to pitch in.'

'No. He's not.' Vale wondered how much Scheider knew about the Basement, SIS's own force of hand-picked

specialists. While its existence was hardly a secret in the closed
community of the intelligence world, not too many outsiders
ever spoke about it. He was assuming that one of them would
be accompanying Angela Pryce on the assignment. But one
was not enough.

'Well,' Scheider continued, 'if you happen to hear of a name
you might use, I could run them through the Meat Grinder in
Langley.'

The Meat Grinder; the CIA's vast but highly selective vetting
software run by a team of IT wizards. It was boasted with some
degree of justification that a name fed in one end could appear
within an hour or two with a full vetting and background rating
suitable for most security clearances.

'That would be very useful, thank you. Except I don't recall
even suggesting I would consider such a thing.'

Scheider grinned knowingly. 'Of course. Understood. But
we've both been round the block a few times, so I guess we
might be thinking along the same lines. If you do get a
name and you'd like to check it out, call me.' With that, he
walked away, his minder preceding him out of the door like
an attack dog.

Vale watched him go, then turned and made his way back
towards Vauxhall Cross. Scheider had been surprisingly perceptive, although as he'd said, perhaps not so surprising given their
shared background. An idea had been bubbling through Vale's
mind as he came downstairs after the meeting. It sprang from
a memorable period while on his first posting in Cold War
Berlin many years ago. Back then, in a burst of unexplained
aggression, British operatives and agents moving back and forth
across the Wall had been targeted by the East Germans for
capture or assassination. Since neither they nor their masters,
the Russians, were given to half measures, it was decided to
set up a team of shadows, unseen and unidentified, to cover the
agents as they moved. Vale had been given the task of monitoring
them. After one or two 'incidents' involving the unexplained
disappearance of East German operatives, the targeting had
ceased and the shadows had been disbanded. The matter had never
been admitted to, the funding channelled through a number of

covert accounts until its origins and goals were lost in a fog
of bureaucratic subterfuge. It was yet another aspect of that less
documented period which meant that certain matters would
never be made public, even under the '30-year secrecy rule'
releases which regularly caused those who studied such matters
a severe rush of blood to the head.

Vale arrived at Vauxhall Cross and cleared security, then stood
for a while in a deserted stretch of corridor near his office,
mulling over Scheider's words. The CIA deputy clearly shared
his reservations about the risks inherent in Moresby's plan, not
least to the people involved. But he'd made it clear in just a few
words that putting in his own people to help was a non-starter,
mainly because of current US commitments elsewhere and
increasing levels of accusation about their role as self-appointed
global police.

He felt frustrated. In spite of his reservations he could see
that the potential outcome of the plan, if successful, was too
good to miss. And to many observers in the corridors of
Whitehall, that would prove sufficiently attractive to outweigh
any risks.

He stared out of the window at the river below, watching a
barge trundle by with two men on board, mugs of tea in hand.
He wondered fleetingly at the simplicity of their life, and decided
that all the sound-proofing and bullet-proof glass and walls of
this place, while conveniently preventing outside noises filtering
in, probably affected some officers' judgement in their relationship
with the outside world, causing a disconnect in more than just
space.

He returned to his desk and picked up his phone. He checked
his watch and dialled a number. It was very early for the person
on the other end, but he knew the man's habits. He didn't sleep
for long and would be up and about already, working on a new
day.

'Sweetman.' The voice was early-morning gruff but alert.
Vale was calling his brother-in-law, an American living in New
York State. Nate had passed through London only a few days
ago, and had told Vale a story that had surprised him. He hadn't
yet had time to look into the details, but now was maybe the

moment when he needed to think outside the square, as some of the hipper officers downstairs were fond of saying.

'Nate, it's Tom. How are you?'

'Hey, Tom, I'm good. You?'

'I'm fine, thanks.' He had never told Nate what he did for a living, but the American was perceptive enough to have guessed that Vale was no ordinary civil servant. He launched straight in with his reason for calling. 'You remember that person you told me about – the one who delivered you to that airport down south last week?'

There was a momentary hesitation as the cogs clicked into place, then Nate said, 'Damn right I remember. How could I forget? What about him?'

'I know you mentioned it already, but I need his name and room number.'

'No problem. It was Challenor. It's engraved on my memory. No idea of his first name. His room was next to mine: three-oh-two. But he won't be there now . . . he flew out the same day as me.'

'Do you know where he was headed?'

'No. New York, I think – at least, that was the impression I got. I was flying to Chicago.' He paused. 'Funny thing was, I asked what his name was, where he lived, where he was going – all the usual stuff when a guy comes out of nowhere and saves your life . . . but he never got round to giving me any detail.'

'That may have been for a reason,' Vale suggested cryptically. He thanked Nate for his help, told him to give a big kiss to his sister, and cut the connection. His next call was internal, to a researcher on the floor below.

'That's all you have – a surname and hotel room number?' It wasn't a criticism; most of the time they had far less to work with.

'That's all.'

'Fine. What level of information?'

'The full card. Names, addresses, next of kin, jobs, what he eats for dinner. The works. Especially his military record. And get a visual on any current location.'

'Got it.'

He sat back and thought things through. The way he saw it, there was only one way to protect Angela Pryce. He couldn't prevent Moresby from sending her out on his proposed op, but he could do his best to ensure she wasn't completely vulnerable. That excluded the specialists SIS had on call, those men and women with Special Forces backgrounds, trained in insertion and extraction work in hostile areas, since it would require too much in the way of counter-signatures and electronic records – none of which he dared use. Moresby would see it as interference and immediately block it.

The only thing he could do was find the mysterious Challenor, a man who could apparently step out of his hotel room into a three-gun kidnap in one of the most dangerous cities in Latin America, and walk away with the intended victim leaving two kidnappers dead and a further two unconscious.

Seven

In my line of work you rarely get to choose who you work with. I pick up most jobs by word of mouth, some via a loose network of former military personnel, spooks and private security contractors trading information on intelligence or security assignments around the world. I vet as many as I can beforehand, but you can't always be too selective. Other times the chemistry simply isn't there and you either suck it up or say no.

It certainly wasn't there with Parillas. But by the time I found that out, I was already in.

Right from the start he made it clear he didn't like working with an outsider. By that he meant non-DEA. When he heard Beckwith mention that I was a contractor, he got all bug-eyed and stared at the intelligence specialist as if he'd gone nuts.

'What the hell – are you kidding me?' He leaned across the table and hissed, 'Since when do we bring in outside help?' He had no trace of a Latino accent, I noticed, although he looked the part for where we were going. Dark eyes, thin face and skin like coffee, a few pockmarks around his cheeks.

'Since we decided the situation demanded it.' Beckwith's response was friendly, but beneath the words, layered in steel. I got the impression he wasn't going to stand having a fight with his colleague about it. 'We brought you in for the same reason; because you won't be known faces. Mr Portman here has never been down south, never mixed it with the drugs gangs, but he's got an excellent record in similar work, so we'd like you to go along with this.'

'What kind of work was that?' Parillas wasn't looking at me, but his hostility rippled across the table in waves. 'Is Portman your real name?'

'He's done stuff you've never dreamed of. Trust me.' Beckwith's voice had gone flat; end of discussion. 'And Portman's the name we're using.'

Parillas nodded, but he wasn't happy. His face had gone tight and I could hear a foot drumming on the floor beneath the table. I put it down to the stiff-shirt attitude of some special agents I'd worked with before, who thought anyone from outside their own sphere of activities was deeply suspect and not to be trusted. I ignored it.

'You read the file?' Parillas asked once Beckwith had said his goodbyes and left.

I nodded. Maybe he'd warm up a little once we got to know each other. Somehow I doubted it. I stood up, eager to get the show on the road. The sooner we moved, the easier it would be to focus on what we shared rather than what we didn't.

Parillas led the way out to a dusty white Land Cruiser that had seen better days. It had some damage to the panels and some flecks of rust here and there, but by the smooth sound of the engine, it had less time under the hood than it looked. I'd seen plenty of similar vehicles in the area already, and had used one or two myself.

Parillas climbed aboard and we took off at a clip, heading south.

'This is an in-out job,' he explained briefly. 'We get to Tijuana in less than an hour, pick up the equipment, then split up. I make the rendezvous and you stay on the outside. Shouldn't take more than an hour, then we leave.'

'What time is the rendezvous?'

'Four thirty on the nail.'

'Suits me,' I said. 'Wouldn't it be better if I stayed close?'

'No. Believe me, in Tijuana two guys moving around together attracts too much attention; the cops down there operate in teams and pairs for safety, and the gangs are aware of that. Single guys looking like they want to make a score or pick up a short date, not so much. You hang back but stay within phone contact and hope this isn't a set-up.'

'Is it likely?'

He shrugged. 'Anything's likely in Tijuana. It's that kind of town.'

'You sound like you've been there before.'

'A long time ago. Problem?'

I shook my head. 'No problem.' Beckwith had told me Parillas was an outsider, like me. 'Give me your guy's name and description.'

He considered it for a moment, and evidently thought it was OK to tell me.

'His name's Louis Achevar. Why do you need to know what he looks like? You won't be eyeballing him.'

'Because if something goes wrong and I have to pull him out, I need to know who I'm looking for. We'll let Beckwith worry about getting him across the border afterwards.'

He looked reluctant, but he couldn't argue with the logic. One of the main points of any operation is having a fall-back plan in case it doesn't go as expected. Beckwith had talked only of success, not failure, and while we were going to be within a short spit of the US border, I was still thinking about ways out if the balloon went up.

'He's a forty-two-year-old runt,' he said. 'Skinny, with glasses, and about five-six. A Mexican Woody Allen, but bald as a coot. If he sees you, he'll run. I ain't kidding – the guy's paranoid. Anybody but me and he'll think it's the cartel come to waste him.'

'So he knows what you look like?'

He hesitated. 'He has a rough idea, sure. He's been told to take a room in the hotel and wait for me to show up.'

'What number?'

'Jesus, you want his inside leg, too?' He puffed out some air, then said, 'Thirty-four, on the second floor. But you're not to go near him, understand? Stay out of it.'

'Fine. I won't go near him unless I have to.'

The idea seemed full of holes to me, but I had no way of knowing what stress this Achevar was under, or what hoops he'd had to jump through to come even this far. All I knew was that insiders, especially middle-ranking insiders who knew too much and who decided to rat on organizations like the cartels or the mafia, were treading a fine line between life and death. And that was enough to get to the strongest individuals.

Parillas nodded and drove on in silence.

We reached the border on the I5 and joined a queue at the highway inspection gate. It was hot and dusty and full of noise and the acrid smell of car fumes hanging over us like a thick fog. Some of the vehicles heading south were beyond the low end of road-worthy, packed with families and pumping out carbon monoxide in clouds. The border agents kept us moving, although it was slow enough to make it uncomfortable. Parillas seemed edgier the closer we got, but he probably knew the risks involved more than I did. Eventually we cleared the border control and were on our way.

'After we pick up the stuff,' he said, swerving to avoid a beat-up and overloaded truck wallowing in the nearside lane, 'I'll drop you off before we get downtown. You head for the hotel and call me when you're close. I want to know exactly where you are.'

'What will you be doing?'

'Checking out the area, watching for Achevar, what do you think?'

I shook my head. He was departing from the plan. 'No. Checking the perimeter is my job. I'm the escort, you're running the meet. I'll scope the area and call you to confirm if it's safe to go in.'

He was ready for that one. 'No way, man. I know this place better than you. You're meant to be in the background, so stay there.' It was odd, but the more uptight he got, the more a trace of an accent came out, accompanied by a faintly nasal tone.

'You know the place? How well?'

'Enough. Believe me.' He clamped his jaws shut.

'What if there's someone there who knows *you*?'

'There isn't. Trust me. It's been too long.' He refused to look at me and was gripping the wheel like he didn't want to let go. The temperature in the car had gone up noticeably in the last few seconds and Parillas was sweating heavily.

Something wasn't right here. 'Like how long? Like a lifetime? A couple of vacation trips?' Then I had it. 'You used to *live* here.'

'No. Yes – when I was a kid. So what? It's been years.' He was angry and defensive.

'Can you guarantee there are no old school friends who never moved on? Neighbours who remember the kid even though he grew up?'

He said nothing and I got the feeling he was wishing he hadn't started this.

'You can't,' I said calmly. 'Which means the quicker you get in and out, the less likely you are to be made by a random passer-by, and the sooner we'll get back on the other side with the information we've come for.'

He shook his head, unwilling to give way. 'I don't know.'

'I do.' I stared hard at him. 'I've done this before – a lot. So how about you trust *me*?'

He looked resentful, but he must have known it made sense. Random was the biggest enemy of planning; a chance encounter, a face from the past – anything like that could put a bomb under the most carefully thought-out scenarios. I wondered if he simply didn't like handing over control, in which case he should have come in by himself. It made me wonder whether Beckwith knew what he was doing.

We followed the highway into Tijuana and Parillas took a turning off which dropped us into a residential and commercial district. He pulled into the car park of a mid-size motel and sat waiting, checking out the few cars around us.

'Our contact will be here soon,' he said, and checked his watch. He still wasn't happy.

Moments later, a pickup with tinted windows slid up alongside us and the driver climbed out. He was fat and friendly looking, with a heavy beard, a man in his fifties. He didn't look at us, but went to the back of the pickup and lifted out a polished wooden box. He placed it on the ground by the back of the truck.

Eight

I t took Vale's researchers less than twenty-four hours to come up with something concrete. Challenor was a cover name, used and discarded after the trip to Bogotá. Vale wasn't surprised. But luck had been with them. They had picked him up on CCTV going through the airport and tracked him to a New York flight, then got him coming off the other end where he'd stopped at an ATM machine. By then his name had become Marc Portman.

This name had yielded three addresses to which he was connected, one each in New York, London, and Paris. Mr Portman seemed to have international connections.

While Vale was waiting for local assets to run visual checks on the three addresses and find out more about the man, he used every channel he could think of to put a block on Moresby's plans for the meeting.

As an experienced former field controller, and given his oversight role in SIS, he was granted the courtesy of hearings most other officers would not have had. Hearings where he could voice his misgivings, doubts and concerns about the dangers to the personnel involved. The people he spoke to were senior managers, each capable of stopping an operation in its tracks on the grounds of safety, necessity or national security, and each with considerable experience in seeing officers go out into hostile territories where casualties were not unknown.

They listened, nodded at each point he raised and considered the implications, even his carefully worded suggestions that not only had Moresby frozen him out of the announcement of the plans, but that the officer selected for the operation lacked the required experience. But each had politely and firmly knocked him back. Moresby, they advised him, had presented carefully considered plans with full risk analyses and outcomes, and the dice had fallen squarely in his favour.

With his final meeting over, Vale retreated to his office and shut the door. He felt humiliated. He was in the middle of the world's most effective intelligence gathering organization and he was powerless to use any of it.

He checked a slim file in his drawer, and scanned the brief report on the man who had saved Nate's life.

Marc Stuart Portman resides in Paris, London and New York. All address titles are held and dealt with by Belnex, an offshore administration company based in Gibraltar, as are various hotel group account cards. Described variously by neighbours as friendly, aloof, a businessman or job unknown, the subject's passport details list him as holding joint American and British nationalities, aged 38, with no next-of-kin and no outstanding physical characteristics. He is slim to compact with dark hair cut short and lightly tanned skin. Enquiries at fitness suites near to his homes reveal use on an ad hoc basis under the above name. Suite instructor in London describes him as fit and strong, focussed but not obsessive in his training regime. Instructor in New York (ex-US Marine Corps) believes him to be former military but says he doesn't talk much and doesn't answer questions. Each reported no obvious tattoos or other military-related body markings.

No records found of education, military service or employment. Search ongoing.

A copy of a passport photo was attached. It showed a man with neat, dark hair, dark eyes and prominent cheekbones. Unremarkable looking and of Caucasian, possibly Mediterranean appearance, he was everyman, save for the directness of his gaze. Vale recognized that type. There were at least a dozen men fitting that description in this very building, some of them specialists in the Basement. They all had the same look. And like them, Portman probably had the ability to merge in a crowd, unmemorable and grey.

Also like them, he could undoubtedly handle a weapon on first contact with deadly effect and come out unscathed.

He picked up his phone and dialled Scheider's direct number. Portman was primarily a US citizen and spent most of his time there. It was logical, therefore, to take up Scheider's offer and see what the Meat Grinder could turn up about him.

'Leave it with me,' the American said. 'We'll get right on him.'

Nine

P arillas made a big show of climbing out of the car and looking down at the box, then lifting his chin as if asking what it was. The fat man said something and Parillas bent to lift the lid up and down as if testing the hinges. For good measure he gave one side a gentle kick before nodding and asking another question.

The fat man went through the motions of haggling, which I didn't think would fool anybody for a second. But maybe it was the way they do things down here. It was their show and probably a perfectly reasonable explanation for strangers meeting in a car park in the middle of the day and making an exchange of some kind.

Parillas handed over some notes and lugged the box on to the back seat of the Land Cruiser, while the fat man waddled back to his pickup and took off.

'We just bought a piece of furniture,' Parillas said, in a weak attempt at humour. 'There are guns and cell phones in the box – all throw-aways. Were the jackets and hats your idea?'

I nodded. Disposable clothing is useful for changing one's profile in tight situations. Followers of a target automatically lock on to colours, clothes and the physical characteristics of the person they're tailing. Switching any of these creates confusion and maybe a chance of getting clear. Changing physical points isn't so easy, but putting on a jacket, taking off a hat, picking up or discarding a bag, are often sufficient to throw off a tail.

We set off again, this time for a kilometre or so, before Parillas stopped to drop me off. It put me five minutes' walk from the hotel where the meeting was to take place. I stretched into the back and opened the wooden box, and took out a 9mm semi-automatic and a spare magazine, a pale linen jacket roomy enough to throw on over my own jacket, and an anonymous baseball cap. A cell phone completed my kit and I was ready to go.

We synchronized watches and cell phone numbers, then I shrugged on the jacket and left Parillas to disappear somewhere quiet until it was time to arrive at the hotel for the meet. I had more than an hour to scope the area, and figured that should be enough to spot trouble if it was waiting. If there were any bogies around and I hadn't spotted them by then, we were in deep water.

As it turned out, I didn't have long to wait. As I approached the hotel, which was in a busy section of town, I saw two black SUVs nosing at walking pace through the traffic. Alone, they might have gone unnoticed in such a crowded street. But keeping pace alongside them were several men on foot, scouring the faces of pedestrians.

I felt alarm bells ringing. This wasn't good. They might have been local dealers for all I knew, putting on a show of strength to win over some turf. Or a local law enforcement team on an exercise. But if so, why here, right now?

I took out the disposable cell phone and hit speed dial to warn Parillas. If they were the cartel, we had no choice – we would have to abort. The meeting must have been compromised, although whether Achevar had already gotten scooped up was an unknown quantity.

The phone rang for a full thirty seconds. I cut the connection and tried again, checking to make sure I hadn't fed in the wrong number.

No answer.

Ten

I t was too much of a coincidence. From Parillas' dismay at finding I was an outsider, to his general air of edginess when he let slip that he'd once lived here, and then his insistence on keeping me away from Achevar – all of that. Now he'd dropped off the net.

It didn't feel good.

I ducked into a doorway and ripped off the linen jacket, dumping it behind a trash can. I stuck the baseball cap in my pocket, as that might come in useful. Then I checked the semi-automatic to make sure it was in full working order. Finding out later that it was a useless piece of junk would be fatal to my chances of getting out of here alive. But it was clean and well used, ready to go.

I figured I had two options: one was to bug out and head for the border, calling up Beckwith on the way to warn him we were blown and I was in need of a fast passage through the control posts. How he got me out was up to him; if he didn't, I'd just have to walk across the border and hope I didn't get stopped. The other option was to stay and find out what had happened. What if Parillas was simply in a bad signal area somewhere, or was ill and couldn't respond? He was hardly my best buddy, but if he was in a jam I couldn't just leave him. I'd made that mistake once before and didn't want to repeat it.

I left the shelter of the doorway and made a circular tour of the block housing the hotel, shuffling along with my shoulders hunched, another wage slave going about his business. The area was packed with small shops, a riot of colour and music and smells, some familiar, others I couldn't place. As I walked I checked the street and the surrounding rooftops. If the area was being blanket-covered by the opposition, who I figured had to be the Cartel, they would have watchers at ground level and high up, strategically placed to follow Parillas' – and my – progress to the meeting point. That way they could lift us both off the street while keeping a bird's eye view of any law enforcement in the area.

I saw two possible spotters fairly quickly. Both with the cold expression of gang members, they were standing on a corner, scanning the crowds and holding cell phones ready to use. I couldn't see any tattoos or other insignia, but that didn't mean much; if they were under orders to be discreet, they would hardly be advertising their presence openly. I walked by them without a flicker and checked out the cars parked in the street, another customary blind spot for placing backup muscle.

By the time I got back near the front of the hotel, I'd seen four more men. The two SUVs I'd seen earlier were now stationary two blocks down from the hotel, their engines off. The men with them were clustered on the sidewalk outside a small coffee bar, evidently waiting for orders.

On my way round, I'd formulated a plan based entirely on surprise and impulse. It wasn't great and my chances of success were limited, but it depended on getting to Achevar and persuading him to follow me. Otherwise I'd have to leave him.

I slipped down a side street alongside the hotel and found a narrow door reinforced with steel plate. A pile of crates holding empty beer bottles stood nearby, ready for collection. I hefted one of the crates on my shoulder and walked inside. I was in the rear of the building, the air thick with cooking smells. A young woman in kitchen whites stepped out of a door ahead of me, spotted the crate and nodded towards a room on the far side, where I could see more crates stacked by the door.

People see what they expect to see.

I dumped the crate in the storeroom and continued along the corridor towards a rack of tourist brochures and city maps. The reception area was close by. I could hear a woman taking a booking just out of my line of sight to my left, marking the reception desk, and got a glimpse of the main entrance and a circular door dead ahead. A sign on the wall pointed to the stairs and elevator.

I made a show of checking out the literature while eyeing the foyer, which had a marble floor and lots of yellow lights reflecting off brass panels, and pots of large exotic plants in the corners.

I heard a man's voice, deep and fast, followed by a laugh. Then a shoulder appeared round the edge of the wall, so close I could have touched it.

It was a security guard complete with shoulder badge and a gun on his hip.

I held my breath. No way would I get past him. I needed the emergency stairway. I turned back down the corridor the way I'd come and saw that the doorway the young woman had come through moments earlier was now closed, and carried a running man sign. I must have walked right by it.

I ducked through and found myself in a lobby at the bottom of a flight of concrete stairs leading up. The air here was stuffy and warm, with no ventilation. Tucked under the stairs and spilling out into the lobby were some damaged chairs, a broken headboard and a couple of electric lamps, and I guessed the fire regulations didn't stretch this far. Before going further, I took out the cell phone and tried Parillas once more.

Still no answer.

I walked up the stairs, my shoes crunching on a fine coating of grit, and hoped there were no security cameras in operation. Just in case, I opened a map I'd picked out of the brochure rack downstairs and held it in front of me with my head down and one hand inside my jacket on the gun.

I passed the first floor landing and stopped to check for voices. Nothing. But it was hard to tell with the hum of traffic and bustle filtering in from outside. As hotels go, it couldn't have been in a busier district. I checked my watch. Four fifty-five.

I continued on up and did the same at the second floor, then walked up to the third and stepped out into a corridor. It was carpeted and well lit, and smelled more like a hotel, with a hint of air-freshener and cleaning liquids. I walked along until I reached another small lobby area with a single elevator and a flight of stairs. I listened for a moment over the void, but couldn't hear anything.

Time to go visit Mr Achevar.

It's always easier walking down from a higher floor to the one you need. That way you get advance warning of anyone waiting, because guards don't always look up; they expect trouble to come from the lower floors. It also gives you the chance to turn and go back up if you need to, because up is generally less busy. The closer to the ground in a public building of any kind, the more likely you are to run into trouble.

I stepped off the bottom stair and checked the corridor. Empty. If Mr Achevar was still waiting, he must be getting edgy.

The door to thirty-four looked perfectly normal. I took out the gun and held it down by my leg, and stood to one side. I knocked.

No answer. I knocked again, slightly louder. Maybe Mr Achevar was taking a nap.

This time the door clicked and moved, then swung open a little.

I smelled Achevar right away.

I stepped inside, following the gun, although I didn't think I'd need it. It was a standard room, with a single bed, TV, a couple of chairs and a writing surface with a drinks tray. There was no sign of the occupant, but it looked as if a hurricane had gone through, tearing the place apart. The bed had been stripped and ripped, drawers opened and the chairs tipped upside down and sliced open. Even the corners of the carpets had been lifted.

I sniffed and felt my gut twitch, and eased round the corner of the bathroom door.

Louis Achevar was slumped in the shower tray. Blood had splattered up the wall and shower screen, lending the scene a pink hue that was anything but soft.

He had died hard, and I hoped for his sake that it had been quicker than it looked. Somebody had hacked off his hands and feet, the latter still in their shoes. They were lying outside the shower, placed neatly side by side, as if he might have stepped out of them before folding himself into a tiny ball and dying. His hands had been placed on his chest, with the fingers dipped into the gap where his throat had been sliced open like a pair of lips.

A towel had been stuffed in his mouth to prevent his screams being heard, and the air was thick with the smell of blood and faeces. Dozens of flies were coming through the air vent in the wall, rushing to settle on the body, where they began feeding greedily off the slick layers of blood.

I heard a police siren blip some way off, and felt the hairs lift on the back of my neck. I didn't have much time. I was pretty sure that if Achevar had brought anything with him to hand over to Parillas, like a memory stick or a notebook, it had been taken. Even so, I had to look. I didn't waste time checking the body; the pockets of Achevar's pants had been ripped outwards and his shirt torn open. So I focussed on the bedroom area, trying to get inside the mind of a man terrified for his life yet determined to hand over information about his employers.

There was nothing. The searchers had done a thorough job, even checking the top of the wardrobe and inside the TV. The only things left were the hotel facilities folder and a local phone directory with a cheap ballpoint pen lying nearby.

My cell phone rang. It sounded too loud in the confined space of the room, and I wondered if they could hear it outside.

I checked the screen; caller's number withheld. I hit the button and listened. I could hear breathing, and some voices in the background. Then another blip of a siren, sounding very close to whoever was calling me.

'Portman?' It was Parillas. 'Where you at, man?'

For a brief second, I wondered if I'd been wrong and he'd genuinely got held up. I said, 'I'm close. Why – are you in trouble?'

'No, man. Everything's cool, y'know?' His breathing was harsh and I wondered why he was calling me 'man' and sounding so hip.

Something wasn't right.

The police siren.

'Are we ready to go?' I asked.

'No. Not yet.' A gabble of voices sounded in the background, then he continued, 'Tell you what, come in to the hotel. It's safe, OK? I got Achevar, but we need to move fast.'

'Got it.' Liar, liar. I shut off the phone and heard shouting outside. I stepped over to the window. I couldn't see the area right in front of the hotel, but people on the far side of the street were all focussed on something further along.

The two SUVs I'd seen earlier were still there, but a police cruiser had stopped alongside them, the driver gesticulating for them to move along. After a moment, he stopped waving and nodded, and drove off, one arm hanging out the window. At that, the men at the coffee bar broke away and began walking along the street. They looked as if they meant business.

Just as I was about to move away, the rear door of the nearest SUV opened, and a man in a pale jacket jumped out. He stood on the sidewalk listening to someone inside, then grinned and slapped the roof of the car before turning and chasing after the other men.

They were all heading towards the hotel.

I watched as the man in the pale jacket caught up with them and clamped an arm across the lead man's shoulders. The movement lifted this one's shirt, revealing the butt of a semi-automatic stuffed into his waistband. Whatever the man in the pale jacket said to him was enough to have him shouting orders to his companions, and they put on a burst of speed, spreading out across the street.

I swore silently. It was a trap. And I'd walked right into it.

The pale jacket was similar to the one I'd dumped in the trash earlier, the partner of the one delivered in the wooden box.

It was being worn by Oscar Parillas.

Eleven

I got out of there fast, snatching up the phone directory on the way. It seemed to be the only thing the searchers hadn't touched. I didn't know if it was meaningful, but I could get into that later.

For now I had to survive the next few minutes until I got clear.

I hit the emergency stairs on the run. This time I wasn't being too careful. Distance was of the essence; between me and the cartel gunmen outside, and distance from here to the border.

As I walked out of the downstairs lobby area I heard raised voices coming from the reception area. One belonged to the security guard. If he was savvy enough to recognize these men for what they were, he'd back off without resistance and let them do what they had to. He wasn't being paid enough to stand up against the cartel.

I slipped out into the side street and walked away from the hotel, a low sun at my back, clutching the directory under my arm. I was running a mental map and working out where I had to go to cover as much ground as I could. My problem was, Parillas knew where I would go and might have already told his new associates to despatch men to the border to intercept me. That was a chance I had to take.

I was at the end of the street and about to turn the corner when a beefy guy in a flashy shirt stepped out of a doorway and stood in front of me, squinting into the sun. He had smooth facial skin stretched over high cheekbones, and black, lank hair. He also had one hand under his shirt and was holding a cell phone in his other hand.

It was one of the spotters I'd seen earlier.

Out in the open was no place for a fight; his colleagues were all over the area and would come running the moment they heard anything. So I held up my hands and walked straight into the open doorway he'd just left, which was little more than a small tiled lobby.

The move threw him. He hadn't expected compliance, so he hesitated in bringing up the cell phone and stepped in after me.

It was a bad move. From staring into the sun, he was now in shadow and struggling to adjust his eyesight.

I dropped the phone directory. It landed on the tiled floor with a loud slap. He was startled by the sound, eyes dropping to locate the source. I used a snap kick to his belly and followed it up with an elbow strike to the side of his head. But he was tougher than he looked. He shook it off and tried to shout, and his other hand appeared, bringing up a gun from under his shirt.

I grabbed his face and drove him back against the wall as hard as I could, slamming his head into the plaster. He looked surprised and I felt a spray of saliva against the palm of my hand. He was stunned but he wasn't finished yet and fought against me. I dropped my hand and cupped it under his chin, this time snapping his head backwards as hard as I could. There was a crack and he went limp, and slid down the wall.

I moved back and waited for sounds of alarm within the building. But there was nothing. The dead man had dropped his gun and cell phone. I scooped them up, kicked the gun behind his body and slipped the phone in my pocket.

It was time to go, before his colleagues began to wonder where he was.

I picked up the directory, walked outside and stopped.

Two men in police uniforms were waiting, guns pointing right at me.

Time seemed to slow right down.

They must have seen the dead guy bring me in here and decided to investigate.

'Hey – you're just in time,' I said, making like the angry tourist. 'This bastard tried to rob me!'

One of the cops, skinny and with eyes as dead as a fish, looked past me, squinting into the lobby. I heard the word *muerte* – dead – and his colleague shrugged a pair of fat shoulders like he could care less.

At which point things went from bad to worse.

Fish-eye flicked his gun for me to turn round, then searched me and took my gun, my cell phone and my wallet. He looked at the directory with a frown, then walked over to a battered sedan at the kerb and tossed it through the rear window. He motioned for me to get in the back.

The car was a piece of junk. I'd seen plenty of undercover cops driving worse, but these two weren't undercover; they both wore creased uniforms and the car was a genuine clunker, with bald tyres and a broken tail light.

I climbed in and the two cops slid into the front, watching me carefully. Fish-eye dropped into the passenger seat and turned to face me, his gun held down between the seats where I couldn't get at it without getting shot. His fat pal signalled for me to place my hands out front and had me cuffed in a second. Then he muttered to his colleague and leaned forward to punch out a number on a cell phone in a holder on the dashboard.

The two-way conversation that followed was loud and excited and in words too fast for me to follow. Then he cut the call and took us away from the kerb and along the street.

It didn't matter what they'd said because I knew I was in a jam. First, I figured these two were multi-tasking for the cartel, and had no intention of taking me in to police headquarters. If they had, we'd still be at the lobby, waiting for the usual song-and-dance array of backup vehicles and detectives.

Second, I'd heard a familiar voice in the background during the phone conversation, and I knew I wasn't going anywhere nice.

Parillas. And he hadn't enquired after my health.

I sat back and waited. Fish-eye, the one with the gun, was too watchful for me to try anything, so I pretended to be despondent and frightened, as he would expect. While I was doing that, I inspected the back of the car. It smelled of greasy food, of dog, of stale cigarette, oil and other stuff I didn't want to think about. A bunch of squashed coke cans, tissue and old newspapers littered the floor, and the worn-through remnants of carpet were sticky underfoot.

I shifted the cans about while pretending to get comfortable and tried to figure a way out. Fish-eye grinned at me and muttered something to his pal. They both laughed and I figured they were already planning how to spend the money they'd be paid for bringing me in.

We were soon out of the main streets and into an area near a rail yard, bumping along a squalid backstreet bordered by small workshops and warehouses, most of them empty and fenced off, with just a few old people and kids stopping to watch us roll by. The car seemed to bottom out all the way, the springs beyond salvation, and I felt my spine beginning to bruise as it came into contact with the floor, by-passing what should have been cushions.

I was formulating a plan, which wasn't going too well, when I realized that one of the coke cans wasn't squashed. I rolled it with my foot. It was full.

The car began slowing and the driver seemed to be considering which empty factory lot to turn into. They argued over it for a while, like it mattered.

I felt my gut go cold. They'd had their orders and taking me in wasn't one of them.

They were looking for a place to dump me.

Twelve

We bumped across a stretch of broken sidewalk and through an open chain-link gate into a large concrete yard covered in trash. The building in front of us looked like an old tyre wholesaler, with Goodyear and Dunlop nameplates rusting off the weathered fascia. Stacks of ancient, rotting pallets were piled haphazardly around the yard.

The driver steered down the side of the building towards more pallets, an ancient Portakabin with a busted-in door, and some old dumpsters piled with metal and rubber trash.

'You mind if I have one of these?' I asked, and showed Fish-eye a flattened coke can I'd picked up in my right hand.

He sniggered, showing me bad teeth, and conveyed my request to his fat friend, no doubt laughing about the crazy *Americano* wanting a last suck of an empty can.

What he didn't see was that with my left hand I'd picked up the full one. It was warm and sticky and covered in hairs, and had probably been rolling around in here for days. I gave it a quick shake, then held it out in front of me so he could open it.

Surprised laughter this time, but he dropped the gun in his lap, took the can off me and ripped open the tab, the way you do.

The can exploded in his face, showering both men in warm, sticky foam and coating the roof and windows. It was enough. Bending the flattened can into a blade, I drove the sharp edge into Fish-eye's face, ripping through his cheek and nose. He doubled over, screaming like a girl, his blood splashing across the car. The driver swore and stamped on the brakes, reaching for his holstered weapon.

Too late.

I snatched up Fish-eye's gun and slammed it into the side of his head, then did the same to the driver. Twice. It was a heavy weapon and knocked both men out for the count.

Ten seconds later I was out of the car and dragging both cops into the Portakabin, where I handcuffed them together in a position only their wives would have recognized. Then I retrieved my phone and wallet.

I took a few moments debating what to do. I couldn't be too far from the border, but getting a cab here would be next to impossible – even if I had a number to call. And right now I had to get out of Tijuana and back to the north as fast as I could.

I got in the car and started it up, trying to ignore every surface now covered in sticky coke. The engine sounded like shit and coughed smoke out the back, but if I could ignore the discomfort and the smell, it would do. I took the same way back out of there that we'd come, until I got back on to a main street and saw a sign for San Diego and a schematic of a border control booth.

One thing I hadn't counted on was the volume of cars heading north. We stopped short by a good few hundred metres, at the back end of several lines going nowhere fast, some vehicles overheating. I guess if Parillas had been driving us back into the US, he'd have made a quick call and we'd have by-passed the lines. But I couldn't do that without starting a riot.

Several drivers were out of their cars, lighting up smokes and taking a drink, chatting with their neighbours or making phone calls. Others had their hoods raised, trying to cool the radiators. If you could ignore the undercurrent of frustration and impatience, it was a regular party atmosphere.

I stuffed the cop's gun under the seat, then got out of the car with the directory under my jacket and a coke can in my hand, and sauntered over to join a group of sleepy-eyed North American college kids. They looked as if they'd had a wild time last night and were regretting it. We exchanged nods and I continued on by, and walked right down the line until I saw a pedestrians-only sign.

Ten minutes later, I was in front of a border control agent and showing her my passport. She took one look at me, saw the coke stains on my clothes and my rumpled appearance, and came to the only possible conclusion.

'Have fun in Mexico?' she queried. Her hard face told me the question was rhetorical.

'I got ripped off by a cab driver,' I said, and threw her a sheepish grin.

She didn't buy it, but gave me back my passport and nodded me through. She had seen plenty of men like me before, so another one heading back north with a sad tale to tell was nothing new.

I walked out the other side and instantly spotted Beckwith. He was standing alongside a black SUV with tinted windows, parked in an official bay. Another guy stood alongside him, scratching at one leg. He was a buttoned-up individual in a tan suit and woolly grey socks, and a recent case of sunburn.

I walked over to join them. Beckwith looked surprised and threw a glance behind me as if expecting somebody else.

'What happened? We heard you got separated.'

Parillas, it turned out, was on his way, happily returning to the north by car. He had reported in and told them I was making my own way back as we'd agreed.

I handed Beckwith the phone directory from the hotel. He flicked through a couple of pages, and when he saw some pen marks against names and phone numbers, he knew instantly what it was.

The other man said nothing, but watched carefully.

'His name's Mr Black,' said Beckwith casually, and walked me away a few paces. 'He's along as an observer.'

'Mr Black.' I gave him a look. 'Really?'

'It's what it says in his passport.'

'Is he as British as he looks?'

Beckwith didn't say, but the slow blink of his eyes was answer enough.

I let it go and gave him a rapid de-brief. He wasn't happy at what I told him; in fact he looked as if he wanted to take out a gun and shoot me on the spot.

'What the fuck are you saying?' he grated, trying not to let the Brit hear. 'Parillas is with the Tijuanas? I don't buy it. You must be mistaken.'

I didn't bother fighting him on it; he was feeling bruised by the possibility that one of his men had gone bad. If true, it reflected on him as lead intelligence officer and the DEA as a whole. Having a foreign observer along to witness the fact wasn't helping any.

'You didn't know he was born in Tijuana?' I said.

He shook his head, but it was obvious by the set of his jaw that he'd already begun to put pieces together and was building a jigsaw. Either someone had made a huge error of judgement selecting Parillas for this job, or Parillas had developed a recent change of heart about his career choice. The final confirmation was when I took out my cell phone and handed it to him.

'What's this?' he muttered.

I showed him. I'd filmed Parillas on the cell's camera from the time he'd emerged from the cartel's SUV to him dropping an arm around the lead gunman's shoulders. That and the way they were grinning at each other was enough to confirm that he wasn't being coerced in any way and knew the gunman a lot better than he should.

Beckwith climbed into the SUV to view the footage in private. I stayed on the outside with Mr Black, who nodded but said nothing. Beckwith didn't need us seeing his embarrassment. He must have checked it three times, the expression on his face going darker with each showing. Then he made a call and two minutes later, a couple of armed border agents appeared and hovered nearby.

It must have been tough, finding out who had been feeding the Tijuanas with inside information. But he wasn't going to try covering it up.

We waited in silence until a familiar white Land Cruiser nosed out from the border crossing and slid into a bay further along. We watched as Parillas climbed out and sauntered across, playing Mr Cool.

When he saw the two border agents walking towards him, he didn't seem concerned. Then he saw me behind the car and stopped dead, his mouth hanging open.

When the two agents cuffed and searched him, he simply looked sick and made no effort to protest. For him the deception was over.

Thirteen

Picking up on a tail is never easy. Forget what they tell you in books or films. The shop window trick is only good in a deserted street with few pedestrians. Too much vehicle or pedestrian movement is unhelpful clutter. And in the area around 31st and Fifth Avenue in New York, clutter is the name of the game.

The other problem is, serious tails rarely work alone; they operate using a box or leap-frog formation with up to four or more people, some on foot, others mobile, constantly swapping over, their movements steered by a controller. That makes the job of counter-surveillance pretty tough; you just don't know where the next watcher is coming from.

Unless the person following you actually wants you to know he's there.

The man behind me made himself known on at least three occasions before I got the message. But just in case I'd picked up a genuine head case with time to spare, I made him work at it a bit longer before I gave up on the game. I was intrigued.

He was dressed smart, in a sports jacket and pants, good walking shoes. English, at a guess, which was more than interesting. I put him somewhere in his late fifties, maybe older, but fit, with combed-back greying hair and a slightly jowly face. In spite of his age he had no trouble staying with me, even when I upped the rate a little and jigged across a couple of intersections to string him out. He seemed to be at home in the area, knowing when to stay on one side and when to cross to take advantage of the traffic flow.

I finally stepped into a Starbucks on Fifth and E34th, and watched him through the steamed-up windows as he paused to study the front of a Korean electronics store on the corner. Then he turned and strolled across the street on the lights. By the way he was moving, he knew there was no need to hurry.

It told me he knew where to find me if I managed to lose him.

He caught my eye as he walked by, and I smiled to show him I knew. Then I went to the counter and ordered two daily brews.

He was sitting at a corner table when I turned round, checking out the other customers. He'd chosen a seat away from the crowd and looked very relaxed.

Even more interesting.

I got sugar and paper napkins and walked over, putting the coffees down and drawing up a chair.

'I'm not sure what I should call you,' he said, inspecting the coffee. 'Is Portman your real name?' He smiled at me and I got the impression of someone who meant me no ill will. Maybe it was the cultured English accent, firm but non-aggressive.

'Portman's fine,' I said. 'Who are you?'

'Tom Vale.' He stirred sugar into his mug. 'Nate Sweetman told me about you.'

It took a second to recall where I'd heard the name. Sweetman. Engineer. Bogotá. Nearly kidnapped. Nice guy, if over-chatty.

'Do I know him?'

'You should – you saved his life. He nearly got FARC'd.' He smiled to show he had a sense of humour.

'Just like that? He told you?'

'We have a family connection. He needed to talk to somebody about what happened.'

'Why you? You know about stuff like that?'

'A little.' He sipped his coffee and looked pleasantly surprised, then sipped again. I let him do his thing and waited. While we'd been going through the preliminaries, I'd been watching the street and the door, checking out passers-by and customers. None that looked like they were with this Mr Vale, though.

'You also know about stuff like that,' he said eventually.

'You think?'

'Well, starting with Nate, who's a very good judge of character, let's look at the facts: you walked into a kidnap attempt and calmly disarmed one kidnapper, shot two with the first man's gun and put down a fourth outside and took his vehicle.' He looked at me with a lifted eyebrow. 'You don't mess about, do you?'

'No point,' I replied. 'Have you seen what they do to people they don't like? They use chainsaws.'

He grunted. 'I admit I thought Nate was hallucinating when he said you paid his hotel bill on the way out. But the hotel confirmed it. Neat. Cool under fire. Which makes me think you're more than just a good Samaritan or a bystander who got lucky.'

'You said "starting with".'

'Pardon?'

'A few seconds ago, when I asked who told you, you said "starting with Nate". It implies you spoke to others.'

'Oh.' He raised a hand in apology. 'Well, I know you don't work for us, so I ran a quick check on other agencies. The only official Portman I found is a senior admin supervisor with the NSA – but she's a busty fifty-year-old with two children and a sick Chihuahua. If it hadn't been for a stroke of luck my people wouldn't have found you so easily. They're very good, but there are limits.'

'Your people?'

'I'll come to that. My main question is, what does this mystery man, this Mr Portman, who pops out of nowhere and disrupts a kidnapping so effortlessly, what does he *do*, exactly?'

I shook my head. 'You tell me.'

He nodded. 'Fair point. I just wanted to gauge your reaction, that's all. The fact that you haven't run screaming into the street is a good sign.' He leaned forward and said, 'I'm with SIS, otherwise known as MI6, London.' He sighed. 'I can't tell you how rarely I ever get to say that to strangers. It's almost a confessional moment.'

'Bless you.'

'Thank you. I've spent my life working in intelligence gathering – mostly as a field controller, running operations. Now I've shown you mine, it's your turn.'

He was either the best fantasist I'd ever met, and a hell of a good liar, or he was telling the truth. It presented me with a dilemma. I could stand up and walk out of here and probably never see him again. Or I could find out more.

I hate mysteries.

'You've got my name, my address. The rest is simple: I'm

a shadow. I run security, evaluate risks and where needed, provide hard cover in potentially hostile situations.'

'Hard cover. Like Bogotá.'

'That was unplanned. But like that.'

'Up close?'

'Not always. Some situations don't allow it. I prefer to work at a distance.' His expression told me he knew what I was saying. Staying back, I get to see more of what's going on around a target. It's easier to intervene that way. Sneaky, too.

'Anywhere?'

'I travel wherever a client needs me and I rarely stay anywhere for long, unless it's to recover from a hot situation, which happens from time to time. Actors call it "resting".'

'So you're a kind of watchman. With attitude.'

'Yes.'

He gave a hint of a smile. 'Was that what you were doing down in Tijuana?'

Fourteen

Forget about Vale being a fantasist; he knew too much. 'How do you know about Tijuana?'

'I lied a moment ago. Occupational hazard, I'm afraid. James Beckwith told us as much as he could without betraying state or departmental secrets.'

'Us? You mean Mr Black?' The guy with sunburn in the SUV.

'Yes, I'm sorry about that. He's an analyst from our Washington office. He was the nearest man I could use in a hurry.'

I let it go. Vale was merely doing his job.

'Beckwith was very unhappy,' he continued in a chatty manner, 'about the Tijuana situation.'

'Professional embarrassment,' I said. 'One of his men went rogue.'

'That explains it. He was impressed with you, however; said you did an excellent job.'

'I try to please.' Beckwith hadn't said anything to me at the time, but he'd pounced on the telephone directory readily enough. I was guessing the late Senor Achevar had found a simple way of passing along information if anything were to happen to him. If you want to highlight names and phone numbers, what better way than to place discreet dots against each one in a telephone directory?

'He mentioned some collateral damage. A certain Mexican group isn't too happy about the results, apparently. They lost an employee and a number of others are now under surveillance.'

'Yes.'

He chewed that over for a moment, then asked, 'What's your current situation? Are you under contract?'

'Not right this minute.' I was between jobs. It got that way sometimes.

'Good. Are there any places you won't work?'

'Not many.' This was beginning to feel like an interview. 'Do I need to write out a resumé?'

'No. I think I have all the information I need.'

'Who else spoke about me?' I wasn't too bothered, but in my business, loose talk can definitely cost lives.

'I'm not at liberty to mention any names. But they both gave you a clean bill of health.'

They. 'Government agencies?'

He smiled. 'All good people, I promise.'

I had to be satisfied with that. 'So what are you looking for?'

'Earlier, you called yourself a shadow. That's exactly what I need. A shadow. Someone adept at staying in the background.'

'Go on.'

'I need you to accompany two of our people on an assignment.'

'Our people?'

'I'll come to that later. I need your agreement first.'

He was being very cautious. 'Is this in hostile territory?'

'Very.'

'Where?'

'I'll come to that, too. Hopefully, it won't come to anything, but I need you to make sure nothing impacts on our people.'

Impact. A word used often in my business, and rarely with pleasant consequences.

'Don't you Brits have specialists for that kind of operation – the Increment or whatever you currently call them?' Most governments have specialist teams for delicate operations. Some are part of the military but not always current serving personnel. The US Navy Special Warfare Development Group (DEVGRU) Seal Team Six is regarded as the elite of the elite, along with the CIA's Special Activities Division. I wasn't sure about the British SIS, or if the Increment had been overtaken by a new designation, but I knew they had one.

'This is not something any of our in-house people could deal with without attracting attention.'

I was intrigued. Vale had already convinced me that he worked for British Intelligence, which implied that he had access to plenty of resources and personnel. Yet here he was looking for an outsider.

'So if anybody goes down, there's no rescue plan.'

'I'm afraid not.'

'Is this deniable?' Deniable meant that if an operative's cover was blown or they got into a bind while on a mission, he or she was on their own. It usually applied where the fall-out from any government launching something on foreign soil would be too loud and messy, such as covert assignments involving spies or black ops teams.

'Our two people will have official status, that's to say, Foreign Office personnel engaged on a mercy mission. But you won't. For various reasons, I need someone so far past deniable they don't even exist.' He stared hard at me with eyes that were beyond cold. 'That means nobody – not even the two individuals involved, unless absolutely unavoidable – must get a sniff that you're out there.'

This sounded deeply personal to Vale and I wondered why. If what he had told me was true, he was an SIS official, aware of, or compliant with, a major operation being undertaken on foreign soil, involving the insertion of personnel. Yet he was running his own side operation off the books, with no traces, no footprints, nothing.

It was a dangerous thing to be doing. So why?

He read my mind. 'I want to protect one of the officers involved but I can't do it officially.'

'Is it illegal?'

'Not the official assignment, no. That has full sanction at the highest level. But I believe it's risky for the potential return. What I'm planning is probably illegal – although I haven't run it past any of our legal experts. I doubt they would approve.'

'I see. What happens if your colleagues find out what you're doing?'

'I would lose my job and in all likelihood serve a prison term.' He looked as pragmatic as he sounded. He'd weighed up his chances and decided to go ahead.

'Is this a UK-only thing?'

'CIA has been briefed on the main operation, but they can't be seen to help. No US citizens are involved. Only one of their officers knows about this, though, although not the full detail. He was one of the people who advised me on your background.'

CIA. I always get nervous around them. Some are very good people, but they use a lot of contractors like me, many of whom are former insiders who decided to go freelance. Given time and certain incentives, some of them have been known to go a little off the reservation when it comes to loyalties.

'Which one?'

'Scheider. He's their London Deputy Station Chief.'

Never heard of him. 'OK. What's so special about your officer that he needs my help? I take it it's personal?'

Vale pushed his coffee away. 'It's not a he, but a she.' He cleared his throat. 'I've made many decisions in the past, Mr Portman, that have involved dangers for field operatives. But I never sent an officer or an asset out that I didn't consider up to the situation. In my opinion this operation is all wrong. It's predicated solely on success and the career ripples for the man running it, without thought for the personnel. I can't put my finger on it, but something about it doesn't feel right.'

'And the field operative?'

'They'll be throwing her away and there's not a thing I can do to stop it.' He blinked. 'Officially, at least.'

Fifteen

The place got busier with the noon crowd, so we walked, taking the quieter streets. It would have been easier to be somewhere inside, but Vale confessed to being a spook of the old school and liked being in the open.

By the time he got through explaining the background, we'd reached the edge of Central Park and I had a fair measure of what it involved. It was the same with military commanders sending out men into the field: some were good to go, others less so. But there were times when you had to use what you had . . . or stand back and watch events unfold. For Vale, this was one of those times. He had no direct responsibility or right of veto over the officer involved, but he wanted to give her a little background 'assist'.

Which was where I came in.

'Why me?' I said, as we crossed a wide expanse of grass.

'You have the right skills.'

'But you don't know me.'

'True. But I know men like you. I've been working with them all my life.' He stopped. 'Why did you help Nate? You didn't have to.'

I wasn't sure how to answer that one.

'I walked into it. I couldn't back away.'

'Balls. I know your type: you never leave a hotel room in a hot zone without checking the corridors first; you never go to bed without having an escape route and you always have access to a spare set of documents, cash or credit to get you out of a jam. Same with walking in the street; you check and double-check. You've been doing it ever since I first spotted you. It's standard operational procedure. In Bogotá you saw what was happening and still you went out and did what you deemed necessary.'

I shrugged. He seemed to have all the answers.

'You saw a situation,' he continued, 'and took decisive

action. You weighed up your chances and made it happen.' He grunted. 'Years ago, I'd like to think I would have done the same. But I know I wouldn't – not every time. It's why I'm still around.'

'You think I've got a death wish?'

'God, no. Suicide jockeys are no good to me; I need a survivor.' He resumed walking. 'You might have a host of inner demons for all I know, but I doubt suicide is one of them. You're too motivated. What happened – did you lose someone?'

I didn't want to answer that. But Vale was perceptive. A light was gleaming in his eyes; he'd seen something in my face.

'I'm right. Who was it – a loved one? A colleague?'

He could ask all day; I wasn't going to tell him.

'A principal, then. Somebody you were charged with protecting.' He pursed his lips and leaned across the table. 'My advice? Get it out; talk about it. If you don't, it'll eat you up from inside. I've seen it happen.'

'Speaking from experience?' It was rude, but he was pushing too hard. Some things are simply not up for discussion.

It was his turn to shrug. 'Very well. Let's leave it.'

'Why are you,' I asked, to change the conversation, 'so against this operation?'

'Simple. Moresby – the man running it. He's going blindly into this without questioning exactly why the other side is so keen to make the contact. It can't be for money – they're getting plenty of that elsewhere.'

'But?'

'They're up to something and I wish I knew what it was.'

'All right,' I said eventually. He still hadn't told me precisely where this was happening, but I was intrigued. I knew there would come a point where he would be unable to say more, where the information would become too sensitive unless I was all the way in. For now, though, it was enough.

'You're in?'

'Almost. What if I get knocked over by a bus?'

'You'll be a statistic.' His voice was matter of fact. 'An unidentifiable casualty of poor road conditions. The one thing I won't do is come to get you.'

'Fair enough.'

He looked keenly at me and we stopped walking. 'What does that mean?'

'I said fair enough. I already work that way; I rely on nobody to pick my face off the floor. Same with exit routes, safe houses and transport.'

'Supplies?'

'Weapons, clothes, documents – anything within reason – I get my own. But I will need money.' It was simpler that way; I didn't have to rely on official channels or supply lines for equipment, and had greater control over any footprints I left behind. And I trusted most of the suppliers I'd been using more than any faceless government department.

'As you wish. The money I can get you, fed through an untraceable offshore fund. Draw it as you see fit.'

'How long do I have before kick-off?'

'Five days. The project's got the green light and the two people are getting in place right now. You'll need to move quickly.'

'OK. Where does all this happen?'

'Precisely? We're not sure yet. But the first jumping-off point we've been given is Nairobi. Our people are to arrive there and will be met and taken to the RV. Our analysts believe the best place for any meeting will be on the coast near the Kenya-Somalia border.'

'Does this operation involve pirates?'

He looked surprised. But it didn't take rocket science; there was very little in that area of Africa other than Somali pirates and some extremist groups and militias. Oh, and al-Qaeda.

'Pirates are involved, yes. But there are others with wider interests. You've heard of al-Shabaab?'

'Of course.' Al Shabaab was an extremist group with links to al-Qaeda, currently said to control large parts of southern Somalia and even into the capital, Mogadishu. They had been pushed back in recent years by the concerted efforts of the Somali Transitional Government assisted by other African forces, but were still a problem, using bombs and bullets to make their point.

'We believe a splinter group of that organization represents the other side of this meeting. They have a large measure of control over any movements in the area, in spite of recent set-backs, so it stands to reason that any discussions or meetings with foreign elements like ours will have been vetted and cleared by somebody with influence. I'll give you the coordinates as soon as I get them. If you get into the region beforehand and sit tight, you'll be in a good position to move in and monitor the situation.'

Somalia. It wasn't the easiest place for a white man to blend in, let alone be invisible. Stretched along the coast north of Kenya, it was a poor country with little reliable infrastructure, and freedom of movement wouldn't be easy. But I'd operated in similar situations before and walked out with everything intact. I was about to mention the problem of moving around when he handed me a memory stick.

'This holds as much detail as I've been able to put together, including maps, road networks, such as they are, and the verified locations of local police and army units, including Kenyan Defence Force supply routes. There's a photograph of the officer who's going in and one or two of the few known faces on the other side. Our officer will have an escort. He's a fully trained close protection specialist, but he's mainly for window dressing.'

'Why?'

'The opposition expect it. It's the one concession Moresby got right. If we sent in a woman by herself, they'd smell a rat.'

'Poor bastard.'

'Yes.'

If things went wrong, the bodyguard wouldn't be able to do much but stand there and pray. No way would the other side allow him in armed, and he'd be outnumbered ten to one at every step. In such situations, it's the bodyguard who gets taken out first. I hoped they were paying him a big bonus.

'Also on the stick is a name and phone number – a local personal contact of mine named Piet De Bont. He's not part of SIS, but he knows the region better than most. He used to be with the South African National Defence Force. He quit to work for animals instead of humans and is now a ranger with the Kenyan Wildlife Service based in Mombasa.' He stared at me. 'He's a good man, but don't count on him running any rescue operation; he'll get you in and out again, but that's all I can ask him to do.'

'I'll bear that in mind. So what's your officer going there for?'

'There are five hostages being held further inland. We don't have a fix on the location and they keep moving them. Two of them are UN officials, one Dutch, one British. So far the Somalis don't know that. They've been there for two months now, shuffled from camp to camp, constantly on the move. We suspect they've been traded through three separate gangs so far, each time at a profit. There's a real danger that the next trade will be their last – to an al-Qaeda cell in the north.'

He wasn't exaggerating the danger; any time al-Qaeda got their hands on a westerner, especially one who was newsworthy, they were quick to make it into a propaganda issue. And that wasn't usually good for the hostage.

UN personnel would be regarded as prime meat.

'We have a chance of negotiating their release,' he continued, 'but it's a slim one. Two weeks ago our office in Nairobi was approached by a man calling himself Xasan. We know that's not his real name – he operates under several aliases. He's a go-between acting for Somali pirates and other extremists. He claims he can negotiate the release of the hostages, but it has to be done on the exchange of gold and face-to-face with the gang holding them. Their leader insists on it. Xasan says this gang has access to other hostages and can act as intermediaries to gain their release, too.'

'If you pay enough.'

'Correct.'

'How much do you trust this Xasan?'

Vale shrugged. 'No more than I trust any of them. He's been around a while and known to have secured the release of several hostages and even a couple of ships. Frankly, we're ready to take any avenue we're offered to get the UN officials back. Moresby and those above him are hoping that if we can start getting a trade going, it could lead to more releases. It will cost us, but that's better than dead bodies floating in the Indian Ocean.'

'And you really think your officer will get anywhere with

these people?' I didn't want to burst Vale's bubble more than I had to, but I wondered if he or Moresby were aware that the Somalis don't negotiate with women.

His next words dispelled that idea.

'That's the puzzle. According to Nairobi, Xasan's instructions were that the gang leader doesn't trust male officials. He thinks they all work for the CIA. It's crazy, I know, but the word is, it's a woman negotiator or there's no deal.'

Sixteen

I checked into the Royal Court in Mombasa and took a few minutes to get my bearings. It was late in the evening, and crossing time zones can be disconcerting, and making rapid decisions on the hoof when you're travel-weary is risky. I drank two bottles of water I'd bought at the airport, then checked my satellite phone for a connection. It all looked good.

Vale had asked for regular reports, but only if circumstances allowed; he was experienced enough to know that operating in hot zones doesn't always permit the casual use of a cell phone as if you were on the street corner back home.

I gave his number a try without checking the time in the UK. He'd be there, I was certain of that.

'I'm at first base,' I said when he answered. It took a while for the voices to travel, and the thing to get used to is the delay when waiting for an answer. It makes for awkward conversations at first, especially when under the stress of an operation.

'Good.' His voice sounded thin. 'You met the wildlife man yet?'

'No. He'll be here in the morning.' There had been a message waiting for me at the front desk. Vale's contact was making his way into Mombasa from his base at one of the national parks. Vale was wary of using names, so we were going to be speaking in indirect terms unless absolutely unavoidable.

'The two travellers are on their way,' he said. 'They'll meet

up with the middle man tomorrow before moving on. As soon
as I know where and when, I'll let you know.'

We ended the conversation and I went downstairs and got a
cab from the rank outside. The driver looked bored and lacking
in curiosity, but glad of a fare. I gave him an address out near
Kilindini Harbour, to the west of the city, and he nodded without
comment and set off.

Mombasa was frantic with pedestrians and traffic, most of it
intermingling in a way that would have had London or New
York's traffic commissioners pulling out their hair by the
handful. It was noisy and colourful and hot, and I was glad I
didn't have to be out there in the middle of it. I had too much
to do.

My destination was a small commercial unit a short hop from
the docks. The area was dark and badly lit, a sharp contrast to
the city centre, which was so full of life. It had a brooding,
alien atmosphere that didn't feel right, even from the inside of
the cab. Groups of men were gathered in doorways, smoking
large, flabby cigarettes and drinking *Yokozuna* or *chang'aa* – the
local illicit and deadly brews of alcohol – from plastic bottles.

They watched us go by with an intensity that had the driver
rolling his eyes at me in the mirror and shaking his head.

'Bad men, sir,' he muttered. 'Very bad.'

'Don't worry about them,' I told him.

'You sure this is where you wanna be, boss?' He turned into
a narrow street between lines of ancient cargo warehouses, dark
and fobidding. 'Not good here, y'know?' The breath whistled
between his teeth as he stopped the car outside a premises
bearing the name Bera Wharf Trading Co. I could feel the fear
coming off him in waves and hoped he wasn't going to drive
off the moment I got out.

I took out some notes and dropped them on the passenger
seat alongside him. It wasn't quite enough to cover the gas, but
enough to keep his foot on the brake until I'd done what I'd
come here for. I showed him some bigger notes for good measure.
'This is yours if you wait.'

He rolled his eyes again and nodded and I got out and
approached the building.

The man who answered the door was as thin as a fisherman's

pole, with a neat goatee beard and half-glasses. He was dressed in a long, white shirt and tight pants, and the overall effect was of an academic stork. The name I'd been given was Ita Khaban, although I doubted it was his real one. According to the man who'd supplied me with his details, part of a network of professionals I used, he could source anything I needed, right up to a Stinger surface-to-air missile, given enough time and money.

Fortunately, my needs didn't yet involve starting a small war.

We exchanged pleasantries, which meant I gave him a name which he acknowledged with a blink of his eyes. Then he stuck his head out the door and checked the street both ways. It looked like he probably did this on a regular basis.

Khaban noticed the cab. 'That is your driver, sir?'

'Yes.'

He turned and called a name. Another man appeared through a doorway behind him. He was a taller, younger version of Khaban, only bigger in the shoulders and carrying a nasty looking sawn-off shotgun.

'My son, Benjamin,' Khaban explained. 'He will stay by the car. There should be no problems.' The way he smiled at me was also a warning not to try anything.

Benjamin stepped past me and stood outside the door, eyeing the street. Khaban left him to it and led me inside, bolting the door behind me.

The area we were in was little more than a metal workshop and storeroom combined, the air heavy with the smell of oil and grease and metal. He sat me down in a tiny office holding a desk covered in paperwork, much of it yellowed by age, and an old photograph of a young British Queen Elizabeth on the wall. He had already received a list of what I needed. It wasn't much, but he looked happy enough.

'I have everything you requested,' he said, his voice a cultured whisper, businessman to businessman. I handed him a folded canvas sports bag purchased from a stall near the hotel, and he poured me some tea and left me to sip it while he disappeared into the workshop.

When he returned a few minutes later, the sports bag was no longer empty.

'If you return the items in good condition,' he said softly, 'I will buy them back from you.'

'At a discount?'

'Of course.'

I checked the contents while he watched, then paid him in cash and said goodbye.

'Thank you, sir,' he whispered before calling his son back inside. 'A pleasure doing business with you.'

Seventeen

SIS officer Angela Pryce stared at the ceiling of the British Airways Boeing 777 and shivered in the blast of air-conditioning. She was impatient for take-off. With an eight-hour flight ahead of her to Nairobi, Kenya, she didn't expect to sleep much. Somehow, leaving London's cooler climate for the hotter atmosphere of Kenya's coast north of Mombasa, where she had been told the temperature was currently topping 31°C, didn't have the attraction it should have done.

Beside her, in the aisle seat, Doug Tober already had his eyes closed and was breathing easily. If the former Special Forces sergeant had any doubts about what lay ahead of them, he wasn't showing it. She hoped his calmness was real and not put on for her benefit. His role was purely close protection, although neither of them was under any illusions about how limited that might be where they were going.

The engines wound up and talk in the cabin began to fall away. A luggage locker fell open with a bang, and a stewardess rushed to close it. A child cried out somewhere near the rear, and across the aisle a very large woman in Kenyan national dress began to pray loudly, drawing responses from those eager to share in requests for a safe take-off and a safer landing.

Angela glanced through the rain-spotted window. The airport buildings looked distant and cold. It reminded her of being sent away to school as a girl, when part of her wanted to leap off the train and run home, while the other part couldn't wait to see what lay ahead for the new term.

She shivered again. She was dressed in a lightweight jacket and skirt, and shoes suitable for all terrains. Since nobody had appeared too certain where she and Tober might end up, she had decided on basic, interchangeable clothes, with spare trousers in case she needed to observe a degree of conservatism for local sensibilities.

She closed her eyes and went over her briefing, trying to pick out potential highlights in the detail. It was no more comforting than listening to the engines winding up and waiting for the first thrust of power to punch her in the back. But it offered a useful distraction for a few minutes.

The briefing room in SIS headquarters at Vauxhall Cross had been busy with maps, schedules, photos and details of the mission ahead. Talk had been muted but firm, concentrating solely on the mission. Nobody, Colin Moresby, Operations Director 4, had stressed, was underestimating the potential diffi-culties that lay ahead. She would be to all intents and purposes alone, apart from Tober, and certainly once they left Mombasa, would be beyond any immediate assistance. But there was nothing they could do about that. Assurances had been given by the other side and that was all they could expect.

'Any show of force on land or offshore,' he had stressed, eyeing her carefully, 'will be construed as aggression, according to Xasan. And they control the region closely enough to detect any intrusions.' That meant no covert backup from units of Special Forces ready to crash in on demand if things got sticky. It was a sobering reminder of what she had undertaken.

She had nodded, aware that they were taking on trust the words of a man with a dubious, if virtually unknown history, who was known for working with the Somali pirates and effecting trade-offs of hostages for money. The knowledge that he had successfully closed more than one such deal, with the safe return of people and ships, was to some, a justifiable claim to credibility. To others it was like approaching a street-corner moneylender rather than a bank. But in the present circumstances, it was all they had.

'We need those people back,' Moresby had continued

smoothly, 'especially the UN personnel. If they get moved further north, they'll be in the hands of extremists and beyond our help.' He meant al-Qaeda, but nobody wanted to hear that name. 'Once gone, I fear we'll lose them until someone, some-where, wants a substantial deal . . . or a huge publicity coup. We can't let that happen.'

'What are the chances,' Angela had queried, 'of them finding out that they're holding two UN people?'

Moresby had looked at Bill Cousins, Controller Africa, to answer that question. 'Higher than we'd like,' Cousins replied. 'Both of them have appeared on UN websites, and both have their photos on the internet if anybody cares to trawl through the archives or check out current photos of personnel in the field. We know al-Qaeda has access to IT personnel and equipment, so they could get lucky and identify them any day. We have to move quickly.'

'We also know,' Moresby added, 'that they are increasingly trawling the net for details on all western hostages, to determine their status and value. If they identify any with position, family or the slightest degree of importance, the price goes up.'

The briefing had continued, going over the plans with great care.

She and Tober were to fly to Nairobi, where they would make contact with a man named Ashkir Xasan. He was the first step in a chain of contacts and agreements going back two weeks – probably longer. It would culminate, if all went well, in the eventual release of the hostages. Xasan would take Angela and Tober via Mombasa to a point on the Kenya-Somali border, where they would meet a group headed by a clan chief called Yusuf Musa. It probably wasn't his real name any more than Xasan's was his, but that was beside the point. Knowing a man's real name in a game like hostage taking was usually the least of one's worries.

'Any queries, Miss Pryce?' Moresby was looking at her, his eyes blank. She felt like standing up and saying, Yes, this whole bloody idea is insane and I don't want to go because I'm terrified we'll both end up dead. But she didn't. She could do this. She'd been trained and could handle herself in crisis situations. And in doing so, would enhance her career prospects in SIS. All she had to do was what most field operatives hoped to accomplish every time they were sent out: get through it successfully and come back in one piece.

'No, sir,' she said, and wondered what Tom Vale would have thought. She also wondered why he hadn't been in on the briefing. 'No questions.'

Eighteen

I recognized De Bont as soon as he walked into the foyer of the hotel, if only because he stood out among the dark suits and floral dresses. He was of medium height, heavy in the shoulders and chest, like a weightlifter, with rust-coloured hair in a brush cut, a spiky moustache and pink, sunburned skin. He was wearing a tan shirt and shorts, which on him looked like some sort of uniform.

He saw me, hesitated for a moment, then came over to where I was sitting.

'Mr Portman?' He held out a hand the size of a small shovel. 'I'm Piet. Hope I'm not late.' His accent was pure Afrikaans, with a faintly harsh rumble in the throat.

'No. Shall we get a drink?' It wasn't yet fully hot outside, which suited me fine, but the air was dry and gritty, and making my eyes sting. I nodded at the bar, which was full of a convention of businessmen and women. 'We need somewhere more private to talk.'

'Sure. I know a nice bar along the street here. Air-con and privacy guaranteed.' He turned on one heel and led the way out of the hotel, into the noisy, traffic-filled atmosphere of central Mombasa. Out here was a different world to the one in the hotel, and we were soon lost among a mass of humanity, honking vehicles and the smell of a busy city. If we'd had the time, I would have enjoyed the atmosphere.

We found the bar and settled at a table to the rear. It was gloomy, cool and deserted save for a barman, the air heavy with the smell of stale tobacco and alcohol. The barman wandered over and handed us a drinks menu without a word. Piet ordered beer and I had coffee. I needed to be awake for the next two days at least and didn't need alcohol to get in the way.

'Tom Vale mentioned you,' I began, 'and said you could help me move around. He said he'd settle the bill.'

He nodded but looked guarded. 'Is Tom still keeping the empire safe?' It was a hint that he knew what Vale's job was. Up close I realized he was older than I'd first thought – somewhere in his early fifties at least – and he'd probably been around the block a few times if he'd served with the South African National Defence Force.

'I don't work for Vale. Just doing a job for him.'

'Sub-contractor, huh? I did that for a while, after the army. Paid well enough but the conditions were shit and there was no pension. Where is it you want to go?'

I told him. The details on the data stick Vale had given me showed a map of the very north-eastern corner of Kenya, where it butted up against the Somali border, about 150 kilometres north of where we were now sitting. The nearest Kenyan town of any note was Kiunga, on the coast. Further north and it was into what Vale had referred to as pirate country.

Somalia.

Piet grunted. 'Long way to go for easy trouble. I'm guessing this is covert, right?'

'Yes.'

'You planning on stopping long?'

'I don't know yet. I hope not. It depends on others.'

He stared at me without expression. 'I figure. How soon do you want to get there?'

'Today would be good. Are the roads passable?'

'The roads are shite, my friend. They're mostly rock, ruts and rubble, and sandstone the rest of the time. They run out, in any case, before you get near that place, so it's overland and tough going. It'd take a couple of days – that's if you didn't break down or run into trouble.'

'What kind of trouble?'

'Poachers, bandits . . . trucks on the wrong side of the road driven by guys high on booze or drugs who don't give a shit. It's not an easy place to travel. Does it have to be today?'

'By this evening – tomorrow morning at the latest.'

His eyebrows lifted and he sank some beer. 'Forget the roads, then.' He checked his watch, which was sunk into the skin of his wrist. 'We can get a flight to Malindi up the coast in a couple of hours, then fly into the Kiunga area this afternoon.'

'Is there a local strip?' I hadn't seen anything on the maps Vale had supplied, but landing strips were often nothing more than a beaten stretch of track or grass cleared of rocks and shrubs. In fact, other than deserted beaches and some dubious tracks, the whole area looked like nothing but scrub, acacia trees, thorn bush and rock-strewn patches of rolling grassland, with palm trees bristling along the coastal stretch. 'I'd rather not turn up where everybody can see me.'

He smiled in a knowing way. 'That's how I work, too, which is lucky for you. Did Tom tell you what I do?'

'Vaguely.' I was guessing as a wildlife ranger he was accustomed to not making his presence too obvious, especially when tracking poachers.

'Good. I'll fill you in as we go.' He drained his glass and stood up. 'You got everything you need?'

'I have.'

Nineteen

Angela Pryce took a dislike to Xasan the moment she set eyes on him. He was short and rotund, with a curly black beard peppered with grey, and lightly tinted spectacles that veiled most of the expression in his eyes. He also smiled too much and seemed intent on staring openly at her legs and chest. When he wasn't doing that, he addressed most of his comments to Doug Tober, who listened but said little. It seemed to be the way Xasan wanted to conduct things.

They were seated in the bar of the Crowne Plaza Hotel in Upperhill, Nairobi, where Xasan had requested their initial meeting in a last-minute email message. Three other men entered the bar with him, two in front and one behind. They took separate tables, but kept their eyes on the two SIS operatives. They were young and slim and neatly dressed in short-sleeved shirts and pants, with large gold-coloured watches on their wrists, and could have passed for casual visitors. But to the trained eye they were too watchful, too intense. The waiters, Angela noted, stayed well away.

She recognized the game, though: it was designed to intimidate, a gentle show of force from the outset.

'Jesus,' Tober growled softly. 'What a bunch of cowboys.'

Angela agreed. The taxi ride from the international airport had been just long enough for Xasan's people to check if the SIS officers had company or not, so this display was simply theatrics.

'Welcome to Nairobi,' Xasan murmured, his voice gentle and measured, as he stopped in front of their table. 'I hope we may conclude our business in a satisfactory way to all concerned. May I see some ID, please?'

They took out their passports and slid them across the table, already aware that arguing wasn't an option. Xasan picked them up and flicked through the pages, comparing photographs with faces. He nodded slowly, giving Tober a more studied look, then returned them, adding, 'Excellent. It is an honour to have members of the Secret Intelligence Service here all the way from London's Vauxhall Cross. It is well placed by the river, is it not? Very scenic.' He waved a vague hand around. 'As indeed is this city.'

'What's the agenda?' said Angela. She wanted to cut short any idea Xasan might have of a guided tour. She knew that simple etiquette meant they were hardly in a position to make demands, but any show of easy compliance would be seen as weakness. Besides, any intel they got now about where they were headed might be useful later.

'As soon as we get word, we go from here to Ras Kamboni. You know this place?'

Tober remained silent, save for a flicker of an eyebrow.

Angela said, 'Isn't that in Somalia?'

'That is correct. You have done your research.'

Angela didn't like it. 'There was no mention before of having to cross the border.'

Xasan shrugged. 'The borders here are . . . flexible, you understand. It is just a few kilometres, that is all. It is nothing. Nobody will notice and the police do not go out that far. Trust me. The man you will meet is anxious that all goes well. You need have no fears.'

'I'm pleased to hear it.'

Xasan didn't react to that. 'There is a place to the north of Kamboni called Dhalib. Beyond that is a house on the coast road, built by an Italian industrialist many years ago. It is comfortable and right on the beach, with very pleasant views. Also –' he wagged a finger – 'absolutely safe for our honoured guests.' He placed his hands together. 'A suitable place for a meeting such as this – a meeting, I hope, that will form the basis for many others.'

Money-grabbing bastard, thought Angela, and stared blankly back at him. No doubt he would be doing well out of any deal struck between the UK, the US and the pirates, with a percentage sticking to his fingers on the way through.

'As soon as you get word?' Tober asked. 'What does that mean?'

Xasan's smile didn't shift. 'We must be patient, Mr Tober. I regret to inform you that there is a slight delay in proceedings.'

'What kind of delay?'

'The gentleman you are meeting has been unavoidably held up by bad weather to the north of here. He sends his most sincere apologies but there is nothing he can do.' He shrugged. 'We are at the will of Allah in these things. Mr Musa has arranged as a measure of his regret that you be accommodated here in this establishment until we can meet.' He waited for a response, but when there was none, he continued, 'It is very comfortable and I am assured that they have a very high standard of western cuisine. However,' he paused and looked towards the entrance of the hotel, 'I must advise you not to leave the hotel under any circumstances. This is for your own safety. Nairobi is not as secure as some other cities, and we would not wish anything untoward to happen to you.' This time his expression seemed loaded with insincerity.

'How long do we wait?' Angela asked. She had worked in

the region before and, like in the Middle East, time was treated in a very different way to anywhere in the west. If Xasan said they had to wait, then that was it. But there were limits.

'Until tomorrow, I think. I will telephone you as soon as I know. Until then, please be comfortable here and enjoy yourselves.'

They watched him walk away, collecting his guards with a flick of his fingers. One of the men trotted out in front of him, checked the car park then turned and signalled that it was safe before Xasan left the building.

'The fat little prick's playing with us,' said Tober.

'Of course he is,' Angela agreed. 'And there's not a thing we can do about it.' She stood up. She needed to report in to London.

Twenty

I caught de Bont giving me the occasional look during our flight from Mombasa, as if checking my reactions. We were on our way to Malindi, about sixty kilometres north along the coast, in a battered cargo plane fitted with removable seats and webbing straps. It was like being thrown around in a hot spin dryer, with unsecured luggage sliding around the floor of the cabin and conversation between the other passengers being carried out in a constant screech.

The truth was, I'd flown in planes like this too many times to be concerned. If it hadn't received its last full service, or somebody had left out a few critical bolts, there was damn all I could do about it. The only thing worrying me was the sports bag under my seat. If a cop or security guard got conscientious and took a look inside, I'd have a hard time explaining the contents.

The aircraft dipped and yawed incessantly, giving us occasional glimpses of brown-and-green swathes of land below, and endless stretches of blue sky above. We'd embarked with little or no apparent organization at Mombasa airport, shuffling up the steps surrounded by people carrying what might have been their lifetime possessions. If there was any aircrew save the pilot, we hadn't seen them.

We were seated separately. Piet was in his normal persona as a park ranger, while I was travelling as a tourist consultant from New York, checking out the coastal and National Parks region for extreme tour organisers in the States. There were plenty of people with the money and time who liked to go off-track to remote regions, so the cover wasn't much of a stretch. I'd also arranged for a business accommodation bureau to answer any calls while I was away, so if someone did think to call up and check, they'd hear a genuine sounding business name and a request to call back another time.

Piet hadn't yet told me how we were going to travel on from Malindi to the border area with Somalia, but I wasn't too concerned, since I figured he had something worked out. By sea would be one way, and shouldn't take more than a few hours, hugging the coast to stay off any local radar. The Somalis pretty much ruled the waves around here, but since their hunting ground was further out, often by hundreds of kilometres, we'd only be in trouble if we ran into one of their motorised skiffs coming in for supplies. White faces close to the border would undoubtedly raise their suspicions.

We hit the ground at Malindi with a bump and careered down the short runway, which was surprisingly smooth. The airport was without frills: an L-shaped, east-west and north-south layout, with a collection of peeling sheds for a terminal, often used by adventurous tourists travelling to the Masai Mara game reserve. Beyond the perimeter, the town, which was substantial, lay baking in the sun, a mix of thatched houses, stucco-type buildings and, in the centre, the tall minaret of the local mosque.

As we turned and taxied towards the terminal, we were watched by a few locals, seemingly unaware of the hazards of walking across the runway when a plane was coming in to land.

I followed Piet down the steps and across the tarmac. The heat was bouncing off the ground in waves, and I didn't much like the idea of being inside a shed for long. So I nodded at the uniformed guard standing by the door, and waved my sat phone. He pointed behind the building across the access road, to a bunch of tables and chairs under some trees where two men and a woman were busy shouting into cell phones.

I walked over to join them, leaving Piet to do his thing, and dialled Vale in London.

'They're in Nairobi, at the Crowne Plaza.' Vale's voice was tinny and faint. The time-lag while using a sat phone was like holding a conversation under water.

'What's the plan?'

'There's been a delay. Xasan, the middleman, says the Somali gang holding the hostages has been held up by bad weather. Their main man is called Musa – his face is on the data I supplied. Xasan and our people will probably be heading out to the RV early tomorrow.'

'Do we know where that is?'

'As a matter of fact, I do.' Vale gave me the coordinates for the town of Kamboni, just inside Somalia. The meeting was to take place in a remote beach-front villa a few clicks north of the town, close to a fishing village called Dhalib.

I was surprised they had been given such precise information so early. The usual way of these things was that locations for meetings were a closely guarded secret until the last minute to avoid compromising the site.

'It's a puzzle,' Vale agreed. 'Particularly since there's been a strong Kenyan Defence Force presence in the region for the past eighteen months, centred on the port of Kismaayo to the north. They were sent in to put a dent in al-Shabaab's activities and to stop them bleeding across the border into Kenya. But why Xasan and his crew have felt free enough to hold any kind of meeting so close to the border is a mystery.'

'Could be they're operating under the radar while the Kenyans are focussed on looking to the north.'

'Maybe. Their National Security Intelligence Service aren't supplying any useful answers, and claim the problem of al-Shabaab has been curtailed.'

It seemed ridiculous that with a military force so close, these negotiations were being allowed to happen without any kind of protection from the army. I said as much to Vale.

'That's not in our control,' he replied heavily. 'Xasan came forward with the plan and we've gone along with it.' His tone made it clear what he thought of that. 'Even if I could, I can't ask the Kenyans for help. There's a risk they'd go in mob-handed and we'd lose the hostages – who probably aren't being held close by, anyway.'

He was right. All it would take was one phone call and the hostages would turn up dead.

'We can't send in our own people for the same reasons,' Vale continued. 'The Somalis have got armed boats in the area, so a seaborne approach would be difficult to hide. And the Kenyans won't take lightly to our interference, no matter what the reasoning.' He went on to explain that the area around the town of Kamboni was still thought to host limited elements of al-Shabaab and other groups, all with strongly suspected links to al-Qaeda. 'If Xasan and his contacts are holding talks here, it's with the tacit acceptance of al-Shabaab – which confirms what we've suspected for some time: that Musa must be one of their main players. Nothing moves in this region without their knowledge and his say-so.'

'Could be a reason for the early release of the location,' I suggested. 'They're checking to see if the news gets out.'

'Exactly,' he conceded. 'Even more reason for you to be careful going in. They'll be watching for you.'

I saw Piet coming across the perimeter road, so I cut the call and went to meet him. He was carrying a gun bag, which I assumed he'd had locked away somewhere secure inside the terminal. He looked relaxed and led me to one side of the terminal building.

'You'll want to see how we go from here,' he said. 'How's your head for heights?'

'Heights don't bother me; it's landings I worry about.'

'Glad to hear it.' He turned his head and nodded. 'Meet Daisy. She's your new best friend.'

'Christ.' Daisy was a surprise, but immediately made sense. I was looking at a microlight aircraft with a V-shaped wing above two open seats and an engine with a large rear-facing propeller.

'She might not look much, but she's my daily workhorse. She's a flexwing, powered by a four-cylinder, four-stroke, eighty horse-power Rotax nine-one-two engine. I tell you that only so you know she'll get us to where we're going better than anything else.' He looked at me. 'You ever flown in one before?'

I had, as it happened. It had been with a madman of an army pilot at the controls, and hadn't ended well. 'Once.'

He grinned and clapped a hand on my arm. 'Great. So you know the drill.'

'Drill?'

'Once you're in, don't move around. If I jump out it's because staying on board is the worst option.'

I watched while he walked round the machine, checking out the rigging and engine. It didn't look much, but if he used it on a daily basis for running the reservation fences and checking for poachers, it was the best I would get. The tyres were bigger than I recalled from the army flight, like giant doughnuts.

He noticed me looking. 'They're called Tundras – they'll cope with most terrains: sand, rocks, grassland – even beach if we get close to the water.' He kicked the nearest tyre, then showed me where to stow my sports bag. 'We can't get your rifle out here – they'll arrest you. I'll put down later somewhere quiet so you can run your eye over it and check the sights.'

'Fine.'

He buckled me in and checked my helmet intercom was plugged in, then climbed aboard in front of me, the machine bouncing under his weight. We had developed an audience. The guard from the terminal building came over to watch, along with a couple of guys in mechanics' coveralls. The guard grinned and held up his thumb, and took a photo of us on his cell phone. A kid of about ten appeared from behind a small storage shed, and Piet shouted and waved at him to keep clear before he got turned to mincemeat.

Getting airborne took seconds, once we were given the all-clear, and Piet levelled out over the town and headed north.

All I could do was sit there and admire the view, while trying to ignore the shattering noise of the engine behind me and a tiny voice of unease that was niggling away at my brain.

The voice continued to niggle for the first hour out of Malindi. Then Piet signalled that we were going down. He circled once, peering over the sides to check the ground, then put us down on a deserted patch of grass and scrub. The landing was bouncy and short, and I figured he knew this area well enough to judge exactly where he could land safely.

I unzipped the sports bag. The longest of the three packages provided by Khaban in Mombasa held an AK-47 sniper rifle. Of Hungarian design, it had an extended barrel compared with the weapon's usual stubby design, a wooden skeleton butt and came equipped with a suppressor, optical scope and bipod. It fired 7.62mm rounds with a declared effective range of up to 600 metres. It wasn't new, but looked clean and ready to go.

I was hoping I wouldn't get to use it.

The next package was smaller, and I put that to one side for later. The third package held a Vektor SP1 9mm pistol with spare magazines. Like the AK-47, it was commonly available in the region and wouldn't point towards the origins of the user if they fell into the wrong hands. There was no suppressor, which Khaban had warned me about, but it was too late to go hunting for one now.

'You planning on starting a war?' Piet was transferring fuel from a spare tank, but had one eye on the guns. With his background, he must have used both weapons himself over the years.

'I hope it won't come to that.'

I looked around. I needed to check the sights on the rifle. We seemed to be in the middle of nowhere, but I didn't want to find a unit of local police popping up if I let off a few rounds. 'Are we alone out here?'

Piet nodded. 'As alone as you'll ever be.' He pointed at a rock about two hundred metres away, and another further back. Both were set against a sandy outcrop with a scattering of dry bushes. 'If you hit those, I'll buy you a drink when we're back in 'Lindi.'

I checked the scope on the AK-47 and inserted a magazine. Folded out the bipod and dropped into the firing position. Wiped the lens and set the butt against my shoulder. It felt familiar and easy. The rock jumped into view through the lens. I breathed out and squeezed off a sighting shot. A puff of sand flew up to the left and back of the rock. A couple of birds followed, disappearing into the sky with shrieks of alarm. I adjusted my

stance and fired twice more. Two hits and a near miss, and bits
of rock flew into the air. I shifted again, this time aiming at the
second rock without adjusting the sights. One hit and a miss.

Piet swore. 'Damn. I shouldn't have been so generous. One
thing, though; you want a piece of advice from an old border
hand?' He was referring to the guerrilla incursions over the
years from South Africa's neighbouring lands. They had become
increasingly bitter and hard fought, and the army had learned
some valuable lessons in bush warfare.

'I'm always happy to listen.' I took out the magazine and
put the rifle to one side.

'Make damn sure you hit what you aim at first time out. The
Somalis don't go in for targeted shots; they spray everything
with as much ordnance as they can get. You don't want to be
on the receiving end, trust me.'

'Why do you mention Somalis?'

'Because at this end of the world, my friend, there's only one
group you'll come up against – and it ain't the Kenyan army.' He
hesitated then said, 'What are we talking about here – pirates?'

'Something like that. Didn't Vale say?'

'Vale doesn't say more than he needs to, which suits me
fine.' He shifted his feet, a sign he had something on his mind.
'I have to say this, Portman – I carry a rifle, too. But it's legal
and for self-defence – not like that thing you got there.' He
nodded at the sniper rifle. 'That's a man killer.'

'What's your point?'

'My point is, I've got a wife and kid in Mombasa and I don't
want to leave them alone in this world. I'll get you in and get
you out again, I'll even come in and move you on further, if
you need it. But that's all I can do. I ain't the cavalry so don't
count on any suicide missions.' He waited while I loaded the
Vektor and fired off three rounds at a spindly acacia tree about
fifty metres away. Two lumps of bark shot off into the bush and
I figured that was good enough.

A man at the same distance would be a much bigger target.

'That's fine with me,' I said. He was right. Now we both
knew where we stood, there would be no confusion if things
got hot. I put the gun under my jacket; the rifle went into a
sling at my side. I transferred the other package and some

essentials along with water, a small medical pack and some energy bars, to a folding backpack, and I was ready to go.

Piet grunted and climbed on board.

As we took off, the earlier niggle that had been tormenting me suddenly mushroomed into something real. I wondered why the airport guard, who must have seen Piet taking off and landing hundreds of times, had suddenly decided that today was a good day to take a photo.

Twenty-One

There wasn't much to do while we flew, save listen to Piet's occasional commentary, check out the scenery, and try not to dwell on the fact that I was sitting in an open bucket seat with bits of aluminium tubing, fabric and wires holding us in the air. I occupied myself instead by counting the number of people or vehicles down below, and wondering what kind of reception committee we might run into if we got unlucky.

'Where do they come from?' I said over the intercom. 'The people on the track.' The ant-like figures were moving slowly in line along a thin trail of bare earth, heading towards Malindi. I couldn't see any signs of habitation and wondered how far they had walked. It was a common enough sight in Africa, where people had to walk kilometres for food, water, medicines or schools – all stuff we take for granted in the west. But it still amazed me every time.

'Some are traders off the offshore islands, like Lamu and Kiswayu,' he said shortly. 'The rest are mainland locals. Any heading south are probably Somali illegals. If they're lucky and miss the army and police patrols, they'll get through to Mombasa and disappear.'

I wondered how he could tell. To my untrained eye the walkers were dots against the landscape. He'd said earlier that we would be flying at 1,500 feet, which gave us a spectacular view of the countryside below, but no real detail save for endless patterns of greens and reddish-brown, of grassland

and scrub through a shimmering haze. Off to our right was a silver sheen where the sun was reflecting off the sea, and I could just about make out the curved scimitar-shapes of sails as local boats moved offshore. The sky above us was a brilliant blue all the way to the horizon.

'Going down,' he said after another thirty minutes. 'There's a section of fence out and I need to check it. If we're being watched it might look odd if I don't.'

We lost height and began to circle round, and I tried to spot the damaged fence, but couldn't. Piet brought us to within a hundred feet of the ground, his shoulders working to keep us level, and I saw we were running parallel to a long stretch of wire fencing. He stabbed a finger out and I saw a gaping hole where the wire had been cut and peeled back. Tyre tracks were plainly visible in the soft earth running in a north-westerly direction away from the coast.

'Poachers,' Piet said. 'I'll have to call it in to HQ.' He regained height again and levelled off, then got on the radio and gave the details and coordinates to somebody on the other end.

'What will happen?' I queried, when he switched off. If Piet was forced to divert or drop me off early somewhere, I'd be behind the band.

'They'll send out an armed patrol. Be lucky, though, if they find them. They could be anywhere. It'll be down to the trackers.'

We flew on until he took us down again, this time just short of the town of Kiunga. We drank water and stretched our legs, and Piet showed me a map of the area.

'We're about ten kilometres from the border. I can drop you about here.' He showed me a position north of the town and right up against the border with Somalia. It would put me about two kilometres from the town of Kamboni. 'I pass this way often enough checking the area around the Kwaggavoetpad and Boni reserves, so the locals know my machine. The area on the other side is a park, too, but I've got no business over there. Any closer than this and the spotters on both sides of the border might start wondering what I'm doing.'

'Spotters?'

'They keep an eye out for army, police patrols and anti-smuggling units, and sell the info to whoever will buy it – including your pirate fellows. Spotters can be farmers, homesteaders, fishermen – anybody.'

'The guard at Malindi?'

He gave me a quick look. 'Why do you say that?'

I told him about the man taking a snapshot on his cell phone. It had seemed such a natural thing to do, I hadn't thought anything of it until we were in the air. In common with others in my line of business, I'm wary of having my photo taken, especially when on assignment on foreign soil.

'He was probably unused to seeing me go two-up,' he said eventually. But he didn't sound convinced. 'Can you manage from there?'

I nodded. It would be easy enough. I'd walked bush country before, and in hostile territory. Some things are like riding a bike; as long as you don't get cocky, you'll survive.

Piet replenished his fuel from the spare tank to avoid having to stop again until he was well clear of the area, then we took off for the last leg.

'We'll be going in low,' he explained over the roar of the engine. 'Anybody down there will hear us but won't see us until we're right overhead.'

As we cleared a line of thin trees and levelled out, this time disturbingly close to the ground, I caught a glimpse of the sea less than a kilometre away to our right. Seeing it all this close was a reminder that this was where things started getting serious.

Twenty minutes later I was alone and on foot, watching from the sparse cover of an acacia tree as Piet took off. Behind me was the border, a vague no-man's land marked by an occasional line of posts running into the distance.

On the other side lay bandit country.

I waited for Piet to get clear, then checked my bearings. Night-time falls quickly in Africa, like God throws a switch, and I needed to get across the border before it was fully dark. But being prepared before you move is a must-do thing. A gun is no good if it doesn't do what you want the first time of asking, and having to search for something vital in the dark can seriously slow you down if you can't put your hand on it right away. I checked my weapons again to make sure they were fully functioning, then opened my backpack.

What I needed first was a lightweight ghillie net. By itself it was no use unless I wanted to catch fish; by adding bits of local foliage, it would become part of the background, under which I would hide if anybody came along. Ghillies were commonly used by snipers and forward observers, some made up in the form of elaborate suits. I preferred something easy to pull over me, yet quick to throw off if I needed to respond suddenly to a threat.

With the ghillie 'shrubbed up', I called Vale. He picked up on the third ring.

'I'm about an hour out from the RV,' I reported. 'I'll be going in on foot, crossing the border in fifteen.'

'Good to hear.' He sounded relieved but concerned. 'Our people are still at the hotel in Nairobi. We've had a man checking flight bookings out of Jomo Kenyatta International for tomorrow but he hasn't found anything yet. If they take an air taxi or a private flight, which is the most likely, we won't know when they leave until too late.' He sounded frustrated at the lack of hard information, and I guessed he was having to take a back seat at SIS headquarters and not ask too many questions.

I sympathized. It would have helped to know more. A lot more. With no idea of how or when his people would get to the coast, I was in danger of going in blind. And if the other side changed the venue of the meeting, I would be left sitting out here with nothing to do and nowhere to go. I couldn't watch over them until I got a visual, but I also needed to be close to the meeting venue early, to assess what forces I was up against. For that I would need to find the villa and get right up close to it before morning.

I shut off the phone and packed it away, then threw the ghillie net over me and set off towards the border.

What I didn't know was that I'd already been spotted.

Twenty-Two

Vale replaced the receiver and looked up to see Moresby standing in the doorway to his office, leaning against the frame. He wondered how much the new Ops Director had heard.

He clamped down on his surprise and said, 'Can I help you?'

Moresby unhitched his shoulder and stepped into the room, kicking the door shut behind him.

'What are you playing at, old man?' His voice was cold, the familiarity an insult. A faint tic was visible in one cheek, something Vale had noticed before when Moresby's emotions were running high. Not a good indicator for a man in his position. Show a sign of weakness in this game, he was tempted to tell him, and the wolves will have you.

'Is something bothering you?'

'You've been to New York.'

'So?'

'I checked your log. You weren't authorized.'

Vale didn't react. There had been a time when he could go anywhere, at any time, at the drop of a hat; it was a requirement of his position as a field officer and agent runner. Now, not so much, especially since people like Moresby had introduced new rules about foreign travel assignments needing authorization, even to 'friendlies' such as the US. It was partly to do with a need for greater control over SIS officers' activities, and to avoid embarrassing questions when the press picked up on something involving intelligence operations.

'I was there on my own ticket. I took leave. Is that a problem?'

Moresby pursed his lips. 'You sure you didn't drop in on our friends while you were there?' He meant the CIA, FBI, NSA and all the other acronyms peppering the US Intelligence community.

'As I said, I was on leave.'

Moresby sniffed and turned his head to study a photo on the

wall. It was a bleak study of the iconic Kaiser-Wilhelm Memorial church in central Berlin, in profile against the evening sky. Vale had been given it many years before by an opposite number in the German *Bundesnachrichtendienst* – the Federal Intelligence Service – after they had worked together on a lengthy and complex insertion operation against the Russians. It had been a wry acknowledgement of shared history and of future co-operation. By return, Vale had sent him a framed copy of Mason's iconic wartime photo of St Paul's Cathedral. They had been friends ever since.

'Scene of one of your triumphs, was it? You and all those other Cold War warriors?' He gave a twisted smirk. 'It's over, don't you know that? Your time has passed. Why don't you retire and leave the rest of us to get on with business.'

Vale sat back, surprised by the venom in Moresby's words. They had never got on well, being of different generations and outlooks – even education. But this was a whole new level of hostility, signalling that the gloves were off. He guessed his continued presence must be getting under the new man's skin.

'I will, soon enough,' he said quietly. 'Is there a point to this visit or are you merely bored?'

Moresby's eyes flashed and his jaw went tight. 'You don't like the way I'm doing things, Vale – and that I can understand. After all, it's a whole new game, isn't it? Things are moving at a faster pace than you and your generation ever witnessed. But that's the world we live in now. I *know* you went into bat against my proposals; I *know* you went upstairs and tried to stop me; I *know* you had a cozy little chat with Scheider the other day. What was that about – sticking a spanner in the works? No, don't tell me – I'm not interested.' He breathed heavily, then added, 'I don't care what you think of me or my plans. And who I send out into the field is no longer your concern. So back off.' He walked to the door, then turned back. 'You've had your time in the limelight, old man. It's time to step back.'

'You've made that quite clear,' Vale murmured. They had been down this road before, only in a more formal and outwardly civilized manner, documented and recorded for posterity, an example of the bureaucratic jousting which Moresby and his kind seemed to enjoy. He saw no reason to prolong it just because teeth were now bared. 'Close the door after you.'

Moresby gave a mirthless chuckle. 'Think you're so hard-nosed, don't you?' His face went tight. 'You get in my way, old man, and you'll find out what hard-nosed really is. I promise.' He walked out, pulling the door closed behind him.

Vale waited until he was certain that Moresby wasn't coming back, then picked up his phone and made a call to the US Embassy. He asked to speak to James Scheider.

Twenty-Three

Inside the citadel that was the US Embassy in London's Grosvenor Square, James Scheider listened carefully to the call from Tom Vale, then said goodbye and cut the connection. The deputy station chief for the CIA looked across his desk at his new assistant, Dale Wishaw, who had just entered.

'Tom Vale, MI6,' he explained. 'The British are running an operation in Somalia, near Kamboni. We were given an eyes-on out of courtesy because of two UN people caught up in the hostage situation out there. The Brits have been made an offer to negotiate for their release, and they've sent out two reps to see if they can work out a deal.'

'UN? That's not good.'

'No. But with no US citizens involved, we get to stand back and watch. The UN people probably work out of the New York headquarters, but can't be seen to interfere unless they make a formal request for us to do so. And frankly, I don't trust anybody in State or the UN to stay quiet on this issue long enough to resolve it. If it got out that talks were being held with pirates, I think the media coverage would sink it dead.'

'But we're talking to the Taliban. What's the difference?'

'The Taliban as a whole have shown willing. This bunch of pirates isn't the same. They could easily get frightened off if the media shows up.'

Wishaw eyed him carefully. 'But you've promised to help?'

'I did, God help me. Limited to over-flight capabilities and supplying whatever intel we can get, using drones for real-time footage of anything that moves.'

'NSA?' Wishaw himself had transferred across from the National Security Agency, the equivalent but far bigger cousin to Britain's GCHQ. With vaster resources and capabilities and, some cynics were fond of saying, fewer official scruples about privacy rules when it came to intelligence gathering, it spent its life and budget trawling the incessant and growing amount of phone traffic, message boards, chat rooms, forums, blogs and websites used by terrorist and other extreme organizations.

'I promised I'd copy Tom separately on all material.'

'How come? Doesn't he already get it?'

Scheider chose his words with care. If any of this ever got out, he would be shipped back home to a senate committee hearing accused of engaging in back-door operations counter to official policy. It was a surefire career killer and one he wished to avoid.

'You would think so, right? I get the feeling Vale's no longer part of the inner circle. This is Moresby's operation and he's new school. Vale is old school and not far off retirement.'

'Problem?'

'Yeah. He has bad feelings about this whole negotiation thing. To be honest, I don't blame him. It smells bad. Why should the Somalis offer to negotiate for any group after months of silence? They don't know that two of their hostages are UN, so why make an exception right now?'

'What does the chatter say?' Wishaw was referring to the buzz and rumour that inevitably peppered the airwaves when something big was in the wind.

'That's the problem: there is none.'

Wishaw blinked. 'What, at all?'

'Not a peep. Whoever's controlling it – this guy Musa, whoever he is – he knows how to keep things under wraps.'

'If Vale doesn't like the plan, why doesn't he say so?'

'He tried. Nobody's listening.' Scheider shifted in his seat. 'I owe him for past favours so I said I'd do what I could.'

'So why look so worried?'

Scheider squinted at him. 'You've never heard of this Kamboni before?'

The younger man looked uncomfortable. 'Actually, I have, but I can't recall where.'

'It's been on the watch list of terrorist training areas for several years, since the Nairobi embassy bombing in '98 and Mombasa four years later. Nothing was proved, but local intel has it as a jumping-off point for border crossings into Kenya and beyond.'

'I'll read up on it,' Wishaw promised.

'You do that.'

'But if it's that hot, why have the Brits agreed to send people in there?'

'Because some hotshot thought it was a good idea.'

'Not Vale, I take it.'

'No. But that's where we come in. He's got a plan running on the side, without Moresby or anyone else knowing. He's sending in a shadow to watch their backs.'

'A shad— you're kidding. Is he serious?'

'Absolutely. It'll be off the books and completely deniable, but he's going for it.'

'How does it affect us?'

'I agreed to run any intel or personnel checks he wanted to make. He came across a name he wanted to use, so I ran it through the database to see what we knew. It came up warm.'

'Anybody we know?'

'Portman.'

Wishaw lifted an eyebrow. 'Now that name I do know. Isn't he one of ours?'

'Not strictly. He's freelance. His background is military. He's very good.'

'It sounds risky.'

'He's done work for a number of approved US contractors and people are happy with that. We've used him, as have other agencies, but strictly on a contract basis.'

'We. You mean Langley?' Wishaw sounded almost shocked.

'Who else would I mean – the Vatican?' Scheider was beginning to wonder how Wishaw had got this far. The younger officer seemed to have a desire to dot all the tees. While not running foul of the appropriate oversight committees was one thing, in this business there were limits. Sometimes sailing close to the line was the only way to move forward. Wishaw, on the other hand, was showing signs of coming down on the wrong side of the fence – the side where the rule-book sticklers and time-servers lived their narrow lives. He was going to have to watch him.

'Of course. I take it that was in Iraq and Afghanistan?'

'Yes, but you wouldn't know it. He's a deep cover specialist; works in the background, makes his own moves, stays loose and off the records. Nobody knows for sure where he got his training – the data doesn't go deep enough. There are rumours he did time with the French Foreign Legion's Second Parachute Regiment, but you know what rumours are like.'

'Can't we ask the French?'

Scheider pulled a lopsided face. 'I tried. They don't talk about their people past or serving. In any case, Portman's proved himself sufficiently over the years, and it's Vale's call, so that's good enough for me. What's up?' he added. Wishaw was frowning.

'I just wondered how come, that's all.'

'How come what?'

'How come we use someone we know so little about.'

Scheider stared at him. 'We use people like Portman all the time, you know that. They're easier to find, require less training and are cheaper to stand down when we don't need them. If it wasn't for the Portmans of this world we'd be in a heap of trouble.' He shook his head in mild exasperation, reminding himself that Wishaw's background in the NSA would have been very different to what he was now experiencing. 'If you have any different ideas, let me know – I could use the input.'

'Sure. And this Portman's gone along with it?'

'Yes. He'll be close enough to touch them. Not that they'll ever know it.' He shook his head in admiration. 'Sooner him than me.'

'What does Vale want from us?'

'Whatever we can supply, like real-time photos and any intel chatter we pick up. But what he really wants, we can't give.'

'What's that?'

'Boots on the ground. Portman's by himself, God help him.'

Twenty-Four

I sensed trouble less than two hundred metres from the border. Using a line of trees as cover, and with the ghillie net over my shoulders to break up the line of my body, I was moving quickly towards the line of posts, pausing every few metres to scout my back trail. I had a faint tickle going on in between my shoulders, which had helped me spot trouble in the past before it hit me. Trouble was, this time I didn't know where it was coming from, or whether the potential threat was man or beast.

I'd asked Piet earlier if there was any danger from wildlife in the area.

'You mean big cats? No, not here. Too close to the coast. Your biggest threat is poachers on their way inland or Somalis looking for tourists to shake down and take hostage. And snakes: mambas and puff adders, mostly.' He grinned. 'Best watch where you sit down.'

I stopped, scouring the area ahead of me. The light was beginning to fade and I couldn't take too long to get across and approach the area around Kamboni. If there was a threat right here, I had to identify it, avoid it . . . or neutralize it.

I eased the AK off my shoulder. The long barrel was cumbersome for close-quarter action, but the suppressor was its main advantage. This close to my target, and with the occasional farm buildings or fishermen's houses scattered throughout the area, an un-silenced rifle shot would be like sending up an air-raid siren.

I waited, convinced someone was ahead of me on the other side of the border. If the Somalis had posted watchers to warn of intervention forces coming this way, it made sense that they would be stationed here, behind me on the Kenyan side, or just into Somalia.

Keeping low and with one eye on the tufts of long grass and spindly shrubs around me, I moved carefully. Ahead of me was a clump of bush, bare of any greenery but thick enough to mask anything waiting inside or behind it. I decided to give it a miss, and moved sideways.

As I did so, a shape rose up out of the grass not ten paces away.

It was a young Somali, dressed in cut-off cotton pants and a loose shirt, with a small bag over his shoulder. He was holding a rifle, an AK-47 like mine, but with the conventional stubby barrel. It looked beaten up and dirty, with a battered magazine and stock. He was no farmer or fisherman, and from the wild expression in his eyes, I guessed he'd been waiting here for some time for somebody like me to happen along.

There was no time for niceties. If he pulled the trigger on the AK, I was done for, even if he missed. I dropped the rifle barrel and fired once before he could get off a shot. The sound was no louder than a slap, and the bullet took him in the chest. He was built like a long-distance runner, all skin and bone, and the bullet was enough to knock him over on to his back. As he fell, I ran forward and followed him to the ground, using the rifle butt to make sure he was dead. It was brutal and personal, but I couldn't afford to waste bullets.

I checked his shoulder bag. No cell phone or radio, just a plastic bottle of water and some dried fish. Field supplies. I breathed a sigh of relief. It meant he wasn't expected to check in on a regular basis, so his silence wouldn't be noticed for a while.

I rolled him into some long grass and kicked some dried vegetation over him. It wouldn't hide him for long come daylight, and the flies that would surely feed on him would eventually attract the attention of larger predators, then men. But it would have to do.

I turned away towards the border and jogged across into Somalia.

The going was easy enough; rough ground for the most part, it was mostly covered in coarse grass and clumps of bush. Even in the gloom I was able to make out sufficient detail to avoid falling flat on my face. But after the experience I'd just had, I stopped more often, watching for signs of movement in case the Somali had backup waiting. I skirted a clutch of small dwellings and crossed a track leading away to the south as quickly as I could. Tracks were too dangerous, even at this time of night. If the locals had all been clued in to keep their eyes open, it made movement even more difficult.

I had to get under cover as a soon as I could.

I stopped to take a drink of water and check my direction from the GPS on my sat phone. I was heading directly east, towards the Indian Ocean. If I continued on this course, I would meet up with the coast road from Kamboni to Kismaayo in the north, and beyond that, Mogadishu, the capital some 400 kilometres away. The village of Dhalib should be somewhere up ahead.

Insects were a problem. I'd hoped they would be silenced by the fall of evening, but they seemed intent on all coming out together and singing my presence. The noise made it hard to discern what was animal movement or human, and distorted the sounds of voices travelling over the breeze from the buildings in the distance.

I pressed on, determined to find the villa and get under cover before it got too dark to see. I came to a track, but this was narrow, heading directly into the interior. I gave it a count of twenty before walking across.

By now I could hear another sound above the insect noises: it was the sea less than 500 metres away. This was the area of maximum danger, where locals would be moving around and where the Somalis would be most watchful.

I veered to the north-east, heading away from the few houses scattered on the outskirts of Kamboni. The ground here was soft, with less vegetation underfoot, and made for easier going. Then I hit the main coastal track, which was wide and flat, beaten down by the movement of traffic. I hunkered down a couple of metres back and waited.

Voices.

I lay down flat, slipping the rifle off my shoulder. I couldn't tell at first where they were coming from. They sounded all around me. I twisted round, scanning my back trail, then checked to the north. Then I heard a burst of laughter and a familiar rattle.

It was the sound of someone slapping a magazine into a rifle.

It was enough to pinpoint the direction, and it wasn't good news. They were standing just a few metres away.

I breathed carefully and felt a prickle of perspiration run down my face. By some miracle of luck, I'd avoided walking into a couple of sentries.

I started to inch away to the north, planning to cross the track further along. Then I stopped as something rustled nearby. I craned my head to see what – or who it might be.

And felt my skin crawl.

It was a snake. A big one, uncoiling from beneath a large tuft of dried grass.

I held my breath. Shoot it or back off? But this close even a silenced shot would be heard by the sentries, and there was no guarantee that I'd hit it. On the other hand, if I tried to move away and it took off after me, there was no way I'd outrun it.

We stayed like that for an age, and I tried not to torture myself with wondering if it was better being bitten by a mamba or a puff adder.

It must have been my lucky night. The snake eventually got tired of the game and slid away towards the track, disappearing into the shadows on the other side.

I did the same, giving the area a wide berth. Once near cover, I stopped again and checked my position. I had approximately half a kilometre to go to the village of Dhalib and a further kilometre to the villa.

Twenty-Five

'There are men in the car park.' Moments ago, Doug Tober had knocked softly on Angela's door. It was 3a.m. and the hotel was quiet.

Angela let him in and padded over to the window. At first she saw nothing; just a few parked and silent cars, and no sign of life other than a scrawny dog trotting along the road past the hotel grounds.

'Under the trees,' said Tober. 'Behind the white Mercedes.'

She saw them; two men, standing very still. They were watching the hotel. Then another figure appeared off to one side, moving across to join them. She couldn't tell if they were the same three men Xasan had brought with him, but she wouldn't have bet against it.

'What do you think they want?'

'They're probably keeping an eye on us to make sure we behave,' Tober ventured. 'It's probably nothing, but best get ready.' He was already dressed, and she noticed for the first time that he was carrying a length of metal tubing in his hand. He caught her look and said, 'Shower curtain rail.' Then he left the room saying he was going to check out the corridors.

Angela stripped off her T-shirt and grabbed her clothes, which were already laid out on a chair. She went into the bathroom and threw some water over her face, then dried herself and dressed quickly. Tober was right to be cautious; if anything was going to happen, they had to be ready.

When she came out, she was dressed in a tan jacket and pants over a white blouse.

A tap at the door announced Tober's return. 'All quiet. It's probably OK but I don't think I'll be going back to bed. Those jokers are out there to keep us unsettled.' He said goodnight and left the room again.

Angela debated calling London again. The duty officer in the ops room would get hold of Moresby if she needed him. But beyond saying there were men watching them, she had nothing concrete to report. She slipped off her jacket and lay down on the bed, and tried not to think about the results of the talks not going well. There were hostages depending on her getting this right, and her own bosses back in London watching to see how she handled it. Dealing with unexpected delays and disruptive tactics by others was all part of the game.

Within seconds she was asleep.

Three hours later, Tober called her on the room phone.

'Xasan sent a message. Kick-off in forty minutes.'

Angela levered herself off the bed and stretched to ease the kinks in her neck. So now it was all hurry. It was part of the game, she reflected, to keep the two of them on edge. After the long journey here, they would already be tired and stiff. Keeping them awake would leave them tired and slow to react in a negotiating situation.

She sent a brief text message to Moresby. *Leaving 40 mins for onward travel.* It was nowhere near specific enough to be of much use, but ballpark was all she had. If Moresby had the

CIA's over-flight cameras going as promised, while they couldn't tell who was on which flight leaving Nairobi, they might be able to track flights moving into otherwise deserted or remote areas like Kamboni.

She switched off the phone with a growing feeling of unease. She was being pulled by forces over which she had no control, but that was part of the job. She went downstairs to the restaurant overlooking the hotel pool. Tober was already at a table, sinking a cup of coffee as if he didn't have a care in the world. She envied him.

They ate in silence, watched over by two waiters, then made their way to their rooms to collect their bags before heading down to the lobby. There were no signs of the other guests.

Xasan was waiting for them. He apologized for the delay and hoped they had passed a good night before explaining, 'We return to the airport now and take a flight to the coast. From there we travel on to the villa by car. We should arrive by late afternoon. It will be perfectly secure.' He said this with a wry smile, as if reassuring children.

Angela said nothing. She couldn't recall having seen an airstrip on the map of the area, but no doubt Xasan knew what he was doing. Either way, she took his last comment to mean that their movements were secure and beyond any means SIS might employ to watch over them.

He appeared to guess what she was thinking. 'The flight will be quicker and more comfortable than by other means, I assure you.'

'Good.' She was tempted to ask why his men had been camped outside the hotel during the night, but decided against it. As instructors like Tom Vale had counselled her in her early days with SIS, never let the opposition know what you're thinking; any knowledge can be an advantage.

They followed him outside and round to the side of the hotel to a Mitsubishi 4WD. There was nobody else around and the air was surprisingly cool. Xasan trotted ahead, a phone clamped to his ear, and began flicking his fingers at the guards, who were leaning against the vehicle watching them approach. The men split up in what was clearly a coordinated move and surrounded Tober, staying just out of arm's reach. Up close, he dwarfed them and looked indomitable.

'What's going on?' Angela demanded. The men were all armed with pistols under their shirts and were clearly not taking chances. But Tober showed no concerns, and signalled for her to stay back. One of the men stepped forward and did a fast pat down while the other two watched. The procedure had been expected, although where they thought he might have acquired a weapon was a mystery.

When the man doing the frisking made a move towards Angela, she shook her head and flashed a steely gaze at Xasan. 'I don't think so,' she said coolly, 'do you?'

For a brief second the middleman looked as if he might insist. But he smiled instead and inclined his head, waving the man away. 'Of course not. My apologies. That will not be necessary.'

'I need to use the bathroom.' She turned to go back into the hotel. In reality she needed to get an update to Moresby.

'I think not.' Xasan's voice stopped her. He was holding out his hand. 'You can use the facilities at the airport. And I must ask for your cell phones. Where we are going, there is no need of them.'

There was a brief silence, and Angela was on the point of arguing when Xasan clicked his fingers. One of the guards pointed a gun at Tober's head.

'Please.' Xasan's voice was a quiet drawl. 'I insist.'

Twenty-Six

I was already awake when dawn came in a rush of cold air off the sea. It was tangy with salt and carried the smell of wood smoke from the villa.

I'd managed to cat-nap throughout the night, waking regularly by instinct to check my surroundings. But there was nothing to see or hear save for the background swish of the sea and the occasional rustle of a night creature.

In the thin light available I made double sure my cover was the best I could get. It had to stand up to more than just a casual survey, although the choices along here were limited. The terrain was low scrub and sandstone, with clumps of dry vegetation and prickly bush, the soft ground pushed into dips and hollows by the elements. I was in one of the dips.

Satisfied my position was good, I ran a quick eye over my weapons before taking a drink of water and chewing on an energy bar. It was too sweet for my tastes, and made me thirsty, but it would keep me going for the hours ahead.

My first sighting of the villa after crossing the Mogadishu road had been a single yellow light flickering in the dark. Beyond it I could hear the sea, a gentle hiss in the darkness. I'd homed in on the light and made my way forward with care, checking the ground every few steps for traps, wires and other man-made obstacles. I'd already seen enough trash lying around to know that the locals weren't too eco-friendly. Old tyres, plastic bottles, coiled clumps of rotting fishing nets, discarded fragments of cork floats and bits of metal too small, thick or rusted to be used for anything else. Any of these were enough to trip an unwary person. The closer I got to the coast, the more I saw.

I'd eventually come to a slight dip in the ground on a slope overlooking the villa. It was little more than a couple of feet deep, but big enough for an observation post. All I needed was some cover to go over the top.

I moved back a ways and gathered a collection of dried branches, then slid into my new home and spread them over me, twisting them together to stop them flying away if a sea breeze sprang up. With the ghillie net over me I was pretty certain I'd be invisible unless somebody actually fell in on top of me.

Next I dug out some of the sand beneath me with a small trowel, then took out a couple of small plastic bags from my backpack. Disposing of waste in a hot zone observation post can be a problem. Flies will soon zoom in on any fresh matter and attract attention.

I carefully scraped away at the earth in front of me to give me a better field of observation and to avoid breaking the skyline. Anybody looking up from the building would notice even a slight movement against the sky, but if I had some soil behind me, I would just about blend in. Once I was happy with my field of fire, I sat back and allowed the sun to do its bit drying the upturned spoil to the same colour as everywhere else.

I checked my surroundings every fifteen minutes, including the villa. The smell of wood smoke was enough to tell me that there were people down there and they were up and about. I had no idea how many, but I'd soon find out if I made the wrong move.

I used the sniper scope to give the building the once-over. It was a simple villa, vaguely European by design and single level, with a flat roof. The walls had once been plastered but were now showing the inner lining of cinder blocks, some crumbling under the combination of neglect and the elements. Tacked to the back was a small outhouse which I guessed had been used in better times to hold a generator.

An attempt had been made to build a wall around the property, but any decent blocks had been taken away once the property had been abandoned. The grounds had no discernible border, but ran into the interior beyond where I was hiding, and extended out on to the beach a hundred metres on either side. And there was no cover anywhere. It put a serious dent in any plans I might have had of getting closer, unless I got lucky under cover of dark. But that was a problem to deal with later.

My sat phone gave a soft buzz. It was Piet.

'Can you talk?' His voice sounded low and gruff. I couldn't hear any engine noise, so I figured he was on the ground somewhere.

'For now. I'm inside the target area.'

'You better get ready for company. I took an early dawn flight, to keep up appearances.'

'And?'

'There's a stretch of track outside Kamboni. You probably crossed it last night. It runs out of the town, then veers directly north, following the border. About four clicks from there I saw a pickup and a group of guys clearing the track. It's been used as a landing strip before, but not for a while.'

'Somebody's flying in.'

'Yeah. I hope you got good cover, man; they'll probably

make a fly over first to check it out. These guys are suspicious, believe me.'

'I hear you.'

It made sense. Fly the SIS personnel in by small plane and truck them to the villa. Anyone else moving in the area, especially in vehicles, would stand out like a camel on a sand dune.

'Where are you?' I asked.

'Running the fence, like always. It's what they expect. At most I'll be twenty minutes out from your position.'

'I thought you didn't want to get involved.'

'I don't. But if things go balls-up you'll be needing a lift. You call and I'll come pick you up.'

I thanked him and switched off. It was good to know I had help out there. As I settled down again, I heard the sounds of an engine.

It was a white 4WD. It came overland from the north-east, drawing a dust cloud behind it, and skidded to a stop close by the villa. Three men got out of the vehicle, and others came boiling out of the building, rifles at the ready and primed for action. When they saw who it was, they waved greetings as if they hadn't seen each other in years. Another man popped his head out of the generator shed at the rear of the villa to see what the noise was about, and I breathed a sigh of relief. If I'd ventured out of my hide I'd have tripped right over him.

I counted nine men, all armed. They were dressed in traditional wrap-around skirts and a variety of western T-shirts or the lightweight *kameez*. With the likelihood of more men on the plane with the SIS negotiators and others on call in Kamboni, it made for a substantial force if anything went wrong.

An hour later, three of the men came outside and stood talking. One of them checked a big gold watch on his wrist, then climbed behind the wheel and took off in a dust cloud. He passed my position two hundred metres away, heading towards the border.

Back to where Piet had seen the track being prepared.

I checked my position and overhead cover. The men in the villa must have got word that the negotiators were on their way in. Time to buckle down and stay still.

I checked through the scope as the remaining men stood chatting. One of them pointed and said something, and I felt the hairs on the back of my neck move.

He was looking right at me.

Twenty-Seven

'We are nearly there!' Xasan turned in his seat and shouted at the two SIS representatives. As he did so, the engine noise decreased and the plane's nose began to drop.

After relieving them of their cell phones outside the Crowne Plaza in Nairobi, Xasan had ordered his driver to take them at speed to the airport. Instead of pulling in at the main terminal, they had driven to a side entrance and through a cargo gate manned by a single security guard. The man had nodded them through without bothering to run a security check. After driving a short distance along an access road past a line of warehouses and hangars, they had pulled up alongside a plane with its engines running, puffs of dark smoke issuing from the engine nacelles.

At a word from Xasan, they climbed out into the acrid smell of aircraft fuel and burnt rubber.

'What the hell is that?' Angela muttered. 'A flying horsebox?'

A chunky, twin-engine design, the plane had seen better times and had the ingrained scars of reddish dust along its undercarriage and on the large rubber tyres and nose wheel. Small repair patches had been riveted at various places on the skin, no doubt concealing incidents in its chequered past.

'Pretty apt description,' said Tober, ignoring a sharp reprimand from one of the guards nearby. 'It's a Skytruck – a variation on the Antonov. They call it a STOL – short take-off and landing. This one's a Polish M Twenty-eight. Good plane.'

She stared at him. Was he showing off or trying to take her mind off the idea of going anywhere in this flying death trap?

He read her mind. 'I've jumped from one just like it – and not because I had to.'

'Where?' She realized she knew nothing about Tober save that he had an extensive background in Special Forces, and was now employed to use those skills on SIS operations.

'In the States, then Venezuela. They can land pretty much anywhere, and unless the pilot woke up this morning and decided this is the day he wants to die, we should be fine.'

'*Quiet*! No speak.' The guard who had spoken before didn't like being ignored. He pulled out his pistol and shoved it towards Tober's head, eyes wide with anger.

Tober looked coolly at the gun, then at the man, and said, 'OK, Bonzo. Will do. But first go fuck yourself.'

'Enough.' It was Xasan, holding out a restraining hand towards the gunman. He flicked a hand to make him go away, then looked at Tober. 'I would remind you, Mr Tober, that you are not the . . . what do you call it – the lead, in these negotiations. You are here as a courtesy. And the use of obscenities is extremely offensive.'

He turned and issued orders to his men, and they all filed on board the plane and took seats in the cabin. Two of the guards sat at the back, their eyes firmly on Tober, while Xasan and the other guard took seats at the front.

The pilot watched them without comment, then turned and got ready for take-off. Minutes later, they were racing down a secondary runway, the airframe around them rattling with the thrust of the engines. After leaving the ground, the plane seemed to hang in the air for too long before levelling off, and the note of the engines changed from desperate to merely urgent.

Angela watched Xasan. He had his head turned away, but she could hear him muttering to himself. She hoped he was praying. The three guards were made of sterner stuff, although innocence probably gave them no idea of what would happen if the aircraft fell apart in mid-flight.

As they began to descend, she caught a glimpse of the ground below and, further on, the startling blue of the Indian Ocean. The contrast between the two was vivid: the ground was feature-less, a brown-green camouflage patchwork with no visible signs of life, while the sea looked inviting and serene. She thought it was deserted, but on closer examination saw a couple of skiffs close inshore and a group of smaller craft with white sails heading out towards the horizon.

The aircraft banked sharply, turning inland, and she saw a villa below, standing alone on a bare expanse of land. Several men were standing around, looking up. They seemed neither interested nor excited. They were all armed.

The plane levelled out and dropped further. This time she glimpsed a sizeable sprawl of buildings in the distance, which she guessed was Kamboni. Moments later, the ground was rushing by, and all she could see was a blur of small trees, brushwood, coarse grass and what looked like dangerously large boulders just feet away from the plane's wheels.

The landing was bruising, the nose rearing up at one point, then going down again with a bump. The aircraft fishtailed alarmingly before the pilot brought it under control, but Xasan's men seemed unaffected, laughing and commenting as they were thrown around in their seats.

A flash of white through the window showed a large 4WD about a hundred metres away, with a man sitting on the bonnet clutching an AK-47.

Tober nudged her with his elbow. He indicated Xasan with a lift of his chin.

The Somali middleman was suffering, his shoulders bowed and lips moving in what could only have been agonized prayer.

As the plane bumped to a stop and the engine noise decreased, Angela couldn't help it. She said, 'Are you all right, Mr Xasan? You don't look so good.'

He didn't respond, but the set of his shoulders told her she had scored a brutal hit.

Twenty-Eight

I checked the AK was ready to go and placed the Vektor within easy reach, the safety off. I made sure I had the spare magazines lined up and free of dust and sand. I had a good field of fire and the advantage of higher ground. It wasn't much, but you work with what you've got.

If the Somalis had seen something suspicious, and came up the hill to find out what it was, I'd have to put most or all of them down before they got here. If I let them get behind me or to the flanks, I'd be dead meat.

The problem was if they all began blasting away. A few isolated shots would be ignored as shooting practice or high spirits. But any higher than normal volume of fire would quickly attract attention from the town. Give it ten minutes and I'd have more trouble than I could deal with.

My mouth was dry with tension. I took a sip of water and waited for the men to move.

A shot whipped over my head, the crack following a split second later. I hadn't seen the shooter throw the rifle to his shoulder, so I was guessing it was a show-off round. The slug hit a rock somewhere behind me and howled off into space. I ducked instinctively, wondering how they had spotted me, and got ready to lay down a few bodies. Spaced as they were, with no direct cover, it would be a turkey-shoot.

Then I heard jeers and laughter. What the hell . . .?

Another shot went by, clipping the twigs above my head. This time there was a clang and I saw the shadow of a rusted tin can leap into the air and bounce away. Cheers this time, and lots of shouting. But no movement towards me.

Bastards. They hadn't seen me after all – they were using the trash around me for target practice.

I risked a quick look. One of the figures was walking up the slope. He was carrying a large plastic bottle with a bright red label, being urged on loudly by his friends all throwing hand signals telling him where to place the bottle.

I got ready. He was heading straight for my position. If he spotted me, he'd be the first one down. Then his friends would follow.

But it would mean the end of the mission.

I watched as the newcomer struggled over the rough ground, his sandals slipping on the shale, all the time grumbling and muttering back at the other men. One of them picked up a stone and threw it, hitting him on the back, and the others laughed.

He was young – about sixteen at a guess – and wearing a thin T-shirt and skirt. He wasn't armed, and I figured he was a general gofer used for menial tasks such as this.

Gofer or not, he had eyes and a mouth and would shout if he saw me. He got to within ten paces of my hide and hesitated. He was looking for a spot to place the bottle, which I could see was half full of water.

Then his eyes flickered past me, ran on for a moment, and settled right back on me.

I breathed easily and centred the sights of the AK on his chest. I was applying the first pressure on the trigger, ready to knock him over, when an ear-splitting roar blasted out of nowhere. Next second the ugly shape of a flying box van passed at about three hundred feet right over our heads, a tremor going through the air and the ground around me.

The kid gave a shrill cry of alarm and dropped the bottle, covering his head with one arm. If he was anywhere near normal, he was probably pissing himself.

The men at the bottom of the slope were staring up in confusion, the shooting practice forgotten. Then they started shouting at the kid, urging him to get back down, and began running towards the house.

The kid didn't waste any time. He galloped down the slope like a gazelle and within seconds they were all out of sight.

I breathed a sigh of relief.

It meant one thing: somebody important had arrived.

Twenty-Nine

James Scheider bit hard on his tongue, telling himself to remain calm. He was in a conference call with CIA HQ in Langley, Virginia, and was just hearing that the promised camera support for the British operation over the Somalia/Kenya border was now in doubt. Across from him, Dale Wishaw winced in sympathy.

'I gave my word on this, Ed,' Scheider said softly, his words aimed at the console in the centre of the table. Forceful language was unnecessary here, as the unit fitted to this room could pick up every nuance and tone in a speaker's voice. 'I agreed that we would give cover for the Brits' operation. You know how important this is. All I'm asking for is a single Hale.' The Hale (High-altitude, long-endurance) unmanned drones were most useful where surveillance and reconnaissance missions were required over extended periods in remote areas. Scheider had suggested using one of these craft because he knew there were at least five currently not assigned to any specific programme.

'Can't do, Jim. Sorry.' Ed Biggelow, one of the Langley-based Staff Operations Officers responsible for supporting field operations, sounded calm, even bored, although Scheider was so far willing to give him the benefit of the doubt. He'd met Biggelow a few times, and had an image of a neat, buttoned-down individual who was probably going to get his ass kicked one day by a field officer he'd let down by being too devoted to the rules of engagement. 'The Hales have been labelled restricted-use only for active operations involving our own field personnel. What you're describing doesn't fit that scenario. Our best evaluation is that if we can avoid the use of direct over-flights in the region, we should do so unless and until the threat impact becomes directly counter to US interests. This is an observation mission only. The best we can do at the moment is a Herti.'

Scheider sat forward so fast, Wishaw thought he was going

to propel himself at the console and grab Biggelow by the throat
all the way down the wire.

'A Herti? What good's that, Ed? It's four years old, for God's
sake and flies like a camel for what – twenty hours max? Hell,
it's not even one of ours!'

'Precisely. It's British. But this is a British operation, isn't
it? I'm sure they wouldn't object.'

'That's not the point. We have Reapers based in the region,
don't we?' He waved aside Wishaw's signal to keep his cool.
The Reaper was one of the most effective drones available,
loaded with cameras and capable of carrying Hellfire missiles
and bombs. 'Dammit, I know we have because I've used them!
Are you telling me I've got to go back to the Brits and tell
them I can't provide intel on the hostages because somebody
thinks it doesn't *fit*? What happens next time we need .*their*
help?'

'Sorry, Jim. That's not my call. If you have any further
intel which pushes this to a higher level, I suggest you take
it further up the chain of command. Let me know what you
decide.'

Scheider stared at Wishaw as the connection was cut, scarcely
believing what he'd just heard. 'Am I in fucking Disneyland?
Did that asshole just tell me to go screw myself?'

Wishaw shook his head in sympathy. 'He offered a Herti,
Jim. It's a good platform. We should take it. If we do, it's up
to Langley to get it in position and start providing us with data.'

Scheider stood up and walked around the room. He had to
calm down. While he did so, he toyed with the idea of pulling
details of Biggelow's financial and credit records and making
them disappear for forty-eight hours. That would make the jerk
sit up and realize there was a real world out there. But that
would hit the messenger, not the people who had made the
decision to counter the use of a Hale.

He sighed and went back to the table, his anger dissipating.
Truth was, this was partly his fault. After hearing what Moresby
was proposing, he'd had serious reservations about the sense
of sending in anyone, let alone a woman, to negotiate with a
prick like Xasan or any of his 'contacts' in such a deeply male
society. Unfortunately, he'd allowed those reservations to seep

into his report and he had the feeling it had been picked up by the analysts back in Langley and passed on up the line.

But he'd made the Brits a promise and he was going to keep it – and the first person he owed it to was Tom Vale.

He took a deep breath. 'OK. You're right. Ask them to get the Herti in the air, will you? You've got the coordinates. We're already behind the mark on this, so make it quick.'

'Sure thing.'

'Before you go, do we have any idea of the local population?'

'No, sir. A couple of thousand is a number we've had for a while, but that's unreliable. It fluctuates all the time, especially since the KDF went through on their way to Kismaayo.'

'Did the Kenyans leave any observers in Kamboni?'

'A small unit. But when things went quiet they pushed them north to join the main force in Kismaayo. There are reports of armed men filtering south into the area during the past few days. It's thought they're al-Shabaab or clan sympathizers, stirred up against what they're calling a Christian invasion.'

Scheider pulled a face. 'Tricky. Can't the KDF stop them moving south?'

'It's almost impossible. They move overland where the KDF is spread too thin, or they come by skiffs or fishing boats. It's a vast area.'

'Are they all hostiles?'

'We have to assume so. The predominant extremist force throughout Somalia is al-Shabaab, in spite of Federal Government and KDF forces having claimed they have control since 2011.' He pointed at the photos, which showed a number of pickup trucks and armed men spread among the buildings. 'These are definitely not Kenyan or Somali troops. They look more like extremists and the groups supporting pirates out at sea. They don't exactly have the numbers to control the area completely, but they represent a sizeable force. The Kenyans are either unaware or unconcerned by their presence due to other commitments.'

'Do we know why they're in Kamboni?'

'No. Our intel is that the KDF are focussing on bigger

problems to the north, and don't give too much credence to small groups elsewhere. That might be true. What we do know is that when the KDF passed through and hit Kismaayo, al-Shabaab melted into the hinterland where they can't be monitored. We thought at first that these new arrivals around Kamboni were the result of being squeezed down there by the troops to the north, but they seem to be moving too freely for that – and they all seem to be armed and fed. They're actually moving in a coordinated fashion, although we still don't have a clear picture why.'

'Could it have anything to do with the negotiations conducted by the British?' Even as he posed the question, Scheider knew that there had to be a connection. Very little was done by al-Shabaab in the region without there being a solid reason. And the thought of gaining kudos of any kind from hostage negotiations would make the al-Shabaab leadership salivate with joy.

Wishaw evidently thought not. 'I can't see how if these negotiations were being kept as secret as you say. I doubt everybody in the region wants individual cells selling off hostages to all-comers. It would weaken their overall bargaining position if the bargaining prices started going down.'

'But they could be non-affiliated hostage-takers, right? This Musa guy may be al-Shabaab, but I bet he'd be happy to trade a fast buck on the side if he got the chance.'

'That's probably true. The independent gangs and clans steer clear of the main religious groups and do their own thing. Even al-Shabaab is made up of different clans with their own interests. I'm just not sure why this particular gathering is taking place.'

'OK. Keep me posted, will you? And see what we've got on Musa. If he's been running things for any time, we might have a voice file. He won't stay silent for ever, and all we need is a match to give us a trace of where he is. Something else is going on here and I'd like to know what it is.'

Thirty

An hour after the plane had flown over, I heard the rumble of an engine from the north. It was the white SUV. This time it was moving slowly over the rough ground, and as it passed across in front of me and pulled up outside the villa, I could see why: it was full of passengers.

A reception committee had gathered and stood watching as the doors opened. I counted three Somalis, all armed, and another man who climbed out and stood issuing orders like he wanted to exert his authority. Unfortunately, his lack of height and sizeable girth seemed to go against him, and none of the men from the house seemed that impressed. Unlike the men from the villa, these newcomers were dressed in light pants and western-style shirts, setting them apart.

The two SIS representatives got out and the reception committee promptly played their part by levelling their guns at them. The woman was slim and of medium build, with dark hair cut short. I didn't need her photo on my sat phone to know who she was. Angela Pryce wore a lightweight jacket and pants, and looked slightly pissed at the number of guns being pushed in her face.

Her minder was a big guy, and looked like he could pick up a couple of the Somalis and swat the rest on to the beach in the background if he got really sore. But he wore the blank expression of a seasoned pro, and I was guessing he must have already worked out that he'd drawn the short straw here if anything went wrong.

After a while, the fat man organized his three goons to get the Brits inside, and everybody followed, leaving two men on guard outside.

The SUV drove away towards Kamboni, leaving a dust cloud hanging over the villa and a sullen silence in the air.

I settled back down to wait and switched on my sat phone, and checked through a file of potential relevant participants supplied by Vale. I found the fat man immediately; it was Xasan, the middleman. None of the other faces looked familiar.

Musa, the man holding the hostages, wasn't here yet. I checked his photo again. He was unusually tall and thin, even for a Somali, with a hawk nose and eyes set close together, and looked oddly familiar, although I was pretty sure I'd never seen him before this photo. The shot had been taken covertly, and showed him at a sidewalk café table with two other men, hunched in conversation over small cups of coffee. Two others stood in the background, watching the street. Musa obviously didn't believe in travelling without protection.

By the time darkness was beginning to roll in, all the signs down at the villa indicated that nobody else was showing up today. First the guards began to look bored, squatting together and talking, their rifles on the ground beside them. Occasionally Xasan would put in an appearance and snap at them. They would stand up and shuffle their feet, but their response was grudging and lacked real respect. I figured he wasn't part of their clan, so didn't rate more than a nod and a grunt.

Xasan himself seemed on edge and would go to the part of the garden overlooking the beach and stare out to sea with the frustrated appearance of a man wanting something important to happen.

I knew how he felt. I was hot, tired and thirsty, and my water reserve was running low. I had to get more or another day out here and dehydration would become a serious problem.

Eventually Xasan went inside. Moments later, the door opened and another figure came out. He was followed by one of the men, who said something and cuffed him round the head before shoving him on his way.

It was the kid who had come so close to stumbling on my OP. He had a bag slung over his shoulder. He ducked his head as he passed the two guards, and headed out towards the track to town, holding one arm tight against his chest, as if injured.

I got him in the scope before he disappeared from sight. He had the bearing of a whipped dog and I was pretty certain his arm had been fine earlier.

It gave me an idea.

I waited for the two guards to get bored again, then slid out of my OP and went after the kid.

Apart from getting water, which I was going to have to steal, I needed to get a line on what was happening inside the villa with the two SIS personnel. I had two ways of accomplishing the second task: one way was hi-tech, the other wasn't.

It was time to try low-tech first.

Thirty-One

T aking the Vektor and Ka-Bar knife, with the ghillie net around my shoulders, I followed the kid along the rough beach-side track leading to town. It was hard, packed dirt for most of the way, with ruts where vehicles had driven out along the coast. It made walking relatively safe in the near dark, but risky if guards had been placed along the way.

I moved off the track at one point when I heard a noise ahead of me, and ran into the wrecks of two skiffs, half buried in wind-blown sand. I had to feel around to get my bearings. The wood was sticking up like rotten teeth, and coarse grass had sprung up between the base boards. I turned back and got on to the track, and hurried to make up lost time.

Fortunately, the kid had slowed down, and I got close enough to hear him mumbling to himself, which I guessed was to bolster his nerves. It meant I'd get plenty of notice and be able to get off the track in time if he came across anybody.

We were soon passing Dhalib, which was in darkness. Little more than a few ramshackle huts clustered above the beach and used by fishermen, it was dwarfed by the nearby town of Kamboni, which began with a few houses and was well spread out. The sea was close by on the left, with the long sleek lines of skiffs just visible against the near-white of the sand, lying on the shore like beached sharks. We passed several low bungalows scattered in a seemingly haphazard manner, some with rough fences, some with lights on from gas or oil stoves or the telltale rattle of generators.

Most of the houses were of a simple plaster construction, with thatched or corrugated-steel roofs and overhanging verandas. Spindly-looking palm trees poked up like curved fingers in between, the only show of vegetation.

The kid was acting more nervous the closer we got to the centre, constantly turning to scan his surroundings. It was probably his first time in town, and I was guessing he'd been told to talk to nobody, to watch his back and stay out of trouble. I allowed the gap between us to grow, using whatever cover I could to stay out of his sight. All the time I was watching out in case I ran into trouble myself.

I lost him when he moved between two houses to avoid a group of men, but soon picked him up again. He'd got well ahead of me and was hurrying, his shoulders hunched to reduce his profile. I put on a spurt and nearly ran into three armed men standing alongside a beat-up Mitsubishi pickup.

I dived sideways into deep shadow. Luckily for me, they were too busy giving the kid a hard time to notice me.

When they eventually let him go, I was ahead and parallel to him, checking his progress through the gaps between the houses. By now I guessed we must be close to the centre of town. The alleyways here were narrow, the houses jammed close together. But everything was deathly quiet, and I figured the presence of the pirates was not universally popular.

Along the way I passed three or four more vehicles, and heard laughter from inside a couple of larger buildings, which I guessed had been taken over by pirates. Experience made me check the back of the vehicles, but none showed signs of carrying spare water containers.

I knew from the map Vale had supplied that Kamboni stood on a small peninsula jutting out into the Indian Ocean. The main part of the town was slightly inland, with a concentration of houses behind the local mosque, which had a commanding position overlooking the water. I couldn't be certain, but my guess was that the kid was on an errand for food. We had already passed a couple of stalls which were closed for the day, and among the aromas of cooking and the more acrid smell of fuel oil, there was a lingering tang of fish.

A flare of light showed me where the kid was heading. It

was a food stall selling fruit, vegetables and – the thing I had come for – bottled water and juices. A number of men were bunched around the front and a couple of gas-powered lights strung overhead gave the scene an unreal edge, picking up the sheen of fruit, packaging, smooth skin . . . and AK-47 rifles. A dog sniffing around the sides of the stall was an added danger.

The kid fronted up to the stall and the men made way for him. I watched as he pointed to some fruit and bottled drinks, and paid with some notes out of his bag. He had trouble using his right hand. Then he turned and began to make his way back through town towards the villa.

I jogged to get ahead of him on the outskirts of town, where we weren't overlooked, but where a faint splash of light made it easy to see me. I took out the Ka-Bar.

I'd thought about this carefully. The kid might run screaming for the hills, but it was a risk I figured worth taking. I was trying not to think about what I would have to do if he freaked out on me, but something told me he wasn't about to go out of his way to help the men who treated him so badly.

I stepped out in front of him.

He was pretty cool, in spite of his earlier show of nerves coming into town. He took one look at me and stopped dead. He made no attempt to shout or run, but eyed the knife in my hand.

'I saw you,' he said calmly, 'watching the house – when the men wanted to shoot at cans.' Hearing him speak English was a stunner. It was heavily accented, and hesitant, but good. I guessed he'd been to college or university, which made him city-bred.

'You've got sharp eyes. Yet you didn't tell your friends I was there.'

'They are not my friends. Also, I did not know who you were . . . and you did not do me harm, even though I saw your gun. Are you French, sir? American? I have not seen Americans here before.'

I considered my reply. Trying to explain why I was helping the two SIS people would take too long, and I wasn't sure what his reaction might be to me owning up to being an American.

Pretending I was French was also risky; their recent venture in Mali had caused uncomfortable ripples throughout the region.

In the end I took a gamble. I went for the middle ground. 'I'm English.'

'Ah. The man and the woman from the plane, they also are the English. Are you a friend of the English, sir?'

'No. They don't know me.' It was an easy truth. But something was bothering me. 'What's your name?'

'They call me Madar.'

'Madar, why didn't you tell the others about seeing me?'

'Because they do not listen to me. I am less than nothing to them, here to do their bidding. They beat me when I do not do something right.'

'They hurt your arm?'

He held up his right hand and winced. 'Yes. The man Xasan did not like some rice I had prepared. He beat me with a stick. I tried to protect myself. They say bad things about my uncle. He was an important man in Mogadishu, a professor of political science in the university. And he liked the English,' he added proudly, tinged with sadness. 'He taught me English and said I would need it one day to travel and work.'

'He's a wise man. Why don't they like him?'

He hesitated and shrugged. 'They tell me I am not worthy of being here because of him.'

'Why are you? It's a long way from Mogadishu.'

'A friend told me I could earn much money coming here.'

'With the pirates?'

'Yes. There is no work in Mogadishu. Many men have come to the coast, like me.'

'And your uncle allowed you to come?'

He shook his head. 'My uncle was killed last year and I do not have other family, save for a sister, Amaani. She lives in Mogadishu. She says my uncle was killed because he criticized those who would hold back our country from its future. I do not know why they would do that.' His breathing was coming in short bursts, and I got the feeling he'd been waiting for some time to talk about it.

I felt sorry for him. There were plenty of militant groups in the region accused of hurling the country back several hundred

years by supporting piracy and allegiances to terrorism. His
uncle must have fallen foul of one of them and it had cost him
his life. It also explained why they were using Madar as some
sort of slave – a punishment by association.

'What about the English – what do they intend doing with
them? Will they trade them on?'

He shook his head. 'I do not know. They do not speak to me
of these things. But I heard them talking. An important person
is coming soon, tomorrow.'

It must be Musa. 'To do what?'

'He is a chief of many people and he will decide what is to
happen to them.'

That didn't sound much like any negotiation I'd ever heard
of. 'Where is this chief coming from?'

'From the north. Everybody here comes from the north.' He
waved out towards the sea. 'He comes on a boat.'

More intel to relay to Vale, although I wasn't sure what he
could do with it. By the time he acted, any boat would be lost
among the other craft on a vast expanse of ocean.

Madar had put down the bag, which was heavy with the
goods he'd bought. It reminded me that I was thirsty. I pointed
at the bag and took out some Somali notes. 'Can I buy some
water from you?'

He nodded. He delved in the bag and produced a litre bottle
of water and a box of dates.

'Will this get you into trouble?'

He shook his head, showing white teeth in the gloom, a touch
of rebellion. 'No. I was told to get what water and juice I could
find. It will not matter how much or how little. They do not
know what can be bought here.'

I handed him some notes and he folded them and slipped
them inside his bag.

'Thank you, Madar,' I said. 'You won't say we met, will
you?'

He shook his head and picked up the bag, slinging it over
his shoulder. 'I must go now. Can I ask your name, sir?'

'Marc. It's Marc.' Most people called me Portman. But for
this kid it didn't seem right, not after he'd helped me like he
had.

He nodded and turned away, and I allowed him to disappear into the dark before setting off after him.

Time would tell if he was going to tell the others about me. I would know soon enough.

Thirty-Two

Angela Pryce stared around her at the inside of the villa and felt an instant wave of unease. The walls were pockmarked and bare of decoration, the plaster having come away in chunks from the underlying shell of rough bricks. What had once been a comfortable, if cheaply made structure of vaguely European design, was now little more than a draughty ruin.

She and Tober had been herded into a room at the front of the property, their every move watched by several armed men crowding in around them. They hadn't been treated roughly so far, but there was undoubtedly a more hostile feel to the atmosphere here. It wouldn't take much, she judged, for something bad to kick off if provoked.

They had been made to sit in rickety hard-backed chairs next to an ancient and warped card table laid out with water, fresh fruit and dried dates. It was a welcome relief after the dryness of the plane's interior, and at Tober's silent urging she had drunk as much water as she could take and eaten several dates. It brought to mind the stern teachings of the SIS survival instructor at Fort Monckton on the south coast, who had counselled all recruits that survival in the field was key, and eating and drinking to maintain energy levels should never be passed up, no matter how dire the circumstances might seem.

A large, brightly-coloured yellow and green flag had been tacked to the wall of the room, partially covering the boarded-up window overlooking the sea. The flag bore the familiar and disturbing symbols of the crossed assault rifles and Qur'an of al-Shabaab, which both the SIS people recognized immediately.

Xasan entered the room and stood watching them eat. The armed men paid him no mind, but whispered among themselves and shuffled their feet. Xasan said nothing, but it was clear that his attitude had changed dramatically since their first encounter in Nairobi. Angela couldn't make out whether he was simply edgy or impatient to be getting on with the talks. This, after all, had been his game from the beginning. But when he spoke to his men it was in a terse manner, and the way he was looking at her and Tober verged on the openly hostile. She wondered if he was putting on a front for the others, and decided to ignore him until something happened.

Another man entered the room. It was the driver of the SUV that had brought them here from the landing strip. He approached Xasan. He was holding a cell phone and showed Xasan the screen. The middleman studied it for several seconds and the man pressed a button. Then Xasan turned his head and stared at Angela.

He walked over and placed the cell phone on the table in front of her.

'Who is this?' He spoke softly, but his voice was clear in the crowded room. The men around him fell silent and turned to stare.

The screen showed two men in a microlight aircraft sitting in tandem. In the background a small cargo plane was standing on a runway, with men loading boxes into its belly. The micro-light pilot was concentrating on something off to one side, while the passenger had his head turned away, adjusting his harness. Both were white, she noted, although the passenger had a tanned look, and was younger than the pilot.

She shook her head. 'I have no idea.'

'Mr Tober?'

Tober said, 'Me neither. Why should we know who he is?'

Xasan studied them carefully. The other men in the room were silent, not understanding but waiting for a reaction.

'The pilot is a park ranger working for the Kenyan Wildlife Service,' Xasan said finally. 'He's an Afrikaans who flies out of Malindi, down the coast. But he does not normally carry passengers.' He pointed at a rifle hanging from a sling by the pilot's side. 'As you can see, he is also armed. Odd, do you not think?'

'Not really,' Tober ventured easily. 'It's pretty standard equipment for a park ranger, I'd have thought. Don't they have a lot
of poachers in Kenya?'

Xasan pursed his lips but did not reply. He did a tour of the
room, hands behind his back. Like a strutting little general on
parade, thought Angela. He stopped in front of them. 'It would
be a grave error,' he murmured, 'for your SIS to have sent any
of your highly-esteemed Special Forces here, Miss Pryce. It
would lead to severe consequences for one of you if they have.'
He turned his gaze on Tober as he said this. 'Very severe.'

Tober grunted. 'One man in a microlight? I know the UK's
strapped for cash, but if they were going to send anyone in, I
think they'd go for a bit more punch than that.'

Angela shot him a warning glance, but Xasan appeared satisfied by the blunt logic. 'You are probably right, Mr Tober.
Perhaps I am being over-cautious and this ranger has simply
brought a visitor to the area.' He tapped his chin with a fore-
finger, then murmured, 'However, better to be safe than sorry
– isn't that what you English are fond of saying?' He tossed
the cell phone back at the man who had brought it in and gave
him rapid instructions. The man grinned and left the room.

'What happens now?' Angela demanded. She flicked a glance
at Tober. The way Xasan was talking didn't sound good.

'You will see.' He turned to his men and gestured at the door.
Two men each approached Tober and Angela, and took them
by the arms. Others crowded in with their weapons ready. 'For
now,' Xasan explained, 'you will wait until we are ready. You
will be fed again in the morning. Do not attempt to resist or to
get away; you are a long way from nowhere and guards have
been posted with orders to shoot.'

'What is this shit?' Tober said quietly. He towered over the
two men flanking him, and they began to look nervous.

'Wait.' Angela held up a hand to prevent any over-reaction
from Tober or Xasan's men. 'Has there been another delay?'
she queried.

'Not a delay, Miss Pryce. A change of plan.' Xasan turned
his back on them, signalling the men to take them away. 'No
more questions.'

They were bundled out of the room into what appeared to

be a rough kitchen at the back, complete with a gas stove and food in plastic boxes. A large wooden trapdoor in the floor was open, revealing a flight of rough stone steps disappearing into the dark. A dank smell came up from below. One of the men handed Tober a flashlight and gestured for him to go down.

Tober hesitated, then stepped into the darkness, followed by Angela.

The trapdoor was slammed shut behind them.

They stood where they were for a few moments on the steps. Tober used the flashlight to investigate their new home. It didn't take long. The basement was a simple square space approximately twelve feet by twelve, with a low ceiling which meant they both had to stoop. Two grass-filled sacks lay on the floor, alongside an earthenware pot of water. A larger pot, which was empty, stood near a blanket screen hung by nails across one corner. It was as much privacy as they were going to get, and confirmed if the two needed it that something about this whole negotiation meeting had changed dramatically. And for the worse.

Tober inspected the walls for signs of another way out. But there were none. They were underground and surrounded by hard-packed dirt and rock. Digging their way out would take days, even if they had the means.

'I should have paid more attention in class,' Angela said, in an attempt at pragmatism. 'I read Arabic and one of the add-ons was a basic course in Somali. I didn't get a single thing they were saying up there, it was all too fast.'

Tober shrugged and kicked the mattresses over, checking for bugs and snakes.

'I didn't read languages,' he said bluntly. 'Didn't really read much English, come to that. But I did six months on armed protection for tankers in the Gulf before joining SIS. It was ninety-eight per cent sun-tan time, so a couple of us got a Somali crewman to teach us the basics. I picked up enough to know what Fat Boy was saying.'

She stared at him. 'Go on.'

His eyes glittered in the flashlight, but his face was blank of emotion. 'He ordered the guy with the camera phone to go find the microlight pilot. He's going to wait for him to make a pass come daylight, then shoot him down.'

She looked stunned. 'But he's nothing to do with us! That's appalling.'

'It is for the pilot. I know some of those guys – they don't bother with parachutes.'

Thirty-Three

There was no noise coming from the villa and no lights. I laid low for ten minutes, tuning in to the night sounds, and eventually picked up the scuff of footsteps as a guard appeared at one corner of the building. Satisfied that nobody was lying in wait further out, I waited for him to disappear and made my way back to my OP.

Before sliding in under the branches, I used a stick to prod around the hollow in case a friendly puff adder had taken up residence. All clear.

I checked the building and surrounding area through the scope. The SUV was parked out front and two men were visible wandering around outside. No sign of the man in the generator shed.

I gave it fifteen minutes to see if Madar had changed his mind about telling the men about me. If he did, they'd soon come boiling out armed to the teeth. But the house remained silent.

I decided it was time to take the hi-tech approach to find out what was going on inside. For that I would need the third package acquired for me by Khaban in Mombasa.

It consisted of a black handset, little bigger than a pack of cigarettes, with a small antenna and tuning dial. With it came a round disk, like a hockey puck. This was the listening bug, fitted with a short wire antenna. The third component was a simple ear bud with a jack plug to fit into the handset. Put together, it was a device for covert audio surveillance of conversations through solid walls. I was well within the maximum operating range of a hundred metres, and with no obstacles in the way to block transmissions, I should be able to pick up on

what was being said. First, though, I had to place the bug
on the outside wall of the structure.

And that meant getting past the guards.

I monitored and timed their movements, but it didn't help
much. They were operating at random, with no fixed patrol times.
One would stay by the door while the other would hoof off round
the villa at his own pace. Then they would change places, sometimes stopping for a brief chat before the other would do his
thing. I tried getting an average time, but it was all too casual to
draw any firm conclusions. I would have to play it by ear.

I checked the lithium batteries were working correctly, then
gathered the various parts together and got ready to move out.
I lifted the overhead branches and slid out on my belly, moving
slowly down the slope and ready to freeze. The listening device
was in my pocket and a Ka-Bar knife in my hand.

I left the ghillie net over my head as a precaution and I
headed at an angle away from the front door. I was aiming at
a point just outside the route taken by the two guards.

I came to the crumbling ruins of the garden wall, which were
little more than knee height, and waited. Moments later, one of
the guards came shuffling round the corner dragging his feet. He
had his rifle over his shoulder, held by the barrel, and was
humming softly, eyes on the ground. It took him thirty seconds
from the time he appeared to the time he vanished again. I waited
some more. Two minutes later the second guard appeared. This
one was even less attentive, and seemed more interested in
chewing on something and spitting out whatever he didn't like.

I took out the bug which came fitted with an adhesive strip.
All I had to do was find a suitable spot on the wall, rip off the
cover and slap it in place. Then it was back to my hide.

I waited for the other guard to do his thing. He came and
went, and the moment he was out of sight, I was up and over
the ruined wall and heading for the front side of the building.

I'd gone no more than three paces when I slammed into a
low obstacle in the dark. It felt like another section of wall, and
I instinctively fell sideways. I hit the ground hard and lay still,
listening and sweating, feeling bruised. I wasn't on the path
used by the guards, but I was close enough to be seen if one
of them chose to take a slightly different route.

As I lifted my head, sub-consciously counting off seconds for the next man to appear, I became aware of a strong smell close by. It carried the stench of rotting matter and human waste, with the telltale buzz of a few late flies.

I'd nearly stumbled into some kind of waste pit.

I felt around in front of me. The wall was about a foot high, and I was thankful I'd instinctively chosen to go down sideways. I was trying to figure out how extensive the pit was when I heard a cough from a few metres away.

It was the other guard – and he was early.

I hugged the rim of the pit, stuffing the bug inside my shirt and grasping the knife. I had nowhere else to go and not enough time to hop back over the garden wall. I held my breath, ready to surge up and take the guard out before he raised the alarm.

I ran the scenario through my head, going over each move automatically. Up, attack, strike, away. I'd have only seconds after silencing him to get out of here.

He approached my position, but instead of continuing on by, he stopped. I heard the rustle of clothing, then the patter of water followed by an echo, and a sigh of relief.

He was taking a leak in the pit.

He finished after what seemed like an age and moved away. As soon as he was gone, I was up again and flat against the wall of the villa, searching for a section of cinder block that was free of plaster. A relatively clean surface would make attaching the bug easier, and picking up voices a lot clearer.

Thirty seconds gone.

I found a section of bare block and rubbed away the dust of the old plaster. I could taste the grit on my tongue, acid and tainted with years of salt spray off the ocean.

Forty seconds.

I ripped off the adhesive cover and clamped the bug hard against the wall, low down behind a clump of dried grass where it would stand less chance of being seen by the guards.

It refused to hold. Damn. I moved it over and tried another spot.

Fifty seconds.

I tried again, this time grinding it hard to get some traction on the rough surface.

It held.

Sixty seconds.

I started back.

'Amiir?'

Jesus – I swung round, reaching for the Ka-Bar.

It was the other guard. He must have got worried by his pal's delay for a comfort stop and come looking for him. He hadn't seen me yet, but was moving out towards the waste pit. Two more steps and there was no way he could miss me.

I launched myself at him.

He heard me coming and tried to step back, but too late. I slammed into him and used my bodyweight to force him to the ground, slapping my hand across his mouth. He was strong, and struggled like a wildcat, trying to wrench his head away and call for help. I could feel his saliva coating my fingers, threatening to lose my hold on him, so I changed my grip and jammed my forearm down hard across his throat to cut off any sound. Then I thrust the Ka-bar in under his ribs, towards the heart.

He struggled briefly for a few seconds, the life draining out of him. Then he went limp and lay still.

It had taken only seconds but I knew my time was up. The other guard would be back soon. I tipped the body over the wall of the waste pit. He was all skin and sinew and weighed very little, and I lowered him as far as I could, then let him go. He dropped into whatever lay at the bottom with barely a sound.

I dropped his rifle in after him. Hopefully, if they found him, it would look as if he'd stumbled in the dark and fallen in.

Thirty-Four

I woke after sunrise and lay still, tuning in, adjusting to the sounds and feel of a new day and thinking briefly about the man I'd killed. It had been him or me, a simple trade-off, but I knew it would be with me for a long while yet.

I forced the thoughts away and listened to birds calling some-where behind me, and the faint hiss of the ocean to the front. It was a strange contrast. I rolled over and checked the villa. It looked out of place along this stretch of coast with its thatched huts and palm trees, and anywhere else it would have been a harmless, if decrepit dwelling long past its use-by date.

Only now I knew better.

I watched for a full ten minutes, wary of moving in case a guard was awake and watching. Nothing moved, which told me they probably weren't expecting company anytime soon, so I slid back down into my hole and dropped some iodine tablets into the bottle of water I'd bought from Madar. I gave it a shake, hoping it would be enough to counter any local contamination.

My sat phone gave a soft buzz. It was Piet.

'How's it going, man?'

'I'm good. Seen anything?'

'That Skytruck from yesterday – it's back in the area.' He sounded pissed off. 'Nearly took me out, coming in out of nowhere at less than five-hundred feet. Soon as I get back to Malindi, I'm reporting him to air traffic for flight violation. If he thinks I didn't get his registration, the asshole, he's got a surprise coming.'

'Can you hold off on that for a few hours?' I wasn't worried about some bush pilot getting into trouble for illegally over-flying the border; but if the Kenyans decided to look into it immediately, which was a possibility with their troops in the area to the north, it could screw with the SIS meeting and put lives in danger. 'I could use the registration, though.'

'Yeah, no sweat.' He read out the number. 'I'll leave it until this evening. Take care and keep your head down. I'll be in the area for a while yet, keeping an eye on things.' He clicked off and I switched on the hearing device and tuned in. Nothing at first, then I picked up a mumble of voices speaking in Somali and the clatter of movement. Early morning stuff, slow and sleep-heavy. No English voices, though.

I checked through the scope. Two guards patrolling, looking like they'd been up all night. One of them stopped by the waste pit and stared at the ground around it, but didn't check inside. Then he stared off towards the beach for a moment before shaking his head and continuing his patrol. It looked like the guard had been posted as a runner.

I called Vale. He sounded as if he hadn't slept much, either. 'Our people failed to report in as scheduled yesterday evening,' he explained without preamble. 'Moresby received a text from Pryce early in the morning, saying they were leaving Nairobi, but he's heard nothing since then.'

'They're here at the villa,' I told him. 'I'm monitoring talk in the building but haven't picked up anything useful yet.' I mentioned what Madar had said about Musa coming in by sea, and gave him the number of the Skytruck. It was up to him what he did with the information.

'Good. I'm not sure what I can do with this without revealing your presence, but I'll talk to the Americans. They might be able to spot the plane's movements on their cameras.' He hesitated. 'Did you say you've bugged the villa?'

'Yes. Thanks to the wonders of the open market in hi-tech gadgets.'

'Christ, you're a tricky bugger.' He sounded almost impressed. 'The bodyguard's name is Doug Tober, by the way. He's ex-Special Boat Service.'

'Good.' Being ex-SBS carried no guarantees that they would get out of the situation they had been placed in, but it did mean Tober was of the calibre to think fast if the situation arose. I just hoped he wouldn't have to.

Vale said goodbye and clicked off and I went back to watching the villa and listening to the audio. There was no sign of anybody leaving to meet up with the Skytruck, and I wondered if it had been told to stay away. At one point Madar came out with food for the two guards. I held my breath as he looked my way for a moment before going back inside. I hoped he wasn't having second thoughts about telling his colleagues about me. If he did, I was cooked.

I studied the terrain around me through the scope, and thought about the area inland. I hadn't seen anywhere better than this on my way into town, but I figured it would be good to have a fall-back position in case things got hairy. Having a large empty space to hide in gave me only a slight advantage if they came looking for me; I'd be able to use the cover of dead ground, and if they got too close, I'd see them coming. But once blown, I'd be out in the open with only that large empty space to run to.

The sun came up and the heat settled on the ground like a heavy woollen blanket. It brought flies and other bugs, and I sipped water in between squirting military-grade insect repellant around me. It was guaranteed aroma-free and had been developed especially for forward observers in hostile territories where alien fragrances would be instantly noted. I hoped the manufacturers had got genuine Department of Defence approval, otherwise I was going to have a bunch of Somali gunmen sniffing around my hide like dogs on heat.

Even the guards began to look lethargic, and I tried not to look beyond the villa at the ocean, where birds resembling gannets were swooping and diving into the clear blue water. Above my head a couple of birds I thought might be drongos flitted about in the branches, and I wished them a long and pleasant stay. Anything that smacked to the guards of normality was fine by me.

Still no recognizable talk from the bug on the house, just a lot of chatter in Somali and the sounds of a bunch of men talking about stuff. Occasionally I heard a drumming sound in the background, but it was impossible to determine what it was.

But I did recognize the sounds of weapons being dismantled and cleaned. Some things sound the same in every language.

It was close to midday when things got busy.

Everything had been quiet for a while, and even the birds had gone to lunch, when I heard engines coming from the direction of Kamboni. I checked my cover and pulled the ghillie around my head and shoulders, and waited to see what was happening.

From inside the house I could hear a babble of voices, and Xasan trying to get some order.

Moments later, two pickups skidded to a stop near the villa. They were full of armed men toting AKs, some wearing bandoliers of ammunition slung across their chests. Something told me they weren't here on a casual outing.

Some of the men inside wandered out to meet them, and they all exchanged greetings and hugs like long-lost pals. Xasan showed his fat face but stayed in the background like a kid who hadn't been invited to the party.

There was a lot of talk, with much gesticulating from Xasan's men towards the area around the building. I took this to be about the missing guard. But it clearly didn't interest the newcomers much, and they soon piled back into the pickups and roared off back the way they had come.

A short while later, as everyone was settling down, a Kenyan military transport plane flew over. The sight of it had the guards and some of the other men running around like chickens, shouting at each other and pointing their rifles at the sky. I watched through the scope as the plane flew out to sea and banked to the right, before making its way back inland and disappearing from sight.

At that point one of the guards decided he'd had enough excitement and decided to take a pee in the waste pit.

He stood there doing his thing and eyeing the scenery, then finally he did what all guys do in these circumstances: he looked down to check nothing important had dropped off.

Then he began shouting.

It took them ten minutes of arguing and gesticulating before they found a way of getting the dead man out of the pit. It involved two lengths of wood and some rope, and nobody seemed too keen on handling the body or the muck it was covered in. They eventually managed to spill it on to the ground, where they stood and yakked over it at length as if it might suddenly spring back to life.

Xasan played no part in the proceedings, but he made it pretty clear what he thought: that some idiots can't walk in a straight line without tripping over their feet. He eventually waved a hand in disgust and waddled away, leaving them to it.

After more talk, three men wrapped the body in an old tarpaulin and took it out of sight, while the others went back inside the house.

Minutes later I heard some banging and shouting through the audio feed, and a very English female voice.

'Why have you got us shut in down here?'

Angela Pryce, and she sounded pissed.

The next voice I heard was in heavily accented English. I assumed it was Xasan.

'You have five minutes to clean yourselves. Then you can eat.'

'What's happening?' Pryce's voice was hoarse and dry and I guessed they had been locked in somewhere since arriving yesterday. It couldn't have been pleasant with the heat and the rough conditions, and whatever they had been fed would have been cold rations. 'What was all the shouting about?'

'Don't ask questions,' Xasan said snappily. 'If you do not do as I say, Mr Tober will be shot. It is your choice.'

'Like you ordered the ranger shot down, you mean?'

Piet.

I grabbed my sat phone and hit the speed dial to call him, thinking Pryce really shouldn't have given away the fact that they had understood Somali. You never, ever let the opposition know you understand more than they think. Once you do that, you've lost whatever small advantage you might have had.

As the phone began ringing at the other end, I heard the distant pops of gunshots drifting in on the air.

Thirty-Five

The shot was a fluke, Piet de Bont figured. Nobody got that good first time, not against a moving target high overhead. It zinged off one of the wheel struts and set off a vibration through the framework, and that was close enough for him.

'Bastard!' He automatically put the nose down, taking the microlight to starboard while searching below for signs of drifting gun smoke. He'd been shot at enough times by poachers to know the signs, and most were merely a warning to stay away. The poachers knew he was in no position to shoot back. They also knew he had radio contact with his base at the KWS and experience told them that it would take time for an armed patrol to get out here. By then they'd be long gone.

But this was different. There were no poachers in this imme- diate area so close to the border – he'd already checked. And the sudden appearance of a bullet hole in the fabric of the wing just above his head meant this was no warning. They were shooting for real.

They wanted him dead.

The engine howled as he struggled to lose height fast enough while getting as far away from the shooter as possible. Over-committing and folding everything around him wouldn't do him any good; with over a thousand feet to go he'd be dead. He looked down, checking for signs of a vehicle; the poachers didn't walk in to pursue their trade, but drove in and out, ready to move fast if a patrol showed up.

Nothing. The heat haze was making everything shimmer, and although he thought he caught a glimpse of a pickup at one point, he'd shifted position before he could zero in on it.

He aimed for a point about a kilometre away, dropping as fast as he dared to give the shooter the impression that he was damaged and going in hard. He wasn't too concerned about the hole; the fabric was unlikely to tear unless it got hit on the trailing edge, then it would rip right through. But damage to the frame was more serious. No frame, no flight.

End of game.

As he coasted in above a section of narrow track, he felt his cell phone buzzing in his breast pocket. Not his base, then; they'd have used the radio. Had to be Portman. He focussed on the ground ahead as the wheels clipped some long grass at the side of the track. It was safe to land here and he'd got a fuel and water cache nearby for emergencies. He came to a stop and leapt out, reaching for his rifle. If the shooter decided to come visit and finish him off, he'd be in for a surprise. Piet knew the bush and was expert at using the most minimal of cover as camouflage. After spending a couple of years on border patrol with the South African NDF, dodging poachers, smugglers and groups of armed intruders, often out for a couple of weeks at a time, he could vanish as effectively as any wild game.

He took out his cell phone and rolled beneath the cover of a dried thorn bush.

'Yeah, what?'

'You OK? I heard shots.'

'Yeah, I'm fine. What makes you think they were firing at me?'

Portman relayed the brief conversation he'd overheard in the villa.

Piet muttered an oath. 'I thought it was poachers. What the hell are these people doing? The moment I get on the radio, they'll have the KWS, army and border patrols all over them.' He took the phone away from his ear for a moment to listen for sounds of an approaching vehicle, but everything was quiet save for the buzz of insects.

'I don't think they were giving it much thought. There's a man named Xasan, a middleman, whose nominally in charge but he doesn't look like he's getting much respect from the men. He was probably trying to show how tough he is.'

'Well, my wing's got a hole in it and I'm pretty sure there's a dent on one of my struts, so your Mr Xasan had better get ready; if I get him in my sights he's a dead man. Daisy cost me good money!'

Portman's dry chuckle echoed down the line. 'Good to hear you haven't lost your sense of humour.'

'Not yet, I haven't. So what's happening with you?'

'Not much. A lot of talk, but I think somebody else is due to come in. Could be why they're jumpy. Stay in touch.'

'Will do.' Piet switched off.

Thirty-Six

It was late afternoon when I saw Xasan step out of the front door. He was followed by two of his men and walked to the edge of the property and stared out to sea, shading his eyes against the dying sun. He turned and looked at them once and shook his head, and I could see he was sweating. Heat or nerves? Moments later they were joined by others who stood in the background, eyes on the horizon.

Then they all got skittish and started looking at each other and slapping arms like it was Mardi Gras . . . or whatever feast

day they liked to celebrate. Even Xasan managed a grim smile
as he turned and tried to join in the celebrations.

I saw what had aroused their attention: three skiffs were heading
for land, their slim shapes head-on nearly invisible without
the aid of the scope. No wonder the security guys on the tankers
had such a hard time spotting them; hugging the waves,
they had virtually no profile and offered little in the way of a
useful target.

By the time they reached the shore, everyone was standing
in a line across the garden overlooking the sand, a ragged
welcoming committee of men waving their rifles like something
out of a spaghetti western.

The skiffs came in fast and smooth, the first one disgorging
three men. The other two beached either side and their crews
each proceeded to unload a number of bags, which I figured
were supplies, and three green metal boxes which looked military in design. I snapped a bunch of photos and hoped Vale
could do something with them.

The men from the lead boat walked up the beach, leaving
the rest to do the heavy lifting. The man in the middle was tall
and thin and carried himself almost regally with long, steady
strides, his eyes straight ahead as if unconcerned with whatever
might be going on around him. And why should he? He was
the boss man.

Yusuf Musa.

He wore a small skullcap with a scarf looped loosely over
the top, and the traditional skirt, *kameez* shirt and a waistcoat.
A belt across his chest carried a line of shells and a slim cross-
strap holding a cell phone like a badge of office. It wasn't
exactly traditional, but I guess if he was important, he could
wear whatever he chose.

As he came nearer and I zeroed in on his face, the feeling
of familiarity that I'd had before suddenly came rushing in on
me.

He was a spit for Osama Bin Laden.

I settled lower in my hide and kept the scope on him. He
approached Xasan and acknowledged him with a curt nod,
giving the fat man something to get excited about at last. They
embraced briefly and Xasan talked volubly, gesturing towards

the other side of the house. When two of the men from the villa broke away and came back moments later dragging the loaded tarpaulin, it was obvious Xasan had decided to get in quick and spill the beans about the dead guard.

I watched Musa's face. As an authority figure, I reckoned he'd be bored by this little exercise in sucking up by Xasan. But I was wrong. His head jerked up at the sight of the tarpaulin and he snapped an instruction which had everyone jumping to attention. The two men carrying the tarpaulin flipping it open so that Musa could inspect the contents.

Then he said something and Xasan pointed to a man standing to one side.

The second guard.

Musa called him forward. The man shuffled over, the others parting to make way for him. Musa asked questions, using a lot of finger stabbing in the air, and the guard replied, looking miserable.

Then Musa held out a hand.

With a chill feeling I knew what was coming.

One of his men handed over his AK. Musa spun it round a couple of times, like a fancy marine guard of honour. On the third spin, he turned it and jabbed the butt viciously into the guard's face, knocking his head back and raising a spray of blood from his smashed mouth and nose. He said something else, but the guard was too stunned to answer, barely able to stay on his feet. With an almost casual air, Musa raised the AK and placed the top of the barrel against the doomed man's forehead and pulled the trigger.

As he did so, he smiled.

The shot was flat and already fading as it carried up the slope to me, like it didn't want to make a fuss about what it had just done. The dead guard was carted away by two men on Musa's instructions, and seconds later I saw it being tipped into the waste pit.

For a long moment nobody moved. It was like they were stuck in the sand, not daring to be the first to break ranks. Then Musa pointed to the beach and some men moved away and fetched the three metal boxes, which they placed on the sand just down from the house. Musa watched them, nodding in approval, and after posting his two companions on guard outside, he followed Xasan into the villa.

I realized that I'd been holding my breath and let it out in one go. I'd seen summary justice before, but never witnessed it done so casually. Musa had clearly been intent on making a point, even stamping his authority on the men. But he'd also enjoyed it, as if it were an act of theatre.

It left me with a bad feeling.

Everything eventually settled down and the two supply skiffs cast off and disappeared towards the south at speed, their powerful engines echoing across the water. They were hugging the coast and probably heading for Kamboni. The new guards went inside and were replaced by two more. Suddenly everything about the place had taken on a fresh buzz, as if the atmosphere had been injected with a sense of urgency.

Two more guards came out after a while and took up positions, this time with a snap and fully alert. One of them, older and darker than his companion, began walking across the rear of the villa, studying the terrain around him and sniffing the air like a hunting dog. His AK-47 had an extended barrel like mine – a shooter's rifle. Unlike the other men, his was cleaned and oiled, and he carried it across his body, leading me to suspect that he'd seen military service somewhere.

I watched as the range of his patrol became wider and wider, moving inexorably up the slope towards me, his face sombre and focussed.

Fifty metres and closing.

This wasn't looking good.

I eased back in my hide and placed the tip of my rifle barrel on the rim, just inside the covering of branches. I made sure the ghillie was in place and made myself as comfortable as I could. If I had to, I could stand up and be on the move faster this way than lying prone. The Ka-Bar was in my belt and I could have it out in a flicker if push came to shove.

Thirty metres.

I could hear the hiss of his breathing now. He wasn't particularly young, and I put his age at forty or more. He had the grizzled look of a hardened fighter, a man who had seen and done things that had earned him his place close to the head man. It made him a more formidable opponent than the guard last night, and I began working out my tactic for taking him down if he came too close.

Twenty metres.

He stopped barely fifteen paces away and looked over his shoulder, taking in the sweep of the beach, the villa, and the line of the coast away to the right. Then he spun and looked across the slope, checking out the ground from left to right either side of my position, quartering it in segments and not missing a thing.

He started forward again before spotting something on the ground. He stopped and bent down.

I held my breath and got ready to move. Had I left footprints at the front of the hide? I couldn't recall. If so, it was a dead giveaway.

But he bent down and picked up something with a flash of red. It was the water bottle dropped by Madar. He examined it, unscrewed the top, sniffed at the contents, then tossed it away.

The bottle landed on the edge of my hide with a dull slap. It teetered for a moment, the water inside sloshing noisily, then tipped over and rolled down, slipping beneath the covering branches. It came to a rest against my leg.

I stayed absolutely still, not daring to blink, my eyes half closed. He was now so close, if he caught as much as a gleam off an eyeball, he'd be in on top of me before I could move.

Then he yawned and rubbed at his face, waving away a fly. My luck was continuing to hold. He had one empty eye socket, the flesh around it twisted and puckered, joining a long scar down the side of his face. An old battle wound.

A voice floated up the slope, and he turned his head.

It was the other guard, calling and waving an arm. He and a couple of other men were walking away from the villa towards Kamboni. They were all armed and looked eager to go. It looked like they had received orders, and I wondered what they were. Whatever they were doing, they clearly weren't going far, and One-eye was expected to go with them.

He turned and walked away, and I breathed easily, thanking

my lucky stars that his eyesight hadn't rivalled the younger Madar's. Maybe now I could snatch a brief sleep.

Ten minutes later I was jerked awake by the sound of gunfire.

Thirty-Seven

It took an effort of will not to overreact. Leaping up in my position would get me killed. Instead I grabbed the rifle and hugged the earth while I tried to locate the source of the gunfire. That's not an easy thing to do when you're crouched in a hole, half asleep and with your head clouded in cotton wool. Sounds get distorted and deflected every which way.

I figured I'd heard at least four or five shots in rapid succession. But they'd been faint, so not from anywhere close by. Then came another burst, and I pinned it down.

Dhalib.

I risked a quick look. Was this an attack? Or had the men with One-eye run into trouble with the locals? The light was still good but beginning to drop, and I couldn't see any signs of activity towards Dhalib. If the Kenyan army or police had decided to pay a visit, and the shots had been a first encounter, no way was I going to hang around. The army would come in heavy-handed and mop up anybody in the area. And that would include me.

Then I saw smoke drifting into the air.

I checked the villa. A single guard was standing near the front door, scratching his butt. He didn't seem concerned by the gunshots or the smoke, so I figured he knew what was going on. But I didn't.

I waited for him to move out of sight, then lifted the cover overhead and slipped out of the hide. It was probably nothing to be worried about, but I had to make sure I wasn't going to be caught in a pincer movement. I crept away towards Dhalib, sticking close to the ground and with the ghillie net over my head and shoulders to break up my outline.

Twenty minutes of slow crawling later, I heard voices and

laughter. The smoke was pungent and black and hanging close to the ground, shifted inshore by the breeze. An occasional slurry of sparks was being pushed into the air, and I guessed I must be close to the huts.

It took me another five minutes to reach the first one. Or what was left of it.

It was too smoky to see much, but it looked like the men had raided the fishermen's huts and got carried away. I figured three of the small buildings had been destroyed by fire and another two were smouldering. The smell of burnt wood and plastic was pungent, overlaid by the heavier stench of burning rubber, which I guessed was from old rubber tyres used as fenders and thrown into the flames by Musa's men.

I crawled closer and found two bodies lying in the bushes. They were older men, lean and stringy, dressed in tattered clothing. They'd been shot several times.

Voices floated up from the beach. I moved back into the bushes and made my way closer to the water.

The pirates were milling around the fishermen's boats, tossing out anything they couldn't use, like nets and floats, and unfurling the sails to check for holes. An engine roared into life for a few seconds before cutting out. Compared to the engines used by the pirates, it sounded feeble and ancient.

A body lay in the shallows, covered in blood, and further along the sand, another man had tried to flee and got cut down.

Musa obviously wasn't playing at being friends with the locals. He must have decided they needed more boats and sent his men out to get them. At whatever the cost.

I relaxed my grip on the rifle. It would have been easy to dish out the same treatment these men had given the fishermen. Satisfying, too. But there was nothing I could do for the dead men without compromising my position, so I slid back to my hide and got busy sending Vale the photos I'd taken earlier. Then I called him with an update. He answered the phone immediately.

'What can you tell me?' He sounded tired. 'These photos are disturbing.'

'It's Musa. He just arrived with more armed men and supplies.' I wasn't sure how to proceed so I said, 'Are you sure this is just a negotiation?'

There was a longer delay this time. 'Why do you ask?'

'Because they look as if they've come for war, and they're already killing locals.' I described what I had just seen in Dhalib – or what remained of it.

He grunted. 'This isn't good.' Like me, he would have recognized some of the boxes unloaded from the skiffs as being of the kind used to carry ammunition, even small rockets. If Musa was planning on stocking up local members of his clan with some extra firepower, his men were in a position, placed behind the Kenyan forces in Kismaayo, to inflict some serious damage on their supply lines. It wouldn't be a prolonged fight, but a quick hit-and-run exercise to unnerve and destabilize the soldiers in the area, followed by a rapid retreat to sea. It explained why he had decided to acquire more boats and why he wasn't concerned about letting a few local fishermen stand in his way. This was part of a campaign and collateral damage was incidental.

'It won't help immediately,' Vale continued, 'but I got some information about the Skytruck. It was on a watch bulletin from the Kenyan and Nigerian border police. The pilot's a Russian, said to fly anybody anywhere, no questions asked. He's been in the region for a couple of years but nobody's been able to pin anything on him yet apart from a couple of minor infringements. Any sign of our two people?'

I told him about the snatch of conversation I'd overheard earlier. He didn't say anything, but I was certain by his silence that he shared the same reservations about Pryce's outburst as me.

'If it all goes wrong,' I said, 'and I get them out, we're a long way from nowhere. I can put Pryce on the microlight, but Tober and I will be on foot in bush country.' I let him work on that one for a bit; he knew the position we'd be in.

'Yes.' That was all he said.

'I know what you said about rescue,' I said, 'but what are the chances of an extraction for Tober?' I was thinking about the Russian pilot and the Skytruck. If he could set down right on the border near here, surely another pilot could do the same.

Vale was ahead of me. 'Close to nil. I'm sorry. I wish I could hire a man to do it but my hands are tied. Piet will have to do what he can.'

At least it confirmed that he hadn't been able to work any miracles behind the scenes.

It made our chances of survival very slim. Always assuming I got Tober and Pryce out safely in the event of trouble, we would still have to get back across the border and keep moving until Piet could make a pickup, followed by a second and third trip.

It would be pushing his luck – and ours – to the extreme.

'There's been a development from our cousins,' Vale said calmly. 'The CIA have failed to get camera coverage of the area. They had an offer agreed, then they were blocked at source. It seems certain elements in the administration don't want to upset the Kenyans by overflying drones, which most people in that neck of the woods regard as attack vehicles.'

With all the news reports of terrorist leaders and others being taken out by drone attacks controlled by keyboard handlers, hundreds, even thousands of kilometres away, I wondered why anybody should be trying to kid themselves otherwise.

'Well, aren't they?'

'Yes. But that doesn't help you or us.' He hesitated. 'What's your position?'

'I'm good. But I've already had two near misses and these guys have shifted up a gear now Musa's arrived.'

'You've had a contact?' His instincts were good, telling him that something bad had happened.

'Yes, but they think it was an accident. You didn't expect this to be trouble-free, did you?'

'I suppose not.' I heard his sigh all the way down the line. 'It would help if we knew what was in those boxes on the beach.'

I knew what was coming next. 'Meaning?'

'Any chance you could take a look?'

Thirty-Eight

Daylight was fading fast when I saw Madar come out of the house. I watched through the scope as he talked to the guards and gestured over his shoulder towards town. He had a bag slung over one shoulder and I figured he'd been given orders to go shopping again. As he walked towards the footpath, he glanced my way briefly and flicked his hand. He probably thought it would look to a casual observer as if he was brushing away flies, but to me it looked exactly what it was – a sign for me to follow.

I gave him a head start in case one of the more switched-on new arrivals had noticed his signalling efforts, then slid out of my hide and followed.

This time I had the Vektor and the Ka-Bar, although their potential for any real protection was limited. If this was a trap, I'd be caught in open terrain against men with rifles. But I didn't think so; Madar was a simple city-bred kid caught up in something over which he had no control and didn't understand. But he wanted an out, which was good. All he needed was a gentle push in the right direction.

I found him waiting for me by the wrecks of the two skiffs I'd seen on the last trip, a short walk away from the huts of Dhalib. Smoke was still hanging in the air and he looked scared to hell. I wondered if it was because of what had happened to the fishermen or something else.

'Mr Marc,' he greeted me politely, although his voice was shaking. 'I am pleased you have come.'

I smiled in an attempt to settle his nerves. If he got too wound up he wouldn't be able to string two words together. 'I got your signal loud and clear. What's going on?'

He looked around and sat on the ground, pulling the bag into himself. It made him look even younger and I felt rough for using him this way. But I had to find out what was happening to the two SIS personnel. I squatted beside him, one eye on the track.

'They say there is to be no talking with the two English spies.'
The words came out in a rush. He looked frightened, and he was
obviously parroting what he'd heard the other men say.

'Did they say why?' This was new. Referring to them as
spies wasn't a good sign. It shifted their position from negotiators to something very different. No talking meant no deal.

Things suddenly didn't look too rosy for Pryce and Tober.

'Before, there was much talk of ransom and barter for some
other people they had taken from a big boat to the north. I do
not know who those people are. But now they say they will not
do this.' His eyes were huge with fright as he looked at me.

'What, then?'

He swallowed, then whispered, 'The tall man who came
earlier in the boat – you saw him?' He made a cross sign over
his chest. The bandoliers. 'He is a very important man.
Everybody says so. It was he who ordered the men to attack
the fishermen and take their boats.'

'I saw. Did he say why he needed them?'

'He told the men that they will be using them as vessels to
strike at the hearts of the unbelievers at sea.'

Nothing different there, then. Definitely a planned campaign.
But what did it mean for the negotiations?

'What else did he say?' Madar was looking sick and I felt
my gut go cold.

'He said the English are to be executed.'

It took a moment for the full shock of his words to sink in.
Jesus.

'How?'

'They are saying we must abide by *adrabu fawq al-'anaq,*
which means strike at their necks.' He made a chopping motion
to the back of his neck. It didn't take rocket science to figure
out what that meant.

'Did he say why?'

He looked unsure. 'It is something they say they must do as
instructed in the Holy Qur'ân. It is an act of payment – of
Zakah – an act of obedience, to please Allah.' His brow knitted.
'I know the Holy Qur'ân, but I do not understand everything
these men are saying. They are also very angry when they say

these words.' He ducked his head in apology. 'I am sorry – I was too frightened to ask why they are doing this.'

'It's not your fault, Madar. You've got nothing to be sorry for.'

I felt numbed by the news, and wondered why I found it so easy to believe what Madar had just told me. Because it was so logical, perhaps. Why else, after all, had this elaborate charade been set up? My mind was already racing ahead, and I could only come to one conclusion about Musa's intentions.

Propaganda.

'What are you thinking, Mr Marc?' Madar sounded worried by my silence.

I shook my head. Now wasn't the time to go internal. I couldn't change Musa's plans, only the outcomes.

'Will they do it, do you think?'

Madar swallowed hard. 'Yes. I am sure. The other men talk and say the tall man has come here for this thing only. He has also called others to come from the town, to see what is being done in the name of Allah. They are very excited by this, I think.'

Witnesses. He wanted others to see it, to validate the event and spread the word. He'd planned a gory spectacular, but without other eyes and voices it would be a non-event. This way the ripples would spread outwards like a shockwave.

So much for negotiations.

'He made me prepare a room in the house,' Madar continued softly. 'I was instructed to clean it carefully and hang a flag on the walls, which he brought with him in the boat. He also brought a camera and a small computer to make disks. The man named Xasan knows how to do these things. He has done it before, I think.'

Musa had told Madar to prepare a killing room. Complete with the usual backdrop of flags for propaganda purposes and a crowd of cheering onlookers, the beheading would be recorded on DVD and shipped around the world for eager followers to gloat over. And making victims of two SIS representatives – one a woman – would ramp up the tension higher than it had ever been. It wouldn't matter a damn to Musa or his followers that the more hawkish elements in the west would demand a high level of retaliation; they would look on any response as merely symptomatic of increasing western aggression and to hell with collateral damage among their own people.

By which time he would be long gone into the Somali interior, beyond reach.

And Xasan would be in the background, making a quick buck from it any way he could.

I needed to know more. 'What was the flag?'

'I am not sure. Someone said it the flag of al-Shabaab, but I do not know what that is. I have heard the name, but only from others.'

Al-Shabaab. If anybody was going to benefit by such an extreme act, it was them. But were they the only ones? And what would happen to Xasan's reputation for trading hostages afterwards? He'd be on every kill list around the world. Maybe it was going to be worth it to him; being in the middleman business was fraught with danger, especially when dealing with unpredictable characters like Musa. This might be his way of getting out.

'Did they say what they are looking for in return?' Propaganda was only one benefit. I didn't hold out much hope of this kid knowing anything, but I was in for a surprise.

'Much money,' he said. 'After the man spoke, the others were laughing and saying how they could buy new engines for the boats, much faster and more efficient, to out-run the foreign ships – and new guns, too. And rocket launchers.' Just for a second he looked almost excited, as if sharing in the possibility of some new toys to play with. Then he looked ashamed. 'Sorry.'

I waved it away. He couldn't help it. Excitement in such a closed environment was contagious. And the chance for these men to have access to more arms and equipment to pursue their piracy campaign was something beyond their wildest dreams.

'Did they say where this money would come from?' I had to ask the question, although I already knew the answer.

He spoke the name softly, as if in awe. Even Madar, a young, innocent boy from the city who did not know of al-Shabaab, had heard of them. 'al-Qaeda.'

So the terror group was using al-Shabaab to do their dirty work for them. But the reaction to the killings would be the same, whether their dead hand was seen on the sword or not.

'You had better go,' I told him, 'before you are missed.'

He nodded and looked relieved. 'What should I do, Mr Marc? This is a bad thing they do.' He nodded towards the ruined huts of Dhalib. 'To the fishermen also. Many people have already left Kamboni. They believe airplanes and soldiers will come and there will be much fighting.'

I didn't want to tell him that was unlikely, so I said, 'At the first opportunity, you should leave. Go home. The only thing waiting for you here is death. How did you get here?'

'By sea. They said that is the only way to avoid the Kenyan army around Kismaayo.' His face twisted at the memory. 'I was sick all the way. They thought I was weak, like a girl, and threatened to throw me overboard.'

'Don't worry about it,' I told him. 'Some of the greatest sailors in the world were often seasick.'

'True?'

'Absolutely. Can you go back that way?'

'Yes. There are always boats looking for men to help. And I can cook.' He thrust his chest out, a boy wanting validation among men.

'Then do that. At least in your home town you have a sister. She will be pleased to see you again.'

'That is true.' His eyes grew large. 'Are you going to attack the house?'

'No. There are too many men.' That wasn't quite true, but I didn't want to give away any plans I might have. 'But if they execute the English, everybody in the house will die. You don't want to be here when that happens.'

'I understand.' He frowned, processing the information. It must have been hard for him to take in, and I wondered whether I'd gone too far. If the thought of the house being flattened really freaked him out, he might run back and warn the others.

'Before you go,' I said, 'show me where the two English people are being held.'

He sank to his knees and drew a square on the floor, dividing it roughly into four sections. He prodded the right-hand square at the front of the house, facing the sea, and said, 'That is the room I have prepared.' He then pointed to the one behind it, at the rear. 'This is where I prepare food. Under this floor are steps into a hole – another room. The English are down there.'

'Locked in?'

He shook his head. 'No. There is a flat door, but always with two guards watching over it. The English have mattresses and water in buckets. It is not a good place. It smells of death.'

'Lighting?'

'They have one flashlight. They asked for candles but Xasan said they might try to burn down the house. He does not trust the big Englishman. I think he is scared of him.'

As well he might be. Tober was in a hell of a situation, but he wouldn't have been picked for this job if he wasn't capable of thinking on his feet.

The situation hadn't been good to begin with. Now it was far worse. I had to let Vale know, although I had no idea what he could do with the information.

'Get out of here,' I told Madar. 'Do it now. When you reach town, keep going and don't look back.'

He stood up and held out his hand. I shook it gravely. He turned towards town and scurried away into the gloom.

Thirty-Nine

Pryce and Tober listened as the talk went on above their heads. The voices were muted by the thickness of the floor between them, but it was evident that somebody important had arrived and that feelings among the men upstairs were running high, like a charge of electricity.

'Musa,' said Angela. She automatically looked towards Tober, although it was so dark down here that she needn't have bothered. And the flashlight had to be saved for later.

'I reckon,' Tober agreed. 'Excitable bunch, aren't they? I'm wondering what the gunfire was about.'

Angela waited for him to say more, but he didn't. She took it as a bad sign.

'You don't think this is going to end well, do you?'

'If I was a betting man, I wouldn't expect good odds, no.'
His voice was surprisingly calm, and she wondered how he
managed it. She had worked with others like him before, but
not in situations quite like this. It made her realize that she had
been incredibly naïve to have gone into this so willingly. What
the hell had she been thinking? She gripped her fists tight to
prevent a tremor running through them, and was glad of the
darkness to hide in. What chances of a career progression now,
she thought? 'Is there going to be any backup?'

A short silence. 'I wouldn't count on it. You know what
Moresby said.'

'Yes.' Moresby had said they would not be in any danger.
Assurances had been given by Xasan and the people behind
him that their safety would be guaranteed. That all they were
doing was talking. Negotiating. Even so, there was a chance,
wasn't there?

'So we'll join the hostages.'

'Most likely.'

She felt a ripple of irritation at the brevity of his responses.
'You don't talk much, do you?'

'Never felt the need. Why – do you think talk will get us out
of here?'

'No. I don't. But it might help . . . to . . . help.'

She heard a shuffle in the dark, and then felt Tober's presence
alongside her. He didn't touch her, but stayed a heartbeat away.

'This any help?'

She smiled and felt reassured. It was enough, under the
circumstances.

'Sorry.'

'Don't sweat it. First op I went on I pissed myself.'

She didn't believe him but said, 'Aren't you scared about
what might happen?'

'A bit. But scared is good; it makes you ready for fight and
flight. You give in to fear and you might as well lie down and die.'
He touched her shoulder. 'Be ready, that's all. When the time
comes, you might get one chance only. If it comes, take it and go.'

'I will if you will.' She touched his hand, grateful for the
support. When he spoke, she could tell he was smiling.

'No worries. I'll be right in front of you.'

Forty

'I want to know what your contingency plans are if you fail to hear from Pryce and Tober within the next few hours.' Vale barged into Moresby's office, past caring what the ops director might do or say. A bad situation had been allowed to deteriorate, and with no word from the two operatives in Somalia, nor from Musa or Xasan, the outlook was looking increasingly grim. They should have heard something by now.

Moresby looked startled, and put down the phone he'd been using. Behind him, lights glowed in the darkness across the river. It was a reminder to Vale that he himself hadn't been home in days and he was running on reserves of energy that would soon become too depleted to function effectively. He'd done it before, many times – but he'd been younger then, with energy to spare. Now things were different.

'What do you mean crashing in here?' Moresby demanded, rising from his seat.

'Sit down, you idiot.' Vale threw himself into the visitor's chair and stared at the senior officer. 'You've fucked up and you know it. You've put two people in the wind and have no way of knowing whether they're alive or dead. It's time to stop pretending you've got a hold on this farce and do something.'

'The first thing I'll do if you don't leave is call security!' Moresby's face twisted at the idea. 'It'll be quite a scene, having someone of your length of service hauled along the corridor and kicked out of the building.' He reached for the phone.

'No, you won't.' Vale stared at him with an air of calm. 'You pick up that thing and I'll activate a prepared internal memorandum copied to the Joint Intelligence Committee giving chapter and verse of the botch-up you've made of this operation.'

'You wouldn't dare.'

'Of course I would. What do I have to lose? I'll list the mission and engagement rules you've trampled over, the complete absence of any risk assessment or support for the personnel involved, and the way you've completely overruled my warnings. In fact, it's my very length of service and experience that's your biggest problem right now. I've been here, remember; I've done it, wrote the bloody book on it – and all without your fancy title.' He leaned forward. 'I know I'll get shunted out immediately as a whistle-blower, probably with an arrest warrant waiting for me before I hit the street. But your career would be over, too. Even the cousins aren't convinced this was a brilliant idea.'

Moresby finally sat down. 'What do you mean?'

Vale's face twitched. 'The cousins? It's what we used to call the Americans?'

'I know that!' A fleck of spittle left Moresby's lips. 'Who said they're not convinced? Scheider promised coverage, so he's on board.'

'Really? What coverage was that?'

'Over-flights, drones with cameras – you were there; weren't you listening?'

'Yes, I was there, but only by chance. That's something else I'll be taking up with the powers that be; the fact that I was excluded by omission when I have a watching brief on all ops.' Vale waved his hand. 'But that's for later. The simple fact is, have you received any hard information from the Americans? Any footage? Details on the ground? Radio traffic from the area?'

Moresby hesitated, then said, 'I haven't seen everything, no. Frankly, I've been too busy. The ops section will alert me if anything develops.'

Vale gave him a pitying look and wondered whether Moresby had ever been down to the ops section since the usual induction tour of the building by all recruits. The operations room in the basement had a twenty-four hour open link with GCHQ taking in their outstations and British embassies worldwide, especially Africa and the Middle East regions. They also collated regular updates from allied sources such as the CIA and NSA. Working on multiple active operations, the ops section analysed and cleaned all information received before passing it on to the relevant directors for further action.

So far, according to the section supervisor Vale had spoken to less than an hour ago, they had received no hard intelligence on the Somali/Kenyan border area, save for some chatter by known terrorist-linked sites and a handful of carefully-worded and obviously coded phone calls in the region which were being followed up and analysed. The supervisor had also mentioned a few brief calls made over an encrypted satellite phone, which they had been unable to unravel due to the sophistication of the system. Vale had expressed vague interest, but nothing more. He knew who was making those calls and calling attention to Portman would serve no useful purpose.

'What's with the look?' Moresby prickled defensively.

'The ops section has nothing. If you were on top of this operation, as you claim, you would know that. You'd have been down there watching the traffic. I happen to know that the CIA have been refused permission to activate any of their Hale drone units, but have offered a lower-grade drone instead . . . which isn't available due to ongoing operational requirements.'

'That can't be.'

Vale stared hard in response to Moresby's incredulous expression. 'I'm afraid it is. Scheider's been stamped on from a great height – something that could have been avoided if you'd activated the Special Ops protocol in the first place. That way they'd have been forced to provide cover under the existing Intelligence Share agreement. As it is, with everything else they've got going on since 9/11, they only have to share information in the normal way. Anything related to this job might get passed across – but only if they happen to be looking for it and see it. You've left that door closed, and with no prioritizing, Scheider's promises have been countermanded.'

'I don't believe it.' Moresby looked furious, but Vale noticed he was making no move to check the facts. *He already knew.*

'So what are you going to do about Pryce and Tober – or are you prepared to see their faces splashed all over Al-Jazeera's next news bulletin?'

For the first time Moresby began to look uncomfortable, as if it was beginning to dawn on him that his planning had been flawed from the outset and was now falling apart.

Vale felt no sympathy for him. 'Well?'

'Nothing. I'll . . .' Moresby wouldn't meet his gaze. 'I'll call

Nairobi, get them to contact Xasan. He's the middleman, he should know what's going on.'

Vale could barely believe his ears. 'Xasan's about as trust-worthy as a snake. He's one of them, don't you see that? He's had his fingers in too many hostage deals, all of them making large amounts of money. We're providing him with goods for his market stall and he's flogging them right back to us; he can't lose.'

Vale stood up and stared at Moresby, trying to judge what the man was thinking. But it was like assessing a window dummy. He just hoped to God that there was something other than self-interested jelly inside his head.

'For Christ's sake do something,' he muttered. 'Before it's too late.' With that he turned and walked out.

Moresby sat immobile for a few seconds, numbed by doubt and the ferocity of Vale's words. Then he shook himself and reached for his phone. He spoke for two minutes, listened for slightly less, then replaced the receiver. A bead of sweat had formed across his brow as the awful realization began to sink that he might have miscalculated in his plans. If what he'd just heard from the MOD liaison officer were true – and he had no reason for thinking otherwise – the SBS detachments on board two Type 23 frigates, with their transport of Lynx helicopters, were still too far away from the coast of Somalia to be of any use for at least another twenty hours.

It was small consolation that he had already reacted, albeit without telling Vale. Alarmed by the silence from Pryce and wary of Vale's potential for causing waves, he'd requested the MOD just yesterday to have the two frigates currently on pirate patrol in the Gulf region to approach the area and remain on stand-by.

Now it looked like too little too late.

Forty-One

When I was sure Madar wasn't going to double back, I turned and walked away from the rotting boats and down on to the beach. I took off my shoes and socks and tied them round my neck to avoid leaving shoe prints in the sand.

The fishermen's boats, I noticed, had been taken away, no doubt for kitting out as attack craft. Only one lay in the shallows, an ancient vessel with its hull deliberately caved in. The pirates' methodology was as old as time, the message bluntly psychological: take from the population what you can use and destroy the rest.

I moved slowly, wary of wandering locals. But the beach was deserted. The only obstacles I encountered were discarded fishing nets half-covered by sand and a collection of plastic bottles washed up on the shore. I stepped carefully over these; exposure to the sun had baked most of them into a highly brittle state, and stepping on them would set them off like a bunch of firecrackers in the night.

The air by the water was several degrees cooler, and I resisted the temptation to wade in for a refreshing dip. I stopped every few paces, listening for movement and straining my eyes to identify some dark shapes ahead of me. They turned out to be another couple of wrecks gradually being absorbed by the sand, and two ancient and rusted oil drums filled with concrete used to tie up boats when rough weather hit the shore.

Somewhere in the gloom was the skiff that had brought Musa and his bodyguards. That was my marker. From there I only had to take a sharp left turn and move up the sand, and I'd find where the men had stacked the three metal boxes.

My main problem was that it would bring me uncomfortably close to the villa, albeit down in a hollow. But that was something I'd have to deal with. I had to find out what was in those boxes.

After a stop-start progression along the beach, I finally saw a vague banana shape against the white sand. I stopped, sinking to a squat.

No movement. I crept closer. Beyond the skiff were two more, returned from their earlier journey.

Satisfied that there were no guards watching, I checked out the first boat. It was sleek and narrow, about twenty feet in length, with some kind of light metal framework and folded canvas lying in the bottom, which I guessed was a dismountable shelter. There were two 5-gallon containers of fuel amidships, and two others holding fresh water. I found bundles of clothing and blankets stashed away beneath the bench seats, and the tools of the pirates' trade – a pile of grappling hooks and rope ladders. A large outboard motor was clamped to the stern and tilted at an angle off the sand.

The other two boats were similarly equipped, and looked ready for spending long periods at sea.

I jumped out of the last skiff and inched my way up the beach until I came to where the boxes had been stacked. They were laid out adjacent to each other but separated by about a foot. Somebody was being very careful to keep them apart.

I wondered why.

I ran my hands over the sides, checking for catches or locks. But they were standard military issue, with simple spring catches and hasps for rapid opening and deployment in battlefield conditions.

I was running one hell of a risk here, because if they were wired with some kind of anti-theft alarm, there was no way I'd spot the mechanism in time. But I figured Musa's men had no worries about thieves daring to steal from them, so I carefully opened the catch of the first box and eased the lid back, slipping my free hand inside to feel for wires.

All clear.

My fingers came into contact with a flat, cold fabric. Plastic sheeting. I ran my hands along to the ends and sides, which were bound with some kind of sealing tape. I counted five oblong strips, each about ten inches long and three wide. I lifted one of the strips and judged it to be nearly an inch thick. When I was certain there were no wires attached, I gently lifted it out of the box, easing it free from its neighbours. It felt reasonably weighty, and solid to the touch, but not hard. I put it to my nose and sniffed. The only smell was a disturbingly familiar one: faintly chemical, like grease, which probably came from the wrapping, it was the kind of smell that hovers around almost any kind of military equipment, from uniforms to heavy artillery. I had a pretty good idea what I was holding in my hand.

It was a strip of C-4 plastic explosive.

I used the strip to measure down the side of the box. If my measurements were correct, the box held approximately 40 of these strips. That was enough C-4 to make a very large hole in something. Or a lot of smaller ones.

I realized that I'd been subconsciously holding my breath. I let it out and replaced the strip, then closed the lid.

The next box was much lighter and not so full. A gentle feel around told me I was holding a slim, tube-shaped object wrapped in soft, cotton-like fabric. It was about four inches long, with a squared-off section at one end, and I knew instantly what it was.

A detonator.

I checked the rest of the box, hoping I was missing something in the dark. I wasn't. I sat back on my heels, worrying. Every detonator needs a power source. Of the kind used in bringing down buildings or bridges, for example, the power is with the operator and involves an electrical charge from a battery. The old method was a plunger; now it's a simple button. With a remote detonator, something like a simple 9-volt battery would be sufficient to power it up and send the required signal to do its job. But it's an extra component involving packaging, storage in transit, checking the wiring and fixing securely in place prior to use. It's messy and open to failure.

Musa had got round that. He had sourced a high-level, ready-made detonator, and the square section I'd felt on the end must be the power source. But you don't just buy that stuff off the shelf of your local Walmart. This level of sophistication had echoes of a military supply warehouse somewhere, and I was betting on Eastern Europe.

I carried on looking. With the detonators were a number of lightweight objects made of a rough nylon weave.

I lifted one out, letting my fingers identify the shape. As near as I could make out it was a pouch. One side was thicker than the other, with a flap at one end covered in a Velcro strip. The thicker side of the pouch was sticky around the edges and backed by a greasy paper strip. I tested the sticky gunk with a fingertip and felt the immediate grab of a powerful adhesive. When I sniffed my finger, I caught a pungent smell that reminded me of PVC glue.

I moved on to the third box. It contained a bunch of cell phones with stubby aerials. More technology. No, not cell phones; there were no keypads. Just a serrated knob next to the aerial, and a button.

Remote triggers.

I closed the last box and sat back. The stuff in these boxes wasn't intended for a normal battlefield engagement. They were going to be highly efficient and lethal IEDs – improvised explosive devices. The pouches were tailored to take the strips of C-4, which would each be fitted with a detonator. By removing the protective strip on the back of the pouch, they could be slapped on to the side of a target. Once safely out of range, a remote signal could be sent from the trigger to set off the bomb.

But what was the intended target? Government buildings? Armoured vehicles? Although C-4 came in a protective covering, I had never seen it so heavily taped at each end. And the plastic sheeting covering the strips felt heavy-duty.

Then it hit me.

There was only one purpose I could imagine for such an elaborate set-up, and that was in extreme wet or damp conditions.

Like at sea.

They were going to attack a ship.

Or maybe more than one. And I knew how they would do it. Using their low-profile skiffs, they would sneak up on a target under cover of darkness and get right alongside. With the adhesive coating, the bomb could be placed just above the waterline. All the bombers had to do then was retire to a safe distance and press the button on the trigger mechanism.

Or threaten to.

The potential for disaster if their threat went unheeded was horribly real. They might not have enough explosive to guarantee being able to sink a large tanker, but if they managed to blow a hole in the side and breached the hold, oil would pump out into the ocean at a furious rate.

Faced with such a horror, and on such a public stage, every shipping company in the world would be forced to comply without a shot being fired.

I gathered together three sets of bomb-making equipment. Placing the detonators in my pockets, I put the C-4 charges in their pouches and the remote triggers in my shirt. It made my skin crawl having that much potential for disaster on me, but I had no choice.

As long as I kept the detonators separate from the C-4 and triggers, I was fine.

I made sure the lids were firm on the boxes and headed up the beach. I had no concrete idea of what I was going to do with my potential bombs, but when presented with weapons in a hostile environment, it pays not to pass up the offer.

Forty-Two

I got back to my hide and gave it a full ten minutes before moving again. If I'd triggered any alert senses in the guards, they were keeping it under their hats and waiting to see what I did next.

When I judged it to be safe, I called Vale. For once there was no answer. I tried again a few minutes later. Probably in conference somewhere.

I used the waiting time to check the remote triggers in the subdued glow of a pocket flashlight covered in gauze. The triggers weren't back-room jobs, put together by guys with missing fingers and using fertilizer and packaging tape. They were state of the art, with the knob on the top numbered, each number matching that of a detonator. A flat button was built into the side of each trigger and covered in rubber. Simple and sophisticated. Turn the knob to the required number and hit the button. All you had to do was remember which detonator was where and make sure you weren't still holding on to one of the devices with the detonator in place when you set it off.

Unless Musa had a few willing suicide bombers among his followers, in which case it wouldn't matter.

I heard the grind of vehicle engines coming. Two sets of headlights were bouncing along the track from town. At the same time I heard shouts from the guards around the building and saw a bunch of figures pushing out of the door and assembling to the rear. In the spillage of light from inside, I could see that they all carried rifles and were spreading out to form a welcoming committee.

Something or somebody had poked a stick into the hornets' nest.

The incoming vehicles were a pickup truck and an SUV loaded with armed men. They stopped a little way out and the men dismounted and walked the rest of the way, while the vehicles turned round and faced back the way they had come.

I couldn't make out much detail amid the huddle of bodies, but when they got closer I saw that two of the men were holding a third by the arms, while another was kicking and slapping him repeatedly. I felt sickened when I realized who it was.

Madar.

From his body posture he didn't look good. The men must have already given him a beating before he got here. He was making noises of protest, his voice thin and desperate, and I wondered what he'd done to run foul of the men in Kamboni. Not that it mattered now.

Then all the shouting stopped and Musa appeared, easing his way through the melee with calm authority. He was shadowed closely by the tubby figure of Xasan.

Musa addressed Madar and got him to lift his chin with a sharp smack of his hand. I was too far off to gauge his tone of voice, but it was clear he wasn't a happy man. Madar didn't say much, but whatever it was got him a sharp slap in the face from Musa, followed by a punch to the chest. Madar folded in two and hit the ground, his cry of pain high-pitched and reaching me up the slope.

For just a second my hand was on the AK, anger coursing through me like acid. This was my doing. A part of my brain was calculating how many men I could take out after killing Musa. He would be the easiest, but after that things would get problematic.

Then I stopped. Instead of reaching for an AK like last time, Musa pointed at the villa and shouted an order. The two men who had brought Madar in picked him up and dragged him inside, while the remainder stood around in silence, waiting for the boss man to speak.

It wasn't long in coming. Musa raised his hands and all eyes were on him in an instant. He spoke calmly and at length, arms still raised, his voice rising and falling like a priest – or, in this case, a *mullah* – before his congregation. Nobody shuffled their feet, nobody moved so much as a flicker. They were frozen still.

When he finished, he pointed towards the east and dropped his hands. They all let out a cheer and began slapping each other on their backs as if they'd won the lottery. Some of the men began making their way inside, while Musa and the remainder walked over to the SUV and the pickup and began piling on board.

I didn't have to have heard or understood what Musa had said; his gestures towards the horizon were clear enough. And now he was off to rally even more support among the faithful. He wanted a crowd for the big event, and thanks to Madar, I knew what that was.

Worse, he now had another victim for ritual slaughter.

Forty-Three

'What the hell's going on?' Angela sat up as the shouting came nearer. The house had been quiet as the men upstairs settled down to sleep, then came the approach of engines and voices calling above their heads. She had heard Tober move in the darkness, then felt his presence close by.

'Something's got them fired up,' he said softly. 'Stay where you are.'

She sensed him move away, then heard the soft scrape of his shoes on the steps leading up to the trapdoor.

'What are you doing?' she hissed.

'Just listening.'

He returned moments later. 'Sounds like they're giving somebody a hard time up there. A kid.'

'Why do you say that?'

'I heard crying.'

Moments later they heard a voice from outside. It rose and fell, the words indistinct but forceful, like somebody giving a lecture. When it fell silent it gave way to a burst of cheering. Seconds later the engines started up and moved away, leaving silence to settle back once more over the building.

The trapdoor to their prison was flung open and a voice cursed, followed by a body hitting the steps and rolling to the bottom. Then the trapdoor was slammed shut again.

'Stay down,' Tober warned her. 'Don't move until I say.'

She heard him move back towards the steps, followed by a groan of pain in the dark.

'Doug?'

'Not me. Wait.'

Another groan, then a coughing sound and a sob. Tober flicked on the flashlight, lighting up the area around the steps and revealing a slight figure lying in a heap.

'It's a kid,' Tober confirmed softly, then looked more closely. 'The one who brought the food.'

Angela shuffled across the cellar and knelt beside him. The youth wasn't moving and at first she thought he was dead. But when she touched his shoulder, he jumped with a cry of fear and shrank away. His cotton shirt was flecked with blood and he had several cuts and bruises on his face. She estimated his age at no more than fifteen or sixteen.

'Christ, what have they done to you?'

She didn't expect an answer, and was stunned when he mumbled softly in English. 'They beat me.'

'Why?'

'I ran away. I want to go to my home.' He sounded miserable and choked back another sob, curling into a ball. 'They say I am a traitor and no better than a girl and will die tomorrow with no honour.'

'What's your name, kid?' Tober asked. 'Where are you from?'

'I am called Madar. I come from Mogadishu.'

'What was all the noise about just now, Madar? The shouting and the cars.'

Madar struggled to sit up, wincing with pain. He hugged his knees and rested his head on his arms. 'Men brought me from town. I asked some fishermen if they were going north, so I could go with them to my home. But they told others who asked me why I was leaving. Then they brought me back here.' He sniffed. 'I do not understand what is happening here. There is much badness. I just want to go home to my sister in Mogadishu. Mr Marc said I should go and gave me money.'

'Mr Marc?' Angela leaned forward. He'd pronounced the name with a slight French intonation. Could this Marc be European?

'Yes. Your friend.'

'I don't understand.' She glanced instinctively at Tober, but he looked just as baffled. What did this mean? Had this kid been put down here deliberately to unsettle them, perhaps to see if they knew about friendly forces in the area? If so, they were going to be in for disappointment.

'He is English, like you. He has guns and hides in a hole very close by. I could almost throw a stone and hit him from here – I have very strong arms. He is very clever; he covers himself with strange netting, but not the same as fishermen use. This has pieces of cloth and some branches.'

'I don't believe it.' Tober's voice was a whisper. 'A ghillie net.'

'He says many bad things will happen to this house tomorrow,' Madar continued. 'That is why he told me I must leave.'

'Why? What's happening tomorrow?'

But the shock of the beating was too much for Madar, and he said, 'I am sorry – I do not know. I feel sick.' With that he turned and vomited, coughing and spitting into the corner.

Angela reached out a hand to comfort him. But he shrugged it off and moved away.

'I don't get it,' she said to Tober, as they moved back to their mattresses and allowed the youth to settle down. 'Is he saying there's a Special Forces guy out there?'

'No idea. There were no contingencies for it. It was a talk, so why bother?' The irony in his voice was evident.

'But the netting – and being so close to the house? It has to be. Who else could do that?'

'Foreign Legion, maybe. They have specialist units.'

'But?'

'Unlikely, if it's one man. And it's a long way from their area of operations. He might be a forward observer for a bigger unit.'

She detected doubt in his voice. 'But you don't think so.'

'Forward observers don't get this close. They stay back and watch, and report.'

Angela felt a flutter of something in her chest. Relief? Excitement? She wasn't sure. But the knowledge that there was somebody out there, close by and highly skilled at concealment, was enough.

It meant that they weren't alone.

'I wonder what the time is?' The thought came out aloud.

'Midnight or after. My timing's shot to buggery locked away down here.'

She tried to put some levity in her voice, but her words came out shaky. 'Really? I thought you guys had internal clocks zeroed to the nearest second.'

'That's SAS,' he replied. 'Bunch of time-keepers.'

'And you're different how?'

'I'm a boat person.' She could hear a smile in his voice. 'SBS are more . . . spiritual in style. We go by the stars.'

'Pity we can't see any.'

'Get some rest,' he said. He switched off the flashlight. 'No point worrying about it until they make a move.'

She stared hard towards his voice in the dark, remembering what he'd said earlier about getting one chance only and being ready to take it. 'You think that time is here, don't you? Our one chance.'

'Yes.' His voice was calm. Solid. 'It looks like it.'

She lay down and tried to sleep, and wondered what the morning would bring.

Forty-Four

At SIS headquarters in London, Tom Vale was jolted awake by his phone. He coughed and rolled off his camp bed, jarring his knee on the floor, and snatched up the receiver from the edge of his desk.

It was Portman.

'There's been a change of plan,' the American announced.

'Go on.' Vale sat down at his desk with a tired sigh. He knew this wasn't going to be good news. Outside the window it was dark, but he didn't bother checking the time. It was the middle of the night and there was nothing he could do, no matter what Portman was about to tell him.

'Your two people are to be executed.'

'*What?*' Vale got to his feet and felt the floor shift. He'd been prepared for something bad but this was far worse than he'd expected. 'Why?'

'Because al-Qaeda want it this way. This was probably the plan all along. Musa's given the order and is stirring up his men. He's calling it *"adrabu fawq al-'ana"*. You know what that is?'

'Yes.' Vale felt sickened. He'd seen the videos. Striking at the neck. Giving it a fancy name didn't make it any easier to stomach. It had all been a lie – and they had fallen for it. 'Do you know when?'

'At dawn. It's to be videoed.'

'Of course it is.' He felt suddenly impotent, as if all his skills and experience and thought processes up to now counted for nothing. Dawn in Somalia was only hours away. 'There's a strike force on the way – finally – but they'll never make it in time. You'd better get yourself out of there.' He had to tell Moresby. It was too late of course, but the bloody man had to know that he could have avoided this if he had given it proper thought. It would mean the end of Vale's career, once Portman's presence was revealed; running private operations was frowned upon these days. But after what was about to happen, he wasn't sure he cared a damn.

'Me? I haven't finished yet.' The words were faint, but clear enough, and carried a tone of optimism. 'What do you know about Musa?'

Vale sat down again, his legs weak. 'What do you mean? What can you do? You'll get yourself killed. You didn't sign up for a suicide mission.'

Portman chuckled softly. 'Really? You should have made that clear. Tell me about Musa.'

Vale fought to rally his thoughts, his brain like mush at the change in developments. 'Uh . . . Musa. He's a powerful clan leader from way back. His family have been clan chiefs for generations, but he's the most extreme in outlook. Educated in Beijing and France, he's said to command quite an army, and his men have been fighting the Kenyans to the west of Mogadishu. Two years ago he torched an entire village he suspected of informing on his whereabouts. Men, women and children – even the animals.'

'And your people are sitting down to negotiate with him?' Portman's disgust was evident.

'Just recently, Musa's been showing signs of mellowing, of wanting to put a stop to the conflict. These talks were thought to be a move towards some kind of normalization.'

'Really? Looks like you got that one wrong.'

'Clearly. What are your plans now?'

'I haven't decided. But you should know that those green boxes on the beach contain a supply of C-4 explosives and detonators with remote triggers.'

'Jesus,' Vale muttered. 'You've seen them?'

'Yes. That's not all. The detonators have an integral power source. No wiring, no mess – just slap on and go.' Portman described them and read out the manufacturer's code numbers.

Vale scribbled down the numbers, his heart sinking. Somehow Musa had found a source of supply that put him a long way ahead of the usual pirate or extremist threat in the region. If these things were now on the open market, it wouldn't be long before they began to turn up elsewhere. Like Afghanistan. Europe. He had to pass on the information as soon as he could.

'I'll be in touch when I can,' Portman continued, breaking in on his thoughts. 'I think you'll know what I'm going to do soon enough.'

'Wait. Portman.' He made a rapid decision. It was based entirely on emotion, but it was all he had left. He couldn't allow Angela Pryce to go through what Portman had outlined – it was too hideous to contemplate. That left only one way out.

'What is it?'

The line crackled. It served to highlight how distant Vale felt right now, how remote he was physically from what he was about to suggest. 'Is there anything you can do for . . . for Pryce and Tober?'

'Like what?' Portman sounded pragmatic, his voice flat, and Vale figured the man knew what was coming. He was a professional.

'If you can't get them out . . . don't let them suffer.' It was all he could think of to say.

'I won't. You have my word.'

There was a click and the line went dead.

Forty-Five

I sat and watched while everything went quiet. What Vale had just asked me to do was a hell of a thing. But I wasn't surprised. Asking for his own people to be taken out by a friendly bullet rather than the blade of a terrorist group would not have come easy to him. No commanding officer likes to be in that position.

The fact was, I'd been thinking along the same lines. If I couldn't get Pryce and Tober out in one piece, the least I could do was to take the initiative away from Musa; unable to get his sick piece of propaganda, it would at least snatch a part of his plans out of his reach.

I gathered together what I needed. Waiting for developments was no longer an option; I had to take the offensive while I still could. And from what Vale had said, help was too far off to do any good. Musa was firing up his men to a fever pitch, no doubt with tales of honour and revenge and a strike against the infidels, with great rewards in heaven awaiting those who assisted him. Once he got them to a certain point, there would be no going back.

I had no doubt now that this must have been his plan all along. The offer through Xasan of negotiations for the release of hostages had been an elaborate ploy. He might not have known that two of the hostages he was already holding were UN personnel, but he knew well enough the value of luring in two members of a top western intelligence agency, one of them a woman, to use as propaganda material. And the extreme nature of the demand had worked; it had played Moresby and his colleagues into thinking Musa was some kind of desperate paranoid, so who should be surprised?

With Musa and Xasan gone, the guards had soon got tired of patrolling and settled down together at the side of the villa. That was fine by me. Laziness was good. I slipped out of my hide, this time taking the AK and the Vektor, with the C-4 strips and triggers in my backpack and the detonators in my pocket. I was loaded down more than I liked, but I'd coped with heavier supplies before. Right now I needed firepower in case things got sticky and I got cut off from my hide.

I by-passed the building by a wide margin and headed for the boxes on the beach. I got to them without seeing any guards and set about helping myself to more supplies.

I assembled two of the explosive packs and placed them under the boxes, then moved out and placed two more halfway down the beach under some old netting and cork floats. The charges were bigger than I needed, but I was looking for as big a bang as I could get. I wasn't aiming for wholesale slaughter, but to disorientate.

I still had the three packs I'd taken first time round, and these I'd reduced in size. I grabbed three more detonators and triggers and added them to my backpack for later.

Next I made my way to the skiffs. These were a problem; they offered a means of escape, but also a means for Musa and his men to move about – and I wanted to avoid that. But since I couldn't use them immediately, I had to look on them as a liability.

I tested the direction of the breeze. It was light and heading offshore. I took a risk that it wouldn't change and opened one of the fuel containers. I splashed some of the contents around the bottom of each skiff and over the engines. The aroma was powerful up this close, but I was hoping none of the guards around the house had a good sense of smell.

The skiffs were too far apart for me to light them all in one go; the moment I showed a flame the game would be up. So I placed a full-size explosive pack in the middle skiff and soaked the sand between it and its neighbours with fuel. I was trusting to luck that the flame from the explosion would move across each side and complete the job.

I threw the empty fuel container aside and jogged back up the beach, and found the track leading towards Dhalib and Kamboni. I picked a point two hundred metres from the villa and laid two more small charges, then made for higher ground above my hide from where I could watch the party. It was too dark to see much detail, but I knew my field of fire was clear, and I was only a short run from the front door of the house. I made sure I had sufficient cover in case of random intruders, then laid out the remote triggers in a row and waited.

I gave it an hour. The few men left in the house would have been left buzzing by Musa's passionate rhetoric, and I needed them to get it out of their system and go to sleep. The last thing I needed right now was a revved-up sentry with heightened nerves and an itchy trigger finger.

When the time came I selected a remote from the row in front of me. Took a deep breath and pressed the button on the side.

Nothing happened.

Forty-Six

For a split second my gut went cold. Damn. What had I done wrong? Had I missed a safety switch somewhere?

Then it happened. The explosion down near the water-line was impressively big. It lit up the beach for a brief second, the flare of light bouncing away across the surface of the sea in the background. The central skiff took off, breaking in half as the bottom was blown out of it, the two ends folding in on themselves. I caught a snapshot glimpse of plastic containers going into the air, then one of the containers carrying fuel exploded in a ball of flame and orange smoke, showering down on everything within a thirty-metre radius. Everything went dark again for a nano-second before another flash came, this time as the fuel-soaked sand around the skiff on the left ignited and burst into flames, followed quickly by the third boat going up like a pyrotechnician's dream.

The two guards outside the villa came awake and began running around and screaming at their colleagues inside. One of them let off a couple of rounds in the general direction of the water, then did the same off to one side, and I guessed the play of light and shadow had fooled him into thinking they were under concerted attack from the sea.

The men inside burst out of the door and raced towards the side of the property overlooking the beach, also firing off random shots into the darkness. I couldn't see them all clearly, but I estimated there were four or five. No problem; them I could handle.

What I couldn't be sure of was how many remained on guard inside, nor what their reaction would be if they assumed they were under attack. Their orders might have been to kill the two prisoners.

I was going to have to move fast.

The men outside were doing what I had expected of them: heading down on to the beach to investigate. In the flickering light coming from the burning skiffs, I counted four, bunched together, rifles at the ready, moving cautiously and ready to jump at the first sound. I was glad I wasn't part of their number; the last thing you need in a group under attack is for one of your colleagues to start shooting wildly.

They reached the burning boats and ran around excitedly, but there was little they could do to stop the destruction. The middle skiff was in pieces and the other two were already beyond help and burning fiercely.

After another fuel container exploded with the heat and shot into the night sky, one of the men seemed to take control and they backed off and hurried up the beach, chattering away angrily.

I waited for them to reach the point where I estimated the old netting to be, then picked up the next trigger and pressed the button.

This time there was no delay. The explosion lit up the villa and caught three of the men with the full blast, knocking the fourth on to his back.

I didn't wait to see what happened next; I already had the AK to my shoulder and was sighting on the two guards who had stayed close to the villa. I fired twice, placing my shots carefully. Then a third.

Both men went down.

Another man appeared out of the shadows and ran around, searching desperately for the source of the shooting. With no sound from the suppressed AK to fasten on, and with the noise of the explosions still ringing in his ears, he must have been thoroughly disorientated. Then he turned and ran towards the building, screaming wildly at somebody inside.

I felt the hairs on my neck stand up. I didn't understand a word he'd said, but the implication was as clear as crystal.

He was telling the man or men inside to kill the hostages.

I couldn't allow him to get back inside; I waited until he entered the flare of light from the door of the villa and hit him with a head shot, knocking him off his feet. He sprawled close to the door, his rifle falling beside him.

Then I was up and off at a full run, my momentum carrying me down the slope past the hide at full speed.

This time I was carrying the Vektor. For what I was about to do, I needed speed and manoeuvrability in a tight space.

And I was no longer concerned about noise; with the explosions and the rifle fire, I doubted anybody within a five kilometre radius was going to dwell too much on the sounds of one automatic pistol.

Forty-Seven

Down in the basement, the percussive effects of the explosion jolted all three prisoners awake. A split second later the sound rumbled by overhead and a thin veil of debris rained down on them from the ceiling and walls as the building continued to vibrate.

'Get ready,' Tober said calmly. He turned on the flashlight again and beckoned Angela to follow him towards the steps. He gave Madar a warning tap on the leg as he passed by. 'Stay close, kid.'

Edging up the steps, he waited, listening for the first sounds of anyone coming to open the trapdoor. The explosion had been some distance away, although he couldn't tell by how much. He guessed it had been a diversionary tactic, to draw the men upstairs outside. He was pragmatic enough to know that if it worked, a rescuer would appear. If it had failed, there might be a brief flare of light as the trapdoor opened, followed by a burst of automatic fire pouring in on them from their angry or crazed captors.

Then lights out.

The men upstairs were shouting in a frenzied panic, and he heard the sound of running footsteps heading for the door to the outside. If anybody was coordinating their response to this surprise attack, they were being ineffective.

The shouting diminished as the men moved away. Two shots sounded close by. Then another explosion shook the structure and somebody began screaming.

The door slammed shut and footsteps sounded near the trapdoor.

A man's voice called out. '*Khaalid*? *Saalim*?'
Silence.

Tober reached up and tested the trapdoor. He had already tried it shortly after being put down here. Now, as then, it was solid. He got his legs underneath him and put his back against the wood. If the gunman upstairs was watching the door, he might be able to take him by surprise. It was a risky thing to do, but better than waiting for the man to open the trapdoor and blast the basement with gunfire.

He heaved, testing the rigidity of the trapdoor, his leg muscles creaking from lack of exercise in the cramped conditions. The door shifted slightly, dust cascading down on his neck, but he couldn't get sufficient power in his awkward position on the steps to really move it.

He had to try again. He handed the flashlight to Angela. 'Take this and stand to one side.'

As he braced himself for another push, he heard a rush of approaching footsteps and a crash as the front door was kicked in. The man on the other side of the trapdoor cried out in alarm, then came a burst of automatic fire.

Silence. Then two shots in quick succession.

More silence.

Tober held his breath and waited, hoping against hope. Even muffled by the trapdoor, he was sure the last shots had come from a semi-automatic pistol. Yet none of the Somalis carried pistols.

Then the trapdoor was lifted, flooding the steps with light, and he prepared to launch himself forward.

Forty-Eight

'You need to see this.' Dale Wishaw hurried into Scheider's office as the deputy station chief was finishing a call. They had both pulled a late-nighter, monitoring three ongoing operations across Europe and liaising closely with other CIA stations and the headquarters at Langley. Wishaw fought off a yawn as he walked over to a high-definition monitor on one wall and switched it on. Instantly the screen was flooded with a sequence of rapidly changing images bearing the unearthly glow of thermal imaging camera footage.

Scheider stood up and joined his assistant. The scene reminded Scheider of a Hamburg nightclub where one of his more lurid informants had arranged a meeting a couple of years ago. What little light there had been was of a nightmarish quality, not helped by the pounding bass and what passed for music. He'd got out of there darned quick but with a blinding headache.

This was no nightclub, however, and whatever was taking place was clearly far more deadly than a few strobing lights and loud music.

'Sorry,' Wishaw murmured, and fiddled with the remote control. 'I'll start again. This is footage taken by a drone camera coming in on a south-westerly heading over the Somali coast north of Kamboni.'

There was a scrolling pattern of dark and light, showing little in the way of ground detail at first. Then Scheider began to pick out the regular pattern of open water, quickly changing as the camera passed over land. Instantly, as if timed to perfection, the scene lit up with dazzling flares of light that bounced around the screen.

'What the hell is that?' said Scheider, although he was pretty sure he knew. See enough explosions at night and you only had a couple of choices to make: were they big bangs or small?

'This is the area around the villa where the SIS people are meeting with Musa,' said Wishaw. 'The larger flares are explosions; my guess is C-4 or similar – the pattern is too spread out for landmines or grenades.' He stopped the film and re-ran it, then pointed to an area at the top of the screen. 'That blank area is open water – the ocean.' Moving the film forward, he shifted his hand lower down, where two indistinct objects like cigars showed up briefly on either side of a flash of light like a giant flower opening out. 'That's the beach. We think two, possibly three fishermen's boats have been destroyed or torched.'

'Fishermen?' Scheider looked sceptical, and Wishaw shrugged.

'Make that pirates. From a mapping run earlier, they were beached close to the villa.' The images shifted and he pointed to a number of white shapes moving around the top of the beach, near what was clearly a building. 'Armed men, some spilling out of the building.' A series of small flashes occurred near each of the dots. 'We can't tell what they're shooting at until we have a full analysis later today, but it looks like somebody engaged them by setting off explosives, then opening fire from higher ground inland as they came out.'

'Do we know where?'

'We do.' Wishaw pointed at the screen again, this time further inland. 'This is the guy right here.'

Scheider stared hard at the image, his heart beating faster. The shooter showed up as a white shape, partially concealed by ground cover.

Portman, he thought. It had to be.

He made an estimate at the distance between the shooter and the sharp dots of muzzle flashes coming from the other men. 'But that's what – about hundred, hundred and fifty metres? He's almost down their throats!'

'He's a lot closer than I'd want to be.' Wishaw pointed at two static white shapes close to the building. 'See here, two men down. He's got them running around like chickens and picking them off one by one. He knows what he's doing.'

Scheider nodded. 'I hope he can keep it up.' He didn't need to see any more and stepped over to his desk. But why had Portman gone on the offensive right now? What had set him off? Had he been discovered or was something else forcing his hand? And where the hell had he obtained the explosives?

'Me, too. There are a lot more men in Kamboni, likely to be affiliated to Musa's group, and they're only a short drive away. If he doesn't move fast he's going to have them pouring in on top of him inside fifteen minutes.'

Scheider felt his gut go tight. If Portman was planning on breaking the two Brits out of the villa, he was cutting it very fine. And any injuries would slow them all down. And where would they run to?

Unless he had other orders.

Jesus, surely . . .?

He turned to Wishaw to blank out the unthinkable idea. 'Make sure Moresby has this footage right away, will you? And copy Vale. I'm going to call him now.'

He went over to his desk and dialled Vale's number.

The SIS man answered immediately.

'Don't you ever sleep?' said Scheider.

'Sleep? What's that?' Vale sounded rough, and cleared his throat. 'Sorry. Too much coffee and not enough fresh air. What's up?'

'Your man's gone on the offensive. He's blowing up boats and shooting people *as we speak*. He's turned the place into a war zone. I'm sending you and Moresby the latest footage just in. I suppose you wouldn't care to share, would you?'

'Um, yes.' Vale's voice was flat, but he didn't sound surprised. 'Portman found evidence that these talks are a scam. There was never any intention of releasing hostages; the negotiations were a ploy to draw in our people.'

'Why?' Scheider could think of only one reason. Targeted kidnaps. The idea chilled him. It put anybody with official status or standing who went through the region in dire peril. But was it likely? 'They can hardly need more hostages.'

'It's worse than that. Musa's got the one he needs.'

'I don't follow.'

'Angela Pryce. He's going to execute her at dawn, along with Tober. *Adrabu fawq al-'ana*. You know what that is?' Vale sounded tired. He'd been right all along about the mission and Scheider felt for him.

'Yes. I know.' As tough as he was, as accustomed to death and the deadly game played out by extremists, he felt himself shrink from the imagery Vale had placed in his mind. 'Jesus, why?'

'Propaganda, making a point – choose any reason you like. They're extremists; what they do doesn't have to make sense.'

'I get that. But how do you know this?'

'Portman got to somebody inside the villa. They've set up a camera ready to burn to DVDs. By tomorrow evening it'll be beamed around the world to every website prepared to take it. Another twenty-four hours and it will be on sale in every radical mosque, shop and bazaar in the region. This wasn't an impulse decision to change the game – this was planned.'

Scheider didn't know what to say. 'What's Portman going to do?'

'He's going to stop it happening.' A phone rang in the background at Vale's end, and he sounded relieved. 'I'm sorry – I think that's me being called to a meeting. It's probably about your footage. Thank you for that, by the way. It's good of you. I appreciate it.'

'Wait.' Scheider was stunned by this turn of events and by Vale's calmness. There was something the Englishman wasn't telling him. Men with Vale's experience didn't give up that easily. 'You've given Portman fresh instructions, haven't you? What did you tell him to do?'

There was a long pause. 'I told him not to let them suffer.'

Scheider's breathing became choked. He thought he'd come across every scenario possible in his time, but not this one. It was nothing short of a suicide mission. There was no way any man could pull this off. 'And he agreed?'

'He gave me his word . . . and I believe him.'

The line went dead.

Forty-Nine

'I've received disturbing reports from our American friends of unusual activity to the north of Kamboni, picked up with live footage from a CIA drone targeted over the area where the meeting is to take place.' The dramatic statement came from Colin Moresby forty minutes later. He was standing behind his office chair, addressing Vale and the controllers for Africa and Middle East, Bill Cousins and Peter Wilby, and the duty MOD liaison officer, Colonel Mike Ventura.

They had all been summoned from their beds by messenger and fast car, and Vale from his office, where he'd been mulling over the revelations of what Portman had told him and now Scheider's camera work.

'What kind of activity?' queried Ventura. A slim man with a stern face and a scar down one side of his neck, the result, Vale had heard, of close proximity to an IED in Iraq, he had the directness typical of most military men and none of the fondness for equivocation of the civil service.

'Explosions and small arms fire.' Moresby leaned forward and touched a button on his desk console, and a wall monitor behind him sprang into life. There was complete silence as the assembled officers watched, until Moresby switched it off again.

He looked, observed Vale, as if it had shaken him.

'Any comments?'

'Could be the Kenyan Defence Force,' Bill Cousins suggested. 'Kamboni's right on their supply route in and out of the area. They might have run into extremists.'

'We asked them that already. The Kenyans are denying any ongoing operations south of the port of Kismaayo, and no confrontations with extremists in the last twenty-four hours.'

'Do you believe them?'

'I have to. They've responded by accusing the UN of an unauthorized incursion, and demanding to be told how we know about the explosions. We're playing dumb, of course, but something's going on and it's right on top of where the talks are taking place.' As he spoke, his eyes settled on Tom Vale for a second before moving on. 'It's possible, I suppose – and I don't discount the view – that a rival extremist group has got into a fight with Musa's people. But until we get confirmation of that, we're at a loss.'

And that, thought Vale, hits it right on the button. You don't know and you didn't think it out beforehand. He clamped his teeth together to stop himself speaking and keep his face under control. Tempting as it was to tell the assembled company about Portman, his private hit man, and the proposed execution of Pryce and Tober, it would serve no purpose. It was still Moresby's operation and throwing that kind of grisly news into the air wouldn't alter anything, short of setting the chickens running round the coop to no avail.

'How did you hear about it?' he asked. 'I thought there were no assets in the area.'

'Until a very short while ago, there weren't. As you know, that was a condition of the negotiations – along with the immediate territory around there.' He smiled thinly and drummed with one hand on the back of his chair. 'But the Americans put up a drone and were right on target to pick up the action as it happened. They're analysing the footage as we speak, but they've given me a heads up on first impressions.'

Jesus, Vale thought grimly, as Moresby's eye caught his for

a split second. He's talking as if he'd had it stitched up all along. But I know different.

'If it's right where the meeting's taking place,' ventured Peter Wilby, 'that's not good news for our people, is it?'

It brought a frown to Moresby's face and he shuffled around to take his seat. 'No. Indeed. But until we get more information, I don't think we should jump to conclusions. These talks always carried a small element of risk, but we know Xasan is keen to make a success of them, and getting these UN people out is a major factor in why we went ahead with it.'

'What are their chances if they've been caught in the middle of a factional dispute?' This came from Bill Cousins. He was referring to Pryce and Tober, not the UN hostages. 'They're hardly likely to be flavour of the month, are they? They'll be shipped north to join the others.'

'Tober's a good man,' Moresby replied sombrely. 'He saw a lot of action in Sangin Province and he's got a very cool head. It's why he was selected for this operation.'

Vale kept his face impassive, although he wanted to jump up and rage at Moresby's posturing. The man was making it sound as if he had personally selected Tober to ride shotgun on a picnic. The former SBS man was indeed one of the best specialist support operatives they had. But he'd been placed in a hideous situation.

'What about the Mogadishu office?' Colonel Ventura suggested. 'They've got a military attaché. Can't he investigate?' A new British embassy had just been opened, heralded by the British Foreign Secretary as a testament to the bilateral agreement between the two countries, especially on the issues of sexual violence – and the worsening growth of piracy.

'It's not fully functional yet,' Moresby replied. 'And our man's being watched too closely. It's making travel beyond the capital very difficult without a fleet of government minders watching his every move, and he's getting little reaction from the Somali government without lots of delays.'

Vale waited for the briefing to end and said nothing, eager to get back to his office. Dramatic gestures or statements right now wouldn't do a thing to help Portman, Pryce or Tober. It was already going to take a small miracle to get any of them out in one piece, and throwing what he knew into the mix, when it was clear little was going to be done to help them, would not improve matters.

He just hoped and prayed that Portman could deliver . . . or follow through on his final instructions.

Fifty

'Follow me and stay close.' I handed Tober the dead guard's AK-47. He stripped out the magazine with barely a pause and fed in a replacement taped to the stock. Angela Pryce followed him out into the light, with Madar stumbling up the steps in her wake. He looked badly bruised but good to go.

Tober had come out of the basement like a bull from a gate, ready to kill. Luckily for me, I'd stepped back and let him see me. He'd looked surprised, then nodded.

'Good to see you, whoever you are.'

'Portman. We have to move fast. Are you all mobile?'

'Yes.'

It wasn't Stanley meeting Livingstone, but we didn't have time for lengthy introductions. Any minute now Musa and his men would come charging along the track from town, alerted by the explosions. Things were about to get seriously hot and we had to get out of here.

Tober found a canvas bag containing spare magazines near the door. He grabbed it and I led the way outside, stopping to pick up another AK. I tossed it to Pryce. She snatched it out of the air without blinking and checked the magazine, then nodded that she was ready.

We almost made it. We were halfway up the slope with Tober hustling Madar along, when the flash of headlights and the roar of engines coming along the track signalled the arrival of Musa's men.

I pointed beyond the hide and shouted to Tober, 'Head that way and keep going until you hit a track. Wait there until I join you.'

He didn't waste time asking questions or voicing what ifs, but gestured to the other two to follow him and set off up the slope at an easy trot.

I made my way to the hide and kicked aside the branches, scooping up my backpack, then moved to where I'd left the last three triggers and the AK. The approaching vehicles were now less than three hundred metres off and coming in fast, the headlights flickering wildly as they bounced over the rough terrain. One or two shots were already coming my way, and I ducked down and waited. The condition of the track wasn't helping their aim any, but a random hit can kill just as easily as a precision shot.

There were two vehicles, the lead one a pickup. I couldn't make out any detail but I guessed they were the same two from before, come to see what the fireworks were all about. From the position of their lights, one was about thirty metres behind the other. Both were travelling fast and eager to get in on the action. Luckily for me, the track was too narrow for them to come in abreast or to split up. But that suited me fine. I waited until the lead vehicle reached a point about eighty metres away, then pressed one of the triggers.

It was guesswork as to whether I'd timed it right, but it worked. The pickup lifted off the ground, the force of the explosion combined with the vehicle's forward speed flipping it sideways and on to its nose, tipping out the armed men in the back. I was hoping Musa was one of them, but instinct told me he'd have opted for the more stately and probably air-conditioned SUV, leaving the lead vehicle to take the first hit.

The driver of the SUV reacted fast. He stamped on the brakes and steered away to avoid running into the wreck of the other vehicle. In the flicker of flames I saw men leaping out of the back and heading for the sides of the track.

I hit the second trigger. The flash was vivid and lit them up nicely, but they were too far away to be badly affected by the blast. Even so, they all hit the deck fast, rolling into whatever cover they could find. If it disorientated them enough to fear further explosions, it would give me time to get clear.

I turned towards the villa and pressed the last trigger. This was the one that was going to seriously piss off Musa.

The two charges I'd wired together were right underneath the boxes containing the remaining C-4 and detonators. The double blast was spectacular, battering the air even where I was standing. Part of the garden immediately in front of the beach disintegrated, rising for a second in the air, then dispersed all over the surrounding area, debris clattering down like hard rain. If it blew out some windows and brought down the front wall of the house, I wouldn't have been surprised, but I didn't wait to admire my handiwork.

I grabbed the AK and got out of there, heading for higher ground, with shouts from Musa's men echoing in the background.

The problem with fighting at night is that your own eyes are as vulnerable to the flash of gunfire and explosives as those of the opposition. I had blank spots in my vision, adding further to the blackness all around me. If confronted by one of the Somalis, it would be bad enough to get me killed, so I majored on getting as far away as I could rather than staying to fight an enemy I couldn't see clearly.

The ground was as rough as I remembered from the other night, but I had the advantage of having been here before; I had an idea what the main obstacles were. I headed back towards my insertion point across the border, hoping Tober wouldn't open fire when he heard me coming.

But he was better than that. I heard a sharp whistle, brief enough to almost miss, and slowed down until I caught a movement off to one side.

I stopped and caught my breath, sucking in air and checking my AK to make sure I hadn't stabbed the end of the suppressor into the dirt, and waited until he showed himself.

'Where are the others?' I asked.

'Up ahead. The kid's struggling so I called a halt. You OK?'

'I'm good.'

'What happened back there?'

'One vehicle and passengers down, another one stopped but the men are out and on the loose. We have to keep moving.'

He grunted and turned away, and we jogged side by side

until we saw a pale flash in the dark. It was Pryce's white blouse. She had taken off her jacket.

'You might want to put that back on,' I told her. 'The guys behind us have good night vision.'

She slipped the jacket on without saying a word. I don't think I'd made another friend, but better that than a dead body.

I checked Madar was OK to move, and he said, 'Yes, Mr Marc. I am sorry to slow you down.' He was a gutsy kid and sounded perky enough, so I clapped him on the shoulder and led the way, leaving Tober to bring up the rear.

We ran across the track and eventually reached the line of border posts. I couldn't be certain in the dark, but I figured we were close to the point where I'd killed the sentry. I gave it another ten minutes of hard walking, then called a halt. Although we were in Kenyan territory, we weren't in the clear by a long margin. Musa's men wouldn't be in any mood to acknowledge the border, and there was the added danger of running into a unit of the KDF on border patrol or an anti-poaching team. They would be armed and ready to fight, and not about to ask questions of a bunch of people sneaking about in the middle of the night.

'We'll rest up here,' I said. 'I've got to make a call.'

Tober was standing next to me. I sensed him looking at me, but he didn't ask questions. Instead he said, 'I'll go and check our back-trail. Won't be long.' With that he was gone, melting into the dark.

I didn't argue; he had some excess steam to work off after being cooped up in the basement, and focussing on doing what he knew best was his way of dealing with it.

'Where's he going?' Pryce asked. She was breathing heavily and sounded as if she wanted to be sick. After what she had been through I wasn't surprised.

'Checking we aren't being followed.' I wondered if she was put out at not being consulted. Tober was, after all, her colleague, not mine, and we hadn't exactly had time to establish any boundaries. 'Don't worry – he knows what he's doing.'

'Like you, you mean? Did Moresby send you?' Her tone was calm and her voice steady enough, in spite of being out of breath, and she undoubtedly wanted to know who the hell I was. It was a natural question but not one I wanted to get into. In any case, having to answer the same questions from Tober later would be doubling up.

I said, 'I'll explain in good time. For now we have to get you out of here.'

I got out my sat phone to call Piet. Dawn wasn't far off, and I was surprised at how quickly time had passed. I needed to get him in here to make the pickup.

Just as I was about to dial his number, I heard a pop-pop in the distance behind us, followed by a burst of automatic fire.

Then silence.

Fifty-One

'Move,' I said, and urged the others to follow me. Madar was ready to go but Pryce wanted to argue. She grabbed my arm and held on.

'We should wait for Doug. He could be in trouble.'

I shook off her hand. 'If he is, there's nothing we can do to help him. If he's in the clear he'll find us. If we stay here and they get past him, they'll be all over us inside thirty minutes.'

I didn't wait for her to agree, but set off after Madar. Pryce followed, but she wasn't a happy trooper.

We covered about half a click, heading over a rise in the terrain and through a clump of bushes and rocks. It was a natural fault in the landscape, and had thrown up debris like giant molehills. Madar had eyes like a cat and avoided the worst of them, so I told Pryce to follow him closely while I dropped back a few metres to cover our backs.

We eventually reached another line of trees where I called another halt. I was worried about Tober. If he'd been caught, we were a good man down and vulnerable. I couldn't see Musa giving up too easily on his plans, and if he thought we were close enough to catch he'd come after us for as long as it took. There was a lot of empty space here, and he probably knew that the chances of his men being compromised in

Kenyan territory were fairly low, especially with the army stretched thin chasing down al-Shabaab fighters.

I dialled Piet's number and heard it buzzing at the other end. Four times, six times, then he answered.

'What did you do, man – start that war?' He sounded remarkably cheerful, letting go of a chuckle through an early-morning throat. 'Where are you?'

It had been clear since hearing of Musa's planned execution that the one person to get out of here was Angela Pryce. She was his most valued trophy, whereas Tober was a soldier, a victim of his job. And Piet could only carry one passenger at a time. I told him where we were and he replied that he was ten minutes away, where he'd been camping out waiting for a call.

'What about you?' he queried. 'And the muscle. Is he there, too?'

'He's coming up behind, plus one other – a boy. He helped us out.'

'Christ, man, you should've warned me – I'd have arranged a *combi* and a picnic basket.' He coughed and said, 'Sunrise is about twenty minutes off. I can't take off in the dark, but once I'm up, I'll spot you if you're out in the open. Just try not to draw too much of a welcome party, right?'

He cut the connection and I put the phone away and checked my weapon. Pryce was doing the same, closely watched by Madar. I don't think he'd ever seen a white woman up close before – and certainly not one who knew how to handle an AK-47.

I left them to it. The more Pryce was occupied, the less time she'd have to dwell on what had happened or to pepper me with questions I was in no position to answer.

I hadn't gone into it much with Vale about what to do if I did come face to face with his two people. The plan was to stay remote and unseen, and come out of the shadows only if they got into trouble. This part had been unforeseen, and was something I would have to ask him.

A few minutes later I heard a brief whistle coming out of the gloom.

Tober.

I told Pryce to stay put. 'Piet's on his way in. If I'm not back by the time he arrives, don't wait. Get on board and tell Madar to make his way back to the coast and find a boat out. He'll know what to do.' I wasn't going far, but if this turned out to be Musa's men playing cute, I had to intercept them before they got too close.

I worked my way back until I reached a spread of open ground, and stopped on the near side, checking out the lay of the land. It wasn't clear enough to see far, but anyone stepping across it would show up. Then I caught a movement directly in front of me, about a hundred metres out.

It was Tober. He was walking easily enough, his rifle slung over his shoulder as if he was on a Sunday afternoon stroll.

I whistled and he raised a hand and broke into a trot to join me.

'They coming?' I asked him.

He grinned. 'They were. I discouraged them.' He hefted the AK and said, 'These things may look like shit but they work fine. Ironic, giving them back their own ammunition.'

I nodded and we set off to join Pryce and Madar.

As soon as we arrived back at their position and Pryce had made sure Tober was OK, she was all over me with questions. I batted away each query with vague responses until Tober sensed I wasn't going to play ball and chipped in with the only question really worth asking.

'What's the plan?' He'd been scanning the horizon as dawn filtered through the sparse trees. Like me, he'd come to the same conclusion based on long experience: it wasn't much in the way of cover, but the one advantage we had was that we could see anyone coming from a long way off. 'Do we have backup on the way?'

I nodded towards the west. 'He's on his way in now.'

He did a double take. 'He? One man?'

'It's all I could arrange at short notice.' I went on to explain that the transport was a microlight and if things got sticky he, Madar and I would have to find another way out. His eyebrows went walkabout, but I could see he understood.

Pryce wasn't so easy to convince.

'That's crazy. I'm not leaving Doug here. We came in together and that's how we'll leave. Anyway, you could call the embassy in Mombasa on your phone. The SIS liaison there will arrange a pickup.'

'It's not as simple as that.' I didn't need to explain to her how most countries were sensitive about cross-border incursions, and that she and Tober were effectively operating in Kenyan territory without the authorities knowing about their presence. But I said, 'With the Kenyans having trouble with extremists in southern Somalia right now, if they find out you've been here without their say-so – and talking to al-Shabaab – they'll probably lock you up out of spite and forget where they put the key.'

'Our embassy won't let them do that.'

I recalled the man with the camera at Malindi airport. 'Maybe not. But it won't end there and you know it. Do you want to take a chance on having your photos spread all over the world's media by tonight?'

They were both staring at me now, and I had their full attention. I guessed that they had been so bound up in the proposed 'negotiations' to free hostages, and convinced by their bosses that everything was above board, neither of them had been suspicious about what Musa's real intentions might have been, nor that there had been no real thoughts given to an exit strategy.

'Musa's hard-core al-Shabaab,' I continued. 'If he can't get you back, he'll do what he can to make trouble for SIS. He'll blow your cover far and wide. I don't know about you, but I'm guessing your bosses won't want that.'

'But he wanted to talk,' Pryce insisted hotly. 'You've gone and blown that right out of the water!'

'There weren't going to be any talks,' I said bluntly. 'It was a ploy by Musa to get you here. And you weren't meant to be going home again, either. Ever.'

Fifty-Two

Pryce wasn't having it. I could feel the scepticism coming off her in waves. But when she saw that Tober wasn't reacting she lost a bit of her bite.

There was only one way to convince her. I called Madar over from where he'd been keeping watch. He scooted close and looked at me for instructions. 'Tell them,' I said. 'Tell them about the room you prepared. Tell them what the tall man was going to do. Everything.'

He didn't want to do it and I could understand why. It was pretty traumatic for anybody, the idea of beheading a live human being. But he told them, anyway. There was no flowery language, either. He laid it out for them in straight, innocent terms, and by his tone of voice they knew he was telling the unvarnished truth.

There was a long silence while they digested the idea. Pryce looked like she wanted to throw up but held it together, eyes going tight. The imagery of what had nearly befallen her was clearly flashing through her mind, but she had the strength of character and training to deal with it.

Tober was more pragmatic. Or maybe he was better at hiding his fears. He shook his head like he'd been told he couldn't go on a weekend pass. 'Would've saved me paying for a haircut, at least,' he said. 'So back to the plan: we get your flyer mate to take her out of here. Then he comes back?'

'No. It's too risky. After the first approach he'll be an easy target. They'll wait for him to come in on another pass and take him out. When he leaves here, that's it.' I looked at Pryce. 'Piet will take you to Mombasa or Nairobi – I'll let him decide. You can go through your embassy or head out on the first available flight.'

'Sounds good to me,' Tober agreed. 'What about us?'

'I hope you're good at walking.'

He scowled. 'Where I come from we call it yomping. And I'm ready when you are.'

'Glad to hear it.' I was familiar with the term, first brought to public ears during Britain's war against Argentina in the Falkland Islands. Yomping was the Royal Marine term for a route march, usually and often over the worst possible terrain carrying full fighting equipment and supplies.

Tober was looking sideways at Madar, who had drifted back to his post. 'I'm not so sure about the kid; he took a battering.'

'He wants to go home to Mogadishu. All he needs is a friendly boat out of here heading north.'

'Great. Where do we . . .?' He stopped. 'You're saying we go back to Kamboni?'

'Yes.'

'Why?'

'It'll be quicker by sea. We can't hang around here in the hopes that your embassy can arrange a pickup; my guess is, they won't be able to, not without causing an international shit-storm. Musa's men will be expecting us to head overland to Mombasa in a direct line from here.'

'I agree.'

'So we do the opposite: we steal a boat and head south down the coast.'

'You're crazy!' Pryce stared at me, then at Tober, who was nodding as if the idea had real merit. 'And you agree with him?'

'Yeah. He's right. Going cross-country would take too long, and I don't much fancy our luck in the bush with no food or water. By sea we'd have more than a fighting chance.' He looked at me. 'I'm with you.'

'Great. Can you handle a boat?' I regretted the question the moment I asked. I'd forgotten his background in the SBS.

Tober merely grinned, saying, 'If it floats I can sail it. If it's got a motor, I can drive it.'

I excused myself to cut short further questions and walked a short distance away to call Vale. I needed to know what we were planning.

He answered quickly and I brought him up to date. His relief that we were all out was palpable. I was right about any extraction plan; he wasn't going to be able to do much to help us out without the Kenyans and Somalis kicking up an international storm in protest when they discovered we were here.

'Getting Pryce out is my prime concern,' he said briskly. 'From what you've said it's clear she's too valuable a target to fall back into Musa's hands.'

'I agree.'

'What about you and Tober?'

'We'll make our own moves,' I said. 'Tober knows what he's doing so we'll figure something out between us.'

'Good. What have you told them?'

'Nothing. But they're asking questions I can't answer. And Pryce isn't going to stop when she gets home.'

'And about the op so far?'

'Only why I had to pull them out, but nothing about who put me here. They have to have something.'

'Fine. Keep it short, tell them you were sub-contracted to keep an eye on them and they'll be briefed fully when they get back. I'm probably going to have to reveal what I've done soon, anyway, but that was always on the cards. I'll keep your name out of it, of course.'

I didn't argue the point. Having my name splashed all over the world of British Intelligence and possibly further afield was something I wanted to avoid. The more I stayed in the background, the better I liked it.

'Listen, Portman,' he continued, 'what I said before – my instructions regarding Pryce?' He sounded strained, even with the delay in transmission, and I could tell he was feeling bad about what he had asked me to do if things had gotten nasty.

'Forget it. It didn't happen.'

'Thank you. I won't forget this.'

Fifty-Three

I re-joined the others, who looked full of questions but said nothing. I sent Madar off a short way with my AK minus the magazine, to keep an eye out through the scope for Musa's men. He didn't need to hear any of this. Then I squatted down so we could talk.

I kept it simple. I told them my name, that I'd been sub-contracted by an officer in SIS to keep an eye on them, and that once I'd heard what Musa intended for them, I'd had no choice but to bust them out.

'You can't talk to anyone about me or what I've just told you,' I added.

'Who says?' Pryce sounded bullish.

'Orders from the man who hired me. You'll be fully briefed when you get home.'

They didn't say much to that. I suppose hearing that their backs had been covered all along, on the grounds that one of their colleagues thought the mission was a bust, was a little hard to take in. Unfortunately Pryce didn't want to let it go. I could see she'd been working through the possibilities. 'If it was somebody in SIS . . . there's only one man it could have been,' she murmured. 'Tom Vale?'

'Yes.'

She tossed her head. 'What the bloody hell did he think he was doing? He thought I needed babysitting, is that it?' She turned on Tober. 'I know that's the only reason you were sent along, to hold my hand. But this?' Her eyes were bright sparks in an angry face. She had recovered well from the exit and the forced march, and I figured that one day she would make a very good senior intelligence officer. Right now, though, she was midway between being relieved to have escaped with her head and pissed for having been, as she seemed to feel, doubted by a colleague.

Tober did the right thing: he looked right through her and said nothing. She was being unfair and she probably knew it, but getting into a fight over it was pointless.

'Vale will likely lose his job when it gets out,' I said. 'So you should go easy on him. Of course, you have every right to be sour at the guy for not wanting to see your life get tossed away on a dead-end operation . . . but you'd be wrong. He made the right call.'

She clamped her mouth shut at that, and I hoped that was the end of it. It didn't last long.

'Why do you do this work?'

'It's what I'm good at.' She could have asked Tober the same question and got a similar answer. He gave me a look and a raised eyebrow but said nothing. Wise man.

She didn't have an answer to that and turned her head away, then came straight back.

'Who else do you work for? You're American, aren't you?'

'Yes. And I work for anybody within reason. Not terrorists, though; I draw the line at that.' By the look on her face I doubted she believed me. The world's full of cynics.

'You're a mercenary.'

I rode that one easily enough. There was a time when it would have been an easy label to pin on somebody – a not-so-veiled insult. Coming from Pryce it sounded petty. I couldn't figure out why she was so hostile, and wondered if it was anything to do with me being an outsider.

'We all work for money,' I told her. 'Me, you, Tober here – and Vale. But some people have the luxury of being able to dress it up in things like duty, honour or patriotism.'

She recoiled a little at that, and I noticed Tober grinning in the background. The bastard was enjoying this.

'Like me, you mean?' Her eyes flashed with righteous anger. 'I don't make any apologies for being patriotic.'

'Nor should you. But don't get carried away with thinking that makes you better than anybody else, or because your boss is the British government. And –' I held up a hand as she looked ready to fly back at me, but kept my voice low – 'don't forget it was you who came here to sit down and talk with terrorists and pirates. Those same people were plotting to take off your head.'

It was a low blow and not a particularly valid point, but I was tired and irritated by her snitty manner.

Tober nodded in approval, then put his head down and closed his eyes. The soldier's prime maxim: when you can't do anything, sleep; because you never know when you might get the next opportunity.

We sat and waited, alone with our thoughts, until I heard the familiar buzz of Piet's Daisy circling round from the north-west. He needed to see us clearly enough to get an ID, so he knew he wasn't flying into a trap. I told Tober to keep us covered and stepped out into the open with Pryce and Madar close behind.

I waited. I could hear the engine but couldn't see him. He was coming in low to avoid being spotted by Musa's men, but it meant the engine noise was dispersed over a wide area. I realized that there was a chance of him flying right over without seeing us.

Then Madar stepped up and whipped off his shirt, and began waving it frantically in the air.

I think he was just excited at the prospect of seeing an airplane. But it worked.

Seconds later Daisy appeared, the engine howling as Piet cleared the tops of a bunch of trees, scaring up a raggedy group of crows in protest. He banked sharply, his bush-trained eyes probably spotting Madar's shirt immediately, and set down on a clear stretch of ground about three hundred metres away.

Fifty-Four

'If you're not Vauxhall Cross,' said Tober, 'what are you?' We watched as Piet and Pryce disappeared over the trees, while Madar crept around in the bush watching out for signs of Musa's gunmen. 'Special Activities Division? One of your black ops units?'

'None of those. Like I told Pryce, I'm freelance.'

'But you're American.'

'So?'

'How did Vale find you?'

I looked at him. His brow was furrowed and I knew what he was really asking. Why an American when the Brits had plenty of their own highly skilled private contractors who could have done this?

It was a good question.

'He heard about some work I did and needed someone unattached. You know the way it goes.' With all the quiet time I'd had since arriving here, I had privately speculated about who else might have put my name forward to Vale, apart from Beckwith of the DEA. It was obviously somebody in the

American intelligence community, but that was a seriously large field to choose from. Whoever they were, they'd been cute; queuing the selection of a freelance operator with no ties and no back-trail gave them clean hands if that operator was picked up. 'What about you?'

He told me about joining the Royal Marines, then applying for selection to the Special Boat Service.

'And I asked you if you could handle a boat.' I pulled a wry smile. 'Consider me suitably embarrassed.'

'Well, it is a sort of entry-level requirement for the job. If you don't do boats, you should join one of the other lot. You weren't to know.' He went on to explain that after spending some years in the SBS, he did a couple of black jobs for SIS and was posted to them on a two-year attachment, working in a team called the Basement.

'Why do they call it that?' I asked, although I figured I knew. Part of getting to know and trust someone you're going to depend on in hostile circumstances is breaking the ice any way you can, even with obvious questions. At times like this, even the trivial stuff counts.

'It's where we operate from: the basement of Vauxhall Cross.' He grinned. 'Just occasionally, they let us out into the daylight to play with stuff.'

'Like this time.'

His face went serious. 'Yeah, well. This was something else. Somebody screwed up. Shit happens, though, right?' He shrugged, although I got the feeling he wasn't going to forget this mission anytime soon. 'You got family?'

'No.' More personal stuff, although I didn't mind him asking. 'Never got round to it. Got close once, but it didn't work out. You?'

'Married, divorced, currently seeing a girl. She'd be royally pissed off if she knew where I was right now. I told her I was in Norway on a training exercise.' He scrubbed at his face. 'Good job I was cooped up in that villa and not getting a suntan, eh? I'd have some real explaining to do.'

'You might have to yet,' I reminded him. 'They do get sun in Norway. Reflects off the snow.'

He gave me a look, no doubt full of questions, but now wasn't the time.

Just then Madar gave a soft whistle. We moved over to join him and scanned the horizon where he was pointing. Trees, shrubs, rocks and . . . movement.

'Two men,' he said quietly, and used the AK to point them out. 'They have guns and are coming this way.'

I took the rifle from him and checked through the scope. Sure enough, two figures were walking towards us. They were a good kilometre away, easily visible in the clear morning air. One of them was looking down at the ground, while his companion had his head up, watching for trouble. They looked like they had done this before.

'Trackers,' I said, and checked the area behind them. I couldn't see anybody else but they were probably out there somewhere. Musa had sent men ahead who knew how to read the ground, and by the way they were moving they weren't having any trouble reading our trail. I gave it another fifteen minutes at most before they were right here where we were standing. Piet's machine landing and taking off had been a dead giveaway.

We set off at a good clip directly east, keeping between the two men and the sun in case we had to turn and blindside them. My plan was to make for Kamboni and liberate a boat. It would mean walking a little further rather than heading directly for the town, but it was a safer way of approaching the beach and seeing what was on offer.

It was thirsty work and getting hotter with each step as the sun crawled higher. I kept a close eye on Madar, although he seemed to have the resilience of youth on his side, in spite of his injuries. But I knew that with youth, when tiredness comes it does so suddenly. I didn't want him collapsing on us.

I also kept watch on the cloud cover. Just before taking off, Piet had mentioned rain coming. I wasn't seeing any signs of it yet but I knew that rain in this region arrived with little warning.

'It'll be short and heavy,' he'd warned, handing over a bottle of water and some energy bars. 'Not monsoon, but enough to get you soaked through. It'll also make your tracks easier to follow on soil, so stick with grass or rocky ground wherever you can. Whatever you do, don't stop, because the guys following you won't.'

'Thanks.' I didn't mind the rain. If it was enough to provide cover, but not stop us moving, we could use it to get further away from the men tracking us, who would be slowed down by having to read the ground for signs once they found we'd changed direction.

'Call Vale as soon as you can,' I told him. 'I'll be in touch later.' I backed off to let him taxi ready for take-off, and with a brief wave, they were gone.

We made good time before the clouds scudded over and the rain fell. It was like walking into a warm shower. At first it was enjoyable; it was my first soaking for days and I relished the feel of water on my skin, which felt cracked and dry. But after twenty minutes non-stop, I was beginning to worry about the men behind us. If they had reached our last position, and worked out our direction of travel, they might be pushing on at a faster pace and not bothering to look for tracks that might have been obliterated by the rain in the hopes of catching up with us.

I put on speed. Tober matched it easily but Madar was struggling until the former Royal Marine hustled him along with one hand on his arm. It was tough on the kid but nothing like what he'd experience if Musa's men caught us.

Most of the going was fairly flat, the harsh soil dotted with brush and coarse grass littered with spiky thorns. I used the occasional elevations in the terrain as cover by going around them, then putting them squarely at our backs, and splitting up for short distances. It was a messy way to travel, but if it messed with the trackers' minds and had them scouting for our trail, it might give us a brief head start.

When we reached a track running north-south, we stopped just long enough to check for traffic, then ran across and into the bush on the other side.

I now knew where we were, even through the curtain of rain. We had angled further south than I'd planned and were uncomfortably close to the villa.

I called a brief halt and explained our location to the other two. Madar looked ready to freak out, eyes rolling at the thought of running into Musa again. I didn't blame him; some of the men had given him a hard time and Musa had a zero-option policy on those who displeased him. I patted his arm to reassure him and explained that neither of us would allow him to get caught. Tober joined in and this seemed to work. Madar looked doubtful but managed a sickly grin.

The next problem was what to do now. We couldn't exactly walk into town and take a boat – we'd be spotted immediately. And I doubted all of Musa's men would have left the area. But finding a place to bury ourselves until darkness fell wasn't going to be easy.

Tober solved the problem with cool logic.

'They won't expect us to go back to the villa. It's not far from there to where the fishermen beach their boats, and it's easy enough to hold for a while if they do find us.' He smiled easily. 'Not great, I grant you, but we don't have a lot of choice.'

I agreed. The idea was sound; going back to the villa was the last thing Musa would expect us to do. The last he or his men had seen of us was hightailing it into the bush, heading due west. And Tober was spot on with the boats: our fastest way out of here was finding a skiff with an engine to carry us south down the coast to Kenyan territory. As long as we got a good head start on any pursuit, we didn't have too far to go.

The only question was, how much of the villa had survived the double blast of the C-4?

Fifty-Five

'*You what?*'

Vale thought Moresby was going to explode. He'd just informed the operations director of Angela Pryce's escape from Somalia. As soon as he'd received confirmation of her arrival with Piet in Mombasa, he'd made arrangements for her onward journey to Nairobi accompanied by two embassy security officials. Then he had made his way upstairs.

He had no clear plan on how he was going to handle the revelation, but given the circumstances the direct approach seemed best. With an SIS officer coming in out of the field under close escort, and reports of the mysterious explosions on the coast already out there, news would soon filter out among embassy staff. The wires to London would be buzzing as the dots were joined up and speculation increased.

'She was lifted out of the area near Kamboni by light aircraft at daybreak and is now on her way back to the UK,' he explained 'What could have been an unmitigated disaster has been averted – at least in part.' He sat down without being invited and waited for the storm to sweep over him.

It wasn't long in coming.

'This is outrageous!' Moresby's face was swollen with rage. He jumped up from his desk and kneed a drawer closed with a bang, sending a bundle of Top Secret papers sliding to the floor. 'What the hell have you done, Vale? If you've compromised these talks I'll have you charged with violation of protocol and abuse of office. You'll be lucky to walk the streets when I'm finished with you!'

'Sit down, Colin.' Vale's voice was as sharp as a whip, and stopped Moresby in his tracks. 'Listen to me and I might manage to save your career. As it is, there's no guarantee that you haven't already lost a fine support specialist with this idiotic plan of yours. I'd stay away from the Basement for a while until it blows over; they might tie weights to your ankles and drop you in the river.'

Moresby sat down, his mouth slack. 'What do you mean? I don't understand. How did you—'

'I ran a black op. Off the books.' There. It was out in the open. The shocked expression on Moresby's face told its own picture. There was no going back now; it was full disclosure and wait for the fall-out. But he wasn't going to wait for Moresby to pick up the phone and call the dogs on him. 'I had no confidence in your plan from the start, not once I heard you'd provided no backup for the two officers going in, nor any workable exit strategy. As soon as I heard who was involved at the other end, I had a feeling it would end badly. So I took steps to protect our personnel.' He brushed a speck of lint from his knee. 'Would you like to hear how before you turn me in?'

Moresby's eyes were like flint. 'This had better be good, Vale. Not that it makes any difference. You're still finished.' He reached out a hand and tapped a button on his desk console, a sign that he intended recording every detail.

'Because I had no faith in the safe conclusion of your plan,' Vale continued, ignoring the threat, 'I hired a specialist of my own. One man to keep tabs on Pryce and Tober and monitor their progress. He remained in the background and reported back to me. He had orders to step in if things went bad . . . which didn't take long, as it happened, thanks to your misplaced confidence in Xasan and Musa.'

'What man? One of ours?'

'His name doesn't matter and no, he's not from the Basement.'

'Who is he? He'll be arrested for conspiracy.'

'His name doesn't matter and you'll never find out who he is from me, so don't bother asking. Off the books means just that. He put himself in extreme danger to protect two of our officers, one of whom I tried to warn you was not yet ready for this kind of assignment. As it turned out, I was wrong about Pryce; she came through it remarkably well – but no thanks to you.'

He stood up and crossed to the window, glad to be on the move. He wasn't concerned about his voice being lost on the recording; the machines in these offices were state-of-the-art and capable of picking up a whisper. 'Xasan was lying all along. There was no intention of negotiating for the release of UN or any other hostages.'

'I don't believe you.'

'Really? Think about it. Why should they negotiate when they can play the long game? And did you never wonder why Musa insisted on a woman officer being sent out to negotiate? It's a little odd, don't you think, in a part of the world where talking to women is unheard of?'

'So what?'

Vale turned and faced Moresby. 'Do you know what the term *adrabu fawq al-'anaq* means?'

Moresby's brow wrinkled with distaste. 'Of course. What of it?'

'It's what Musa was planning for Pryce and Tober – complete with cameras.'

He watched Moresby's face go through the process of

translation and imagery. When it finally hit home, Moresby looked horrified. 'No.' His voice sounded choked.

'An execution, no less.' Vale continued brutally. 'A double beheading – and all for propaganda. Think how that would have played out in the media: two SIS personnel, one a woman, beheaded in Somalia because we sent them into certain danger with no backup and no guarantees. The press would have had a field day.'

'I don't believe it. Where did you get such a ridiculous notion? Musa was ready to talk about the release of hostages, including unbeknown to him, two key UN personnel. If we hadn't followed that offer, we could have seen them fall into the hands of al-Qaeda. Would you have preferred that? OK, so it was for money. But don't be so bloody naïve, Vale, thinking we can't use money if that's what it takes to get people free. That was my decision and I stand by it.'

'Good for you. But if Musa was offering to sell hostages, why did he arrive at the villa with a boat of armed men and a heavy supply of explosives? And why did he meet up with more armed men in the town of Kamboni if all he was planning was a talk? What he was planning, quite apart from the cold-blooded execution of two SIS officers, was to supply his men with the means to attach remotely detonated bombs to the hulls of ships as they sailed into the Gulf. You've studied military history; you'll know all about the ST Grenade, or sticky bomb.'

'Yes. So what?'

'Well, it seems Musa must have read some military history, too. He got hold of a supply of C-4 and some very sophisticated detonators with remote triggers. He was planning to house them in waterproof pouches covered in a powerful adhesive and attach them to ships – most likely tankers – close to the waterline. You can probably work out the rest. The threat of detonation alone would have been sufficient to get him what he wanted, which would have been considerably more than any hostages would have brought him.' He took a breath, then ploughed on. 'They're adapting their tactics, can't you see? And each time they do their methods become more extreme, more dangerous and infinitely more threatening on a global scale.'

He took a slip of paper from his pocket. It held the code

numbers Portman had taken from the detonators and triggers. 'These are the manufacturers' codes. Somebody somewhere, had been selling the latest equipment to terrorists and pirates. You might care to look into it.'

Moresby was beginning to look sick, Vale noted. He stared at the code numbers and gave a deep sigh. When he spoke, his voice sounded dulled by shock. 'How do you *know* all this?'

Vale decided to pile on the pressure. His career was shot now, anyway, so he might as well go down all guns blazing. 'The explosions picked up on the drone footage Scheider sent you were the result of Musa's bombs being destroyed.'

'How?'

'The man I sent out there saw the explosives being off-loaded; he checked the boxes and made the connections; he saw Musa and Xasan, he saw the armed men. He witnessed Pryce and Tober being taken in as prisoners and managed to speak to one of the people in the villa. They told him what was to happen. He took the only course of action open to him: he neutralized the threat and broke Pryce and Tober out of the cellar where they were being held prisoner. This was at great personal risk to himself, I might add.'

He stopped, wary of over-dramatizing. He had said his piece; now he had to stand back and wait to see what happened.

He left Moresby looking stunned and made his way downstairs. He needed some fresh air and exercise. He knew of one route from the front entrance and back that would take twenty-three minutes, another that would take forty-five. He decided to take the longer route and stop for coffee along the way.

Fifty-Six

The villa looked deserted. But I wasn't taking any chances. In spite of what we thought, Musa might have left guards in place in case we did the unthinkable and came back. From a vantage point three hundred metres away, we studied the area carefully until we were certain that nobody was around.

The wrecks of the three boats were clearly visible down at the waterline, and the smell of burned wood, fuel and plastic was bitter on the tongue. The two boats on the outside had been stripped of their engines, which meant they had probably escaped the worst of the fire. The one in the centre was little more than a pile of matchwood in the water.

I switched the scope on to the building. The front door was closed. There were no signs of guards anywhere that I could see, no signs of a fire for cooking, and no SUVs loaded with armed men. Maybe Musa and his men had packed up and gone, having decided to cut their losses.

As a final precaution I took out the earpiece and listened. The bug was still active but I got the fuzzy sound of a dying power unit.

To keep Madar's mind occupied, I handed him the earpiece and told him he was our eyes and ears while we moved closer, impressing on him the responsibility involved.

'Just listen,' I told him. 'You might hear voices instead of the hissing noise. And watch for any men coming from town along the track.'

He nodded seriously and put in the earpiece. 'What shall I do if someone comes, Mr Marc?'

'Can you whistle?' I mimed putting two fingers in my mouth.

He nodded enthusiastically. 'Of course. Very loud.' He made a move to demonstrate, but I grabbed his hand to stop him.

'I believe you. If you see anybody coming, do that – but one time only. We'll hear you. Then stay right here until we come to get you.'

Tober and I took it in stages, one moving while the other watched. I went first because I knew the lay of the land. I dog-legged down to the garden wall and listened carefully, then on my signal Tober played leap-frog and got to the villa wall. We gave it two minutes, then I took over and covered the door while he ran past to the edge of the garden overlooking the beach to check the dead ground below.

'That's some priceless damage you did there,' he muttered, when he came back and gave the all-clear. He sounded impressed. 'Blew the beach to shit and back.'

He was right. The smell of explosives and burned wood was

much stronger now, catching in the back of the throat. The C-4 had taken a huge bite out of the beach and the ground directly in front of the villa, but the building had been shielded from serious harm by the overhang of impacted sand beneath the garden boundary. Even so, part of the roof shingles had been torn away and some of the upper cinder blocks cracked by the proximity of the blast.

We went inside and did a quick check of the rooms. We were in for a shock. It was clear that Musa and his men were continuing to use the place as a base. The al-Shabaab flag was hanging across the window in the front room, with clothes and other supplies scattered around in boxes. Spare magazines of AK ammunition were stacked against one wall along with two shortwave radios and a case of Russian-made smoke grenades and a crate of rocket launchers. The crate markings had been obliterated but the launchers looked like RPG-7s or a later derivative. I checked through the window and saw boxes of grenades stacked right outside. The thought of all that explosive power so close by made my back itch.

I checked the basement. It was empty and smelled like a cesspit.

'We can't stay here,' I said. 'There's nowhere to hide.' It was also a disaster zone waiting to happen.

Tober nodded and looked longingly at the grenades. 'We could leave them a little surprise package. One trip wire and all gone.'

'Nice idea, but it would tell them we were still around. Maybe later.'

I helped myself to a bottle of water and some dried fruit from one of the boxes of supplies, then walked over to the window overlooking the beach and eased aside one corner of the al-Shabaab flag. The glass was cracked and filthy, and by some miracle it had survived intact. I rubbed away some of the dirt, and felt an instant kick in my gut.

Two skiffs with armed men on board were just offshore, coming in fast and leaving curving white furrows of foam behind them.

'Time to go,' I said urgently. 'Keep the house between us.'

We sprinted directly for the slope, running past the hole I'd been hiding in before. Once we reached high ground and could be sure we weren't being observed, we hunkered down and watched as the two boats slid into the shallows and the men began to offload more supplies. It looked well-rehearsed and it was obvious they were here for a long haul. Each boat carried four men, and while two stood guard with AKs, eyeing the extent of the beach and the terrain inland, the others dragged boxes up the sand to the villa.

When we had seen enough and the men had disappeared inside, we angled round and picked up Madar, then headed further inland until we saw a copse of trees. It wasn't much, and was uncomfortably close to the coastal track and too far away to keep an eye on the villa, but it would have to do. Perfection doesn't always come as part of the package.

We sat out the rest of the day, which meant working hard on keeping Madar quiet for the first few hours. I had two energy bars left in my backpack, which helped. Now he was with us he was like a dog with two tails, as if he thought we were bomb-proof and it would give him the same protection. Thankfully, though, he still hadn't recovered fully from his beating at the hands of Musa's men, and tiredness eventually took over and he crashed out.

'What do we do with him?' Tober asked, when Madar began snoring softly. 'We can't take him with us and we can't leave him here – he'll get himself killed.'

'What I said before: we get him somewhere where he can get a boat heading north. Not all the men in Kamboni are Musa's goons, and one of the fishing boats will be happy to have a free deck-hand.' It wasn't the perfect solution, but Madar was bright enough to make his own way. In any case, there was no way we could see him all the way home. He was going to have to do some fast growing up.

Tober and I took turns to watch the track while the other catnapped. The sum total of activity for the day was three vehicles, two heading north, one south, and five small motor-bikes loaded with produce, bouncing along through the ruts and potholes. Nobody stopped to investigate the trees, but we both went on high alert each time, ready to take anybody down who came too close.

I debated ringing Vale with an update. But there was nothing to tell him. He knew roughly where we were, and would know by now from Piet that Angela Pryce was on her way. Beyond that he was as powerless as we were. I decided to leave it and conserve battery power.

By nightfall we were edgy, thirsty and eager to be off. Madar was up again, his energy reserves back to normal, and asking endless questions about what we were going to do next and when. I figured the only way to bring him down to a safe level was to move towards Kamboni, and let a touch of natural fear take hold of him. At least then he'd be easier to keep quiet and do exactly what we told him.

It was time to roll.

There was thin cloud cover, which allowed some starlight and a watery moon to show through. That was good and bad; good because it gave us some vision, bad because it made us easier to spot. We set out in file, me on point and Madar between us. I had a slight advantage over Tober, having seen the general layout of the area, which wasn't a hell of a lot.

The air was still, with just the buzzing of insects to disturb us and clamping down on us in clouds, sticking to our faces and clothes. I got adept at spitting them quietly off my lips every few seconds, and tried hard to ignore the feel of them moving through my hair and tickling my scalp.

The closer we got to the sea, the cooler it became, and the louder the hiss of the waves brushing the beach. It sounded peaceful and serene, a holiday trailer, and it simply couldn't last.

It didn't.

Fifty-Seven

Musa had decided to box clever. Going ahead of the other two to scout the land, I found guards had been posted some way out from the villa. They looked more alert than their predecessors and I guess his trackers had reported in that some of us were still on the loose. He was taking no chances.

Good for him but bad for us.

I walked back and angled away from the area, following a parallel path along the coast towards Dhalib, but not so close to the track from the north. Being caught out by men in vehicles would see us quickly run down and surrounded, and we didn't have enough ammunition for a protracted firefight.

Even moving slowly and stopping every few metres for a listen and to let the other two catch up, I eventually ran into trouble.

It came in the form of a sentry taking a bathroom break.

He shouted in surprise and rose up in front of me, clutching his skirt in one hand and a rifle in the other. There was no time for pleasantries; I had just enough time to loose off a shot from the AK. It took him high in the shoulder and spun him round, but he was a tough bird and hollered out to his friends before I could smack him down with the rifle butt.

Too little too late.

Answering shouts came from the darkness behind us, and a shot sounded as one of the men got excited and drilled a shadow. It wouldn't be long before they were swarming around us and our way out was cut off. We had to move fast.

I whistled and got a reply from Tober, and an even louder one from Madar. Darned kid was going to get himself killed – but at least he was awake and alert. Seconds later they caught up with me and we began running south.

We arrived at the cluster of huts that had once been Dhalib. It still smelled of fire and death, and there was a taste of ash lingering in the air, but the bodies had been taken away. Now it was merely a ghostly place with no sign of life. Given time, I figured it would simply blow away with the next strong wind and be forgotten.

We left the ruined huts behind, but it was obvious from the distant shouting that Musa's men weren't far off. They couldn't know who they were looking for, nor how many, but they must have found their man and were operating on the logic that at least Tober and one other were out here, and were armed and ready to fight.

I slowed down to let Tober and Madar catch up. The kid was game enough, but he hadn't the strength for a full-on run and Tober was having to hustle him along, which slowed him down, too.

I had to think of some way of delaying the pursuit, and giving us a chance to get clear. I could have done with a couple of packs of C-4 right now, but that was wishful thinking.

I grabbed Tober's arm and said softly, 'Head along the coast until you get to the first few houses. Madar will show you. Dig in somewhere on the beach and I'll catch up with you.'

'What are you going to do?'

'I'll spook them and lead them off the other way.'

He nodded and I stepped back towards the track and the incoming pursuers, sinking to one knee while the other two disappeared into the gloom. I was hoping Tober would get them both clear and not stay around to help me. It was pointless us all getting caught.

The first man came out of the dark like a runaway train, his sandals slapping on the hardened ground. He was grunting with excitement, his face shiny with sweat and desperately wanting to be the one to catch us.

He was lucky; he was going to be the one to live.

I waited until he was right on top of me, then stood up and hit him with the butt of the AK, hard enough to drive the air from his lungs but not to knock him out completely. I needed him conscious enough to be aware of what I was doing so he could tell his colleagues.

I snatched up his AK and called out into the dark, making sure he saw that I was looking directly to the west, inland and away from Kamboni. It was a piece of theatre, but I wanted him to think I was following others away from the town into the bush.

As I ran off I heard him trying to holler for backup from his friends, who could only have been a short distance behind him, and the answering chatter of men arguing over the direction I had taken.

Just to make sure they got the message, I shouted again and fired a short burst from the fallen man's AK towards the voices, then hit the ground. I was just in time; the answering fire was thick and fast and sounded like a small war as they let loose in my direction, bullets snapping angrily past me.

I waited for the excitement to die down, then jumped up and ran for several minutes, jumping scatterings of thorn bush and tangled grass more by instinct than sight. After I'd covered enough ground I shouted again and fired another burst until the magazine clicked on empty.

The Somalis responded in like terms, but this time the firing was lighter and seemed to be going in several directions at once. The sound of my shots must have been confusing in the darkness, and the excitement of the chase would have allowed them little chance of figuring out exactly where I was. But they had also learned by now to be cautious, which was going to work in my favour.

I tossed the empty AK to one side and carried on running. This time I headed south, aiming directly for the town and the beach beyond and hoping I didn't run into someone smart who'd figured out what I was doing. I was hoping the diversion would take the men enough time to sort out to give me a chance of catching Tober and Madar and figure out what to do next.

Fifteen minutes later I saw the shadows of buildings to my right, and came across the main coastal track. I had hit Kamboni head-on. I veered off slightly left and skirted a long thatched bungalow, keeping low and trying not to trip over anything in the gloom.

The smell of dried fish was very strong now, with the underlying fresher tang of the sea. I moved between two more long houses siding on to the beach and protected by a line of palm trees, then knelt down to get my bearings.

A dog barked in the distance, and the sea hissed across the sand and bubbled out again. Apart from that, it had the cold, dead feel of a ghost town. I wondered how many people were here, reluctant to leave the few possessions they had in the world.

I checked the beach, looking at the boats moored close to the waterline. I knew Tober would have gone looking for a way out of here as a matter of instinct.

And where there were boats, he would be, too.

Fifty-Eight

I spotted Madar first. He was moving along the waterline, keeping low and checking the boats which were moored in a row, their rigging down. He seemed to be by-passing a lot of solid looking craft, and I wondered why. Then it hit me: Tober would have told him to look out for one with twin engines.

That automatically ruled out boats belonging to the local fishermen. If they had engines at all they were small and probably far from new, held together by repeated tinkering and lots of prayer. Only the pirates could afford the fancier machines required to get them in against their targets in rough seas and away again if they encountered resistance on board or an armed naval patrol vessel.

I stayed where I was and checked out the beach either side, listening for sounds of pursuit coming from among the huts behind me. Going out to meet up with the two others might attract unnecessary attention, and I could do more useful work watching their backs.

Tober appeared, stopping every few paces to check his back trail, then giving each boat the quick once-over in case Madar had missed something. I made sure nobody was behind him, then followed a parallel course through the passageways among the huts, keeping the beach within sight.

Kamboni was on a promontory shaped like the head of a hammerhead shark, with the uppermost part of the hammer forming the protective arm of a natural bay. Most of the town was set back slightly inland, with a few buildings and the local mosque closest to the water at the centre of the hammerhead. I hadn't ventured that far, but from a satellite shot Vale had provided, it seemed that all the boats were moored in the bay, where they would be less vulnerable from storms along the coast.

I paused to watch as Madar approached a large boat in the shallows. We were getting very close to the area around the mosque, which I guessed might have some kind of watchman in attendance. If he carried on much further, he would run out of beach.

Then I stopped moving and lifted the AK. A figure had stepped out from the houses and was walking down the sand. I couldn't see a rifle but he had something bulky over his shoulder. I checked through the scope to see what it was.

A rolled fishing net. And he was heading for the boat where Madar was standing.

Madar saw him too, and stopped, sinking to his haunches in the water. I looked to my left. Tober had frozen, hard up against another boat.

I heard voices.

The man had spotted Madar. But he wasn't shouting in alarm. I held my breath, finger light on the trigger. I didn't want to kill the fisherman just for being in the wrong place at the wrong time. But if he started yelling, we were in big trouble.

Madar stood and walked towards him. The man dropped his netting on the sand by the boat, then stretched his back and looked up at the stars. Next he pointed to the stern of the boat and said something.

Madar stepped forward and picked up the net, heaving it on board.

I waited, wondering what he was doing. Could it really be this simple? Had Madar stumbled on his way out of here? If so, Tober and I were down one problem and free to make our own way out, too.

Madar turned and looked along the beach and gave a short whistle. Tober stood up and moved forward to join them, and stood listening before he turned and waved to me.

He was good. He'd known I was here all along.

I jogged down the beach and saw Madar was grinning, looking like an excited puppy about to go on an outing.

'Mr Marc,' he whispered. 'This is Tawfiq.' He indicated the fisherman, who didn't seem that surprised to see two armed white men on a remote beach in his country. If he thought anything he certainly wasn't saying. Up close, I could see he must have been in his sixties, with the build of a marathon runner, a scrub of white beard and deep-set eyes.

'He is a good man,' Madar continued, 'and says the other men are very bad and will bring nothing but trouble to Kamboni. He believes the Kenyan army will come soon and attack the town, and many may die. That is why he is leaving. It has happened before when the pirates come; they bring nothing and take everything. I have asked him if he will take me with him to the north.'

He rapidly translated for Tawfiq, who nodded and replied in a guttural burst of his own.

'What did he say?' I asked. 'Can you trust him?'

'Yes. He says he dares to go out at night because he has a bigger boat and knows the waters like his own hand. The others are like women with the courage of goats. His cousin's son who helps him is not well and he says he will take me as a deck hand but I will have to work hard or he will throw me overboard to the sharks.' He grinned again. 'I do not think he means that.'

'Let's hope not. Does he need money?' I didn't want to insult the man, but I couldn't take advantage of his kindness.

Madar spoke to him, and the old man looked nonplussed. I dug out some notes and handed them to Madar. 'You deal with it. Tell him if he doesn't take you home, we will come back and sink his boat.'

I'm not sure Madar passed that on, but the man seemed happy with the money.

Madar turned to Tober and shook his hand, then to me and hugged me briefly. 'Thank you, Mr Marc,' he muttered, his voice choked. 'You are a good man, too.'

I hugged him back and slapped him on the shoulder. He was a decent kid and I hoped he made it.

Tober and I helped push the boat out until it floated free, while Tawfiq and Madar climbed aboard and got busy, the fisherman telling the kid what to do in a calm, practiced voice. The sail went up and filled gently, and the boat was soon moving with deceptive grace into deeper water.

Then we heard a shout, followed by gunshots.

Fifty-Nine

Tober and I raced up the beach to put distance between us and the departing boat. If Musa's men thought we were on board, they'd have a fleet of fast skiffs out and be all over Tawfiq and Madar in no time. And I didn't think they'd stop to ask questions.

The shooting had come from between the huts to the northern end of town. It meant we had to head for the centre if we wanted to avoid a full-on confrontation. It was probably heading deeper into trouble, but right now we were short on choices.

I heard the roar of an engine and saw light sweeping through the buildings, and remembered the pickups I'd seen before. Some of Musa's men were camped in town, and had evidently got word of our presence. They would be joining in the search by now, and every minute that passed meant the net around the town would be growing tighter.

We pounded through a network of narrow passages between the huts. Twice men appeared out of doorways and tried to stop us. Each time we ran through them. It was brutal, close-quarter fighting, but if anything Tober and I had the advantage of surprise and momentum. We eventually found ourselves by the side of the town's mosque. Just as we did so, a figure appeared round the corner and ran head-on into Tober, who smacked him down with the butt of his rifle.

Another man appeared, this one swinging up an AK and letting off a couple of rounds before I could stop him. I knocked him over with two quick shots and pointed off to our left towards the lower edge of town, away from the sound of shooting and the searchers' lights.

Tober got the message and headed off fast, barrelling his way between two ragged lines of huts. I followed a couple of paces behind, ready to turn and defend our flanks.

It was difficult to see clearly ahead of us, and we didn't always get it right. At one intersection we saw what appeared to be clear space between two buildings, only to crash through a wall of palm fronds surrounding a small plot of land. The noise was considerable and raised a volley of shouting from towards the beach as the pursuers zeroed in on our location and began closing in, letting off an occasional round to show they meant business. We were forced to duck as we ran down the lines of huts due to the overhanging canopies brushing our faces, which slowed us down, and all the way I could hear the slap of running feet on the other side as the men closed in. If they got ahead of us, all they had to do was run down an intersection and cut us off.

As we turned a corner and raced across a triangle of hard ground, we found two men with rifles blocking our way and yelling at us to stop.

It was bad news: Musa must have issued orders for us to be taken alive.

Tober and I opened fire together, both taking out the man nearest to us. He crashed sideways through a hut wall and disappeared, while his companion thought to hell with orders and sent a spray of wild gunfire our way. I felt something tug at my shirt and the canopy close to my head was blown apart in a shower of palm frond fragments, wood splinters and dust. I returned fire and the Somali fell hard, losing his gun in the process.

I looked round at Tober and felt my stomach go cold.

He'd been hit and was down on one knee.

Even as I watched, he grunted and fell forward in slow motion, instinctively trying to minimize the fall by putting out a hand. But he wobbled as he came half upright and I knew that wasn't good.

I reached out and grabbed his collar, pulling him with me and heading for another narrow alley with lots of shadow. There was no time to stop and ask how badly he was wounded; if he stayed on his feet for another few minutes, that was good enough for now.

Suddenly the whole area was lit up by vehicle headlights, and a spotlight beam thrashed around before fastening on to us. I responded by instinct, flicking the selector and emptying the AK's magazine at the vehicle, chopping out the spot and one headlight and hearing a man go down screaming.

I dragged Tober away under cover of a bungalow, letting go

of him just long enough to change magazines, and felt a searing pain across my ribs as a stray round burst through the wall of the building. I recalled what Piet had told me about the Somalis' rule of engagement, how they go for the spray option with little thought for selective targeting.

It obviously worked for them some of the time.

We skidded along the nearest wall, tramping over domestic debris in the process, and somehow found ourselves inside a small hut. It was some kind of storage shed, full of nets, cork floats and stuff I couldn't work out, and stinking of stale fish. Right then it was the sweetest smelling place I'd ever been in.

I lowered Tober to the floor. 'Where are you hit?'

He coughed, which didn't sound good. 'In the side and the leg. The leg's not bad but I think the bullet in my side might have done some damage. It feels like one good cough and you'll see my guts on the floor.'

Checking a wound in the dark is not to be recommended. I told him what I was going to do, but I was shaking with tiredness and the rush of adrenalin. He swore silently as my fingers brushed against the swollen area of skin around the bullet wound, and I felt the slick wetness of blood seeping out of him and running down his side. I felt round the back but there was no sign of an exit wound.

All I could do was get it strapped up. But right now wasn't the time or the place. We had to get out of here before Musa's men closed in and found us by a process of elimination.

'You should bug out,' Tober muttered, his breathing ragged. 'No point us both getting chopped.'

'Yeah, right,' I said. 'Keep up with that crap and I might save Musa's men the trouble and shoot you myself.'

'It's no longer your fight, Portman. You did what you had to – you got Pryce out.'

'Matter of fact, I got paid for both of you. Now shut the fuck up unless you have a miracle plan to get us out of here.'

He tried a chuckle but it didn't quite come off. 'What happened – you left a mate behind once and never forgot – is that it?'

'Something like that. Any bright ideas?'

His head lolled to one side and I figured he was going into

shock. But his survival instincts were still kicking in. 'Boat. It's the only way. Get me a boat and I'll tell you what to do.'

He was right. First we had to find one we could use. 'Did you see any on the beach with engines?'

'A couple. But they weren't great.' He coughed and clutched his side. 'The hulls looked heavy and the engines were light-weight. The Somalis would catch us in no time if they called up one of their assault skiffs. They may look like shite but those things can really move.'

I decided to check them out for myself. It was risky but anything was better than staying here and waiting to be caught. 'Come on,' I said, giving him my arm. 'We're off to the beach.'

He heaved himself to his feet. 'Oh, goodie. It's been ages since I had a day by the seaside.'

We stepped outside and stood in deep shadow. Voices sounded all around us, the configuration of the huts making it difficult to pinpoint precisely where they were coming from.

Safe to assume all over.

I checked the nearest alleyway, which I estimated ran roughly in a north-south direction, dog-legging between huts and bunga-lows. From the map in my head I reckoned we needed east to west, with a slight kink south to fetch us close to where the nearest boats were moored. I set off, holding Tober's arm until he shrugged it off, and led the way past two bungalows until we came to a narrow intersection. This was about right to turn east towards the beach.

Our one advantage was, nobody had told Musa's men that a hunting party had to be quiet if they wanted to catch their prey. With all the hollering, the roar of vehicle engines and the occa-sional shot being fired as somebody spooked at shadows, we knew exactly where they were, and could plan our route accordingly.

Well, almost.

As we slunk past a small hut, I heard a sudden intake of breath in the darkness and a shot was fired so close it lit up the night around us.

Sixty

We got lucky; the shooter was as surprised as we were. His finger must have tightened on the trigger as he brought up his gun and the round slammed harmlessly into the hard-packed earth at our feet. In the flash of light I saw a shocked face above a bandolier of shells and a white shirt, and a pair of bug eyes staring back at me from less than three feet away. I was too close to bring the AK level, so made do by chopping him under the chin and stashing him back inside the hut under a heap of netting and canvas.

We hurried on and hit the beach a few minutes later, emerging between two long bungalows lit by flickering oil lamps. I kept my fingers crossed that the people inside were fishermen and not Musa's men looking for a taste of glory.

Tober squatted next to me and pointed at a group of five boats in the distance. They were about three hundred metres away across open sand, which is a long way to go with a wounded man losing blood, and being chased by a bunch of trigger-happy gunmen.

But we had no choice.

'Three of those have got engines that looked in working order,' he whispered, and stifled a cough. 'The rest are useless.'

Working order might not be enough to do it, but it was better than the alternative. 'Good. Can you make it that far?' He sounded bad and I wasn't sure I could carry him far; he was a big guy to throw over my shoulder.

'I'll beat you any day,' he muttered sourly.

We set off for the boats, our feet sinking into the softer, sun-dried sand at the top of the beach. It was hard going, especially for Tober, but the sooner we got down on to the harder surface, the easier it would be.

We were about halfway across when whatever thin cloud lay overhead shifted away completely as if a puff of breeze had been thrown up by the fates. Then a shot came sizzling past our heads and a man shouted, followed by others. As we turned and looked, two vehicles burst out through a thin fence at the far end of the beach, throwing wood and palm fronds into the air and charging straight towards us. The lead vehicle had two headlights, while the one behind had only one. We'd met that one already; now he was back for a rematch.

'*Go!*' I shouted, and pushed Tober towards the boats. I needed him to find one that worked and to get the engine started.

But he wasn't having any of it. 'Too far,' he gasped. 'It'll take too long and they'll be all over us before we leave the beach.'

I glanced towards the charging vehicles. He was right: they were moving too fast and would cut us off in seconds. The light of the second one lit up its companion and showed a bunch of armed men clinging on to the back, and among them, something long poking into the night sky. Then a man stood up behind it and swung it down towards us and I felt my blood run cold. I'd seen that profile before.

It was a heavy machine gun.

Jesus, what else were they going to bring to the party?

'Here.' Tober jerked a thumb at his shoulder and knelt down heavily on the sand, putting his fingers in his ears. He was indicating that I should use him as a firing platform.

Good plan.

I laid the AK across his shoulders and dropped to one knee, pushing the muzzle as far forward from Tober's head as I could. I sighted on the lead pickup, which was the most dangerous.

The gunner beat me to it. The muzzle flickered crazily as each round left the barrel, the yammering sound of the shots rolling across the bay towards us in a frenzy of firepower.

The air around us turned crazy as the shots went over our heads in a deadly stream, snapping through the night. But the gunner was too keen to show what he could do and didn't wait for the truck to hit firmer ground; the pickup was bouncing too much for him to get a bead on us and he had an unsteady platform beneath him. We both ducked instinctively, and I turned my head and watched as a stream of shots curved downwards beyond us and kicked up sand at the water's edge . . . and ripped through the very boats we had been heading for.

The devastation was total. The heavy shells tore the wooden

hulls apart like papier maché, throwing a shower of wood chunks, torn canvas and punctured engine casing into the air. The shots that missed the boats with engines continued on by and chopped through the remainder, rendering the entire fleet beyond use.

I turned and sighted back on the pickup, and felt Tober settle and take a deep breath to steady himself.

I aimed at the gunner first. If he got even half lucky with that thing, we'd be reduced to dog meat. I fired twice and saw him punched back off the pickup as if he'd been slapped aside by an invisible hand. Then I aimed at the other men and hosed a brief burst at them, watching them jump or fall as they lost their tenuous hold on their ride.

The pickup swerved wildly, its lead offside tyre digging deep into the sand. The driver struggled to correct but he'd been frightened by my shots coming close by over his head and sensing his colleagues jumping ship. In trying to regain control, he only managed to over-correct. The vehicle swerved again, this time more violently and turning the other way. Only now there was no way he could hold it. With a groan, it flipped, showing us its underside before slamming down on it back and rolling twice before coming to rest on one side.

The second pickup driver did the one thing he shouldn't have done in the circumstances: he slammed on the brakes and pulled to a stop.

'Firing,' I warned Tober, and squeezed the trigger. The shot punched straight through the windscreen, knocking the driver sideways. The engine roared like a wounded beast, but the pickup didn't move.

Driver down.

I grabbed Tober's gun and fired a burst at the rear of the vehicle. After the silenced AK, I needed the noise of hot gunfire to demoralise the men further. It worked. I saw figures jumping clear and racing back along the beach away from us. I fired a short burst over their heads, then dropped the rifle and took out the Vektor.

Time to get us out of here.

I walked towards the pickup, my heart pounding with blood and my head singing from the gunfire. As I got close, I saw movement behind the windscreen and caught the glimmer of metal.

Rifle barrel.

I fired twice, aiming for a spot at the bottom of the screen. The shots punched through the metal surround and blew off the windscreen wiper blade, and the rifle disappeared.

When I got closer, the driver was slumped in his seat, his face towards the sky.

I couldn't see any passengers but I wasn't taking any chances. I fired two rounds from the Vektor at the passenger side of the cab, then walked off at an angle, waiting for someone to pop out from hiding.

Nobody did.

I opened the driver's door and pulled the man out on to the sand. He stared up at me with dead eyes. I jumped in and drove towards Tober. He was sitting where I'd left him, holding his side and shaking his head at me, but grinning weakly. I got him into the passenger seat and securely wedged in, then drove north along the beach and headed as fast as I dared along the track towards Dhalib and the villa.

'Where we going?' Tober grunted.

'Back to where there are boats with good engines,' I replied. Back to the hornets' nest.

As we bumped over the rutted ground, Tober's head lolled against the back of the cab. He was trying to hold on but his grip was failing. He gave me that weak grin again and said, 'You've done this shit before, haven't you?'

Then he passed out.

I was close to Dhalib before I dared risk pulling off the track and heading inland for about half a click. I found a dip in the landscape behind some scrubby trees, where the pickup would be invisible, and parked with the truck's nose pointing towards the villa. It wasn't a great location but I didn't dare risk driving off too far for fear of getting stuck in a gulley. With Tober's condition and Musa's men almost certain to be scouring the area looking for blood after all the damage we had done, I needed to be ready for a fast getaway.

Before that, though, I had to check on Tober's wounds and call Vale.

Sixty-One

'What are you going to do?' Moresby looked beaten, his voice dulled and tired as he looked across his desk at Vale. It wasn't quite the response Vale had been expecting; he'd been anticipating more venom and wondered if Moresby was playing him. Not that he was going to trust the man further than he could throw his desk; even wounded animals can fight back.

He'd spent the day waiting for news from Portman and talking to the SIS liaison officer at the embassy in Nairobi. Pryce had been delayed by bad weather out of Mombasa, and the local security officer had advised against trying to speak to her until she was safe in the embassy's secure suite. In between, he attended to two other operations he was running and a third where he was first stand-in. The hours had been eaten away surprisingly quickly, and it was only now that he'd been able to go back to Moresby to find out what the man had done since their last meeting.

The answer, it turned out, was almost nothing. In fact, Moresby seemed nearly paralysed by indecision, pushing papers around his desk in a seemingly random manner as if hoping to find an answer buried in their midst.

'How far away are the frigates?' Vale asked him.

Moresby's eyes flickered. 'I don't know – several hours, last I heard.'

Vale picked up Moresby's phone and slid the handset across the desk. 'Get on to the MOD and find out their best estimate. We need those Lynx choppers in the air as soon as they get close enough.'

Moresby shook his head. 'But the Somalis—'

'Screw the Somalis,' Vale barked, cutting him off short. 'We can worry about territorial niceties later. If they had better control of their coastline, none of this would be happening.' He reached for his mobile and punched in the speed dial number for Portman's satellite phone.

It rang but there was no reply.

He let it ring out for a full minute, hoping against hope that Portman was either in a dead zone or unable to answer securely due to outside circumstances.

He cut the connection. Even if the Lynx and their detachments did arrive, it would take time to locate Portman and Tober – if they were still alive. Better to concentrate on Pryce and make sure she could give a full account of what had happened.

He stood up and walked towards the door.

'Where are you going?' Moresby called after him.

He turned his head but didn't stop. 'I'm going to make sure that we at least have one person coming out of this alive.' He wanted to add that he was going to talk to Scheider, but he didn't trust Moresby not to wake up and jump in first and tell the American to keep out of it. Once he recovered his equilibrium, Moresby would be looking to rescue the situation and start the process of clearing up the mess. And that would entail making sure that there were no embarrassing stories circulating afterwards. 'Don't wait up,' he added, before closing the door firmly behind him.

He returned to his office and slumped behind his desk, exhaustion beginning to invade every fibre of his body. If he didn't get some proper sleep soon, he'd start to unravel like a badly-spooled ball of wool. And that would suit Moresby just fine.

His phone rang and he picked it up, nearly dropping it in the process. Christ, he felt like an old man. What the hell was he still doing this for? It certainly wasn't for the money or the kicks. Perhaps this call was going to put a stop to it.

'Vale.'

There was a slight delay, then a familiar voice floated down the line.

Portman.

He sat up immediately while the American brought him up to date in a few terse sentences stripped to the bare bones.

'We had a couple of hot contacts, but we're out and away. Tober's taken two. He's mobile for now.'

'Badly?'

'He's got one in him and I think a busted rib. He's lost some juice but I'll patch him up as best I can. He's tough – he'll make it.'

'How will you get out?'

'By sea. We'll aim to head down the coast and make landfall somewhere near where Piet keeps Daisy.'

Vale caught on immediately. Malindi. The town was located on a small bay and easy to spot from the sea. The airport was about a kilometre inland. The two men could get a flight from there to Nairobi. 'It's a long way down.'

'It'll take a few hours, but any further north and they'll stand a greater chance of picking us up. Once at sea we'll lose ourselves. If not we'll hug the coast as much as we can. I'll call you later.'

'Do that. There are two frigates on the way with marine detachments, but I can't tell how long they'll take.' Vale didn't want to add that policy and politics might actually get in the way and prevent them from getting too close to Somali or Kenyan land; Portman had enough on his plate without negative information putting a dent in his spirits. 'Thank you, by the way, for getting Pryce out.' It was the least he could say under the circumstances, and he hoped he would be able to enlarge on it at a later date.

'All part of the service.' Portman sounded almost cheerful, and Vale wondered how the man kept going under the circumstances, with no backup and no guarantees other than his own skills and experience to draw on. But then, he'd been like that himself once, back when nothing seemed impossible and danger was a welcome break from tedium.

'Once we're out of here,' Portman continued, 'you might have one of your flying robots take a close fix on the coordinates of this place.'

Robots. He meant drones.

'I can do that. But why?' He couldn't – not directly – but he knew a man who could.

'I think they're making it a base for operations in the south. It's filled with supplies. Be good if it fell over, don't you think?'

Vale breathed out. So Musa hadn't moved out yet. It meant he was planning on staying in the area for a while. And while shipping off the Kenyan coast might feel it was safe down there, away from the traditional pirate hunting ground around the Gulf, they would soon find out how wrong they were. He wondered if the government was aware of that. Plainly the Kenyans weren't planning on doing much to tackle the pirates just yet.

He toyed with the possibilities, the rights and wrongs, the moral imperatives of taking the fight to Musa's front door. Whether he could get the UK's own recently set up Remotely Piloted Air Systems drone team to do it, or persuade the Americans to use one of theirs, was a big question. If he could, it would certainly send a very clear message to others like Musa, who might try to do what he had done: You can be reached. Whoever and wherever you are, you can be touched.

'Leave it with me,' he said. 'I'll see what I can do.'

'Fine. But give us time to get clear first. I'd hate to see one of those Hellfires coming in head-on.'

Vale nearly choked when he realized what Portman was saying. 'You mean you're actually right *there*? How close?'

'Close enough to start a war.'

Then he was gone.

Sixty-Two

'Jesus,' Tober muttered, watching as I produced a small green box from my backpack and flipped open the plastic tabs. 'You came ready. Were you a boy scout in a former life?'

'No. I didn't rate the uniform.' The box contained a basic gunshot trauma kit. I'd hoped I wasn't going to have to use it, but the dice falls the way it does.

We were about a click away from the villa, and I was being ultra-careful with the use of a small LED flashlight to see what I was doing. Tober was sitting propped against the rear wheel of the pickup, which should hopefully shield us from anybody looking out this way. It would also be easier to hear somebody approaching than it would inside the cab.

I lifted the lid and took out shears, rubber gloves, bandages and some vacuum-packed wipes, and did my best to gently clean the area around the wounds with the addition of iodine for good measure. I slapped on gauze packs and trauma wound dressings and wrapped a bandage as tightly as I dared around his torso and tied it off, then did the same for his leg.

He didn't say much, didn't even grunt at what was surely painful, but nodded when I'd finished. He looked pale but game to go on. I handed him some cephalexin tablets to ward off infection, and he swallowed them without question. It wasn't certifiable medical treatment, but if I could stop him bleeding out and keep any bacteria at bay until we got some proper help, he stood a good chance of making it.

'How does it look?' he queried, touching his side and hissing in protest as the movement stretched his ribcage.

'It could have been worse,' I told him.

'How?'

'It could have been me.'

He smiled through the pain and mimed a weak punch at my head. Battlefield humour; it works every time.

'So who was the one you left behind?' he queried. He was talking to keep himself alert. 'The one you're cut up about?'

I didn't want to answer but I needed him awake, too. 'I was leading a four-man unit in a mountainous region. We'd been given bad intel and got ambushed and split up. One man went the wrong way and got shot, but we only found out later.'

'That wasn't your fault.'

That was true, but it felt like it. We were all highly trained in escape and evasion, and capable of looking after ourselves. In such situations each of us was expected to make our own split-second decisions. But sometimes training isn't enough. You need luck, too.

Tober didn't pursue it. Maybe he knew what it was like. 'You rang London just now?'

'I did.'

'I take it they're not sending a Chinook to give us a nice comfy ride home, then?'

'Not exactly.' I told him what Vale had said about the frigates being a long way off, and didn't layer it with sugar. He was experienced enough to know what the political situation was, and that if there was going to be a fast pickup, it would have happened by now. We were going to have to make our own way out of here and the sooner we started, the better.

'Fair enough,' he murmured. 'Shit happens, right?' He lay back and was soon breathing evenly, if a little heavy. It didn't sound great but at least he was still alive.

Perspiration was making my ribs itch. I'd almost forgotten about the bullet skimming my side, and checked it out. I found a two-inch burn mark and a faint smear of blood. Not even a flesh wound. But it was going to hurt like a bitch later on, so I dabbed it with iodine and slapped on a plaster to prevent infection, and swallowed a couple of cephalexin tablets just in case.

Next I moved out a short distance and took a few minutes to check our perimeter, using the scope to pick up any light clothing or movement where there shouldn't be any. But everything was quiet and there were no signs of pursuit. I returned to the truck and found Tober awake and wincing with discomfort.

'You OK?'

He nodded. 'Yeah. Stings a bit when I laugh, that's all.' He gestured away with his chin. 'We good out there?'

'We're fine. No signs of a search but we'll need to make a move soon. Can you stay awake for a while? I'm going to check out the boats near the villa.'

'Sure thing, boss. Find us a good one, will you?' He told me what to look for: plenty of fuel, all the leads and cables in place and how to find them, and some water. 'We could be out at sea for a while,' he finished, 'so don't pick us a dog, right? I don't swim so good with holes in me.'

'I promise.' I handed him the Vektor, which he'd find easier to use than the AK, and left him to it.

Sixty-Three

Vale rang the embassy in Nairobi, where Pryce was waiting for a transfer to the airport and a military flight out. He was put through to the military attaché, Colonel Prior, to check security was in place, and asked to speak to Pryce.

'She's exhausted,' Prior told him. 'Can't you leave it?'

'If I could, I would. Put her on.' Vale's tone was civil, but only just. Having a solicitous army officer get in his way was the last thing he needed.

Angela Pryce came on. She sounded tired but alert.

'I won't keep you long,' he told her. 'I know you've been through a lot.'

'That's OK, sir. How can I help?'

'Tell me what happened. This is a recorded briefing, so keep it short and to the point. You know the drill.'

She hesitated, and he sensed the puzzlement in her voice. 'Sir, shouldn't I wait to speak to Mr Moresby about this?'

She was correct; operationally, she should be reporting to Moresby or one of his nominated de-briefers. The same with Tober, to cross-match the information. Asking her to speak to himself first was a violation of his remit, but since he'd already blown that out of the water from the start, what was another infraction along the way?

'Of course. And you will. But I'd like an outline first – especially about your escape . . . and how you saw the situation developing.'

When she replied, the tension in her voice was clear. 'Haven't you asked Portman that question?'

'I'll come to that later. Tell me what happened, from the time you arrived in Nairobi. It's important.'

'Very well.' She cleared her throat and Vale punched a button on the desk console and sat back to let her talk.

Ten minutes later, her voice tailed off with tiredness and, he guessed, a degree of shock at reliving the experience.

'I'm sorry I put you through that,' he told her. 'But it was necessary.' He didn't need to remind her that she would have to go through it again when she arrived back at Vauxhall Cross – and in more rigorous detail. Debriefing was a necessary evil for all operatives returning from an assignment and she would have gone through the process enough times already to be aware of the format.

'I understand, sir. Is there any news of Doug Tober?'

'He's still out there, but that's all I can tell you. He's being looked after, I promise.' He had his fingers mentally crossed as he said it. In spite of Portman's assurances, any medical problems could change dramatically within minutes, especially with untreated wounds. Tober was tough, as his job demanded, but he wasn't in the best of locations to be walking around with holes in him.

'Who is Portman?' Pryce's words brought him back. 'He's not one of ours, I know that.'

Vale wondered how much to tell her. Not that it made much difference to himself if the attack dogs came after him following his talk with Moresby. But the less he revealed about Portman the better; he owed the man that much and more.

'He's someone I sent out to watch your backs,' he said simply. 'A professional shadow.'

She was silent for a second, then said, 'Thank you. I'm glad you did. He sounds American. Is he one of their black ops people?'

'To be honest,' he said candidly, 'I'm not sure what he is. Does it matter?'

'No.' She sighed down the line. 'I suppose not. I'd like to thank him one day, though. And apologize. I was snarky when he first got us out; he must think me an ungrateful bitch after all he did.'

Vale chuckled. He could imagine it. 'Don't worry – I'll make sure he knows.'

He replaced the phone and sat back. He felt adrift, unable to decide on the next course of action. So much now depended on Portman and Tober making their way out of Somalia any way they could. What could he do to help them?

He reached for a sheet of paper in the centre of his desk. Under the right circumstances, it was the kind of document which, in a certain light could be used to end a career. In this case, Moresby's.

He read it through again. It was a briefing document which had come his way through uncertain channels. Six months ago, a proposal was put before a Special Committee on Security to actively pursue certain groups involved in kidnapping in the Gulf region, effectively to neutralize them. The operation was code-named 'Adventure', after, it was suggested without irony, the legendary pirate Captain Blackbeard's last boat at the time of his death.

The proposal suggested using a small but highly mobile group of former special forces personnel with SAS and SBS back-grounds, supported by drone coverage and a rapid reaction force stationed offshore. Ostensibly there for public knowledge to counter pirate activity, in reality they were to be used as added firepower as and when needed.

The budget would be considerable and highly secret. Several precedents would be used for employing such personnel and tactics outside the remit of the MOD and approved government procedure, but for the most part the lines would be suitably blurred.

There had been criticism of the scheme from the Joint Intelligence Committee, but in the face of a growing threat, it was making its way through the various committees and looked like getting the nod.

The person with overall responsibility for selecting the targets and focussing the Adventure on them was generally recognized as someone with an intelligence background and with access to and familiarity with the latest intelligence resources, in the UK and elsewhere. One cynical observer had already suggested that the person in charge would be catapaulted up the totem pole to honours and status, and would almost certainly be a lead contender as a future Director of SIS.

A keen backer of the scheme and, it was said, the initial proposer and almost certainly the first name in the hat, was Colin Moresby.

Vale was uncertain. If he was honest, it was a scheme for which he felt empathy. Too much ground had been lost over recent years by bowing to legislation and political correctness; ground that was going to be hard to win back from extremists and rogue elements assisted by naïve law makers.

Had Moresby been secretly using the possibility of SIS losses in the meeting with Musa as a springboard to gaining full approval for his plan – for 'Adventure'? If successful, it would undoubtedly have made his career. Or was Vale's own desire to see the man brought down leading him to see things that were not really there?

He reached behind him and dropped the sheet of paper in the shredder, where it vanished into tiny fragments. If he had any time left, and had to reserve his scheming for anybody, let it be the real enemy.

He picked up the phone. As Portman had suggested, he knew the coordinates of the villa. He also knew the resources available to do what was needed. All he had to do was find a way of asking.

Sixty-Four

Walking through the bush at night is not as idyllic as it might sound. Sure, there's no traffic, no street lights and no man-made noises like air-conditioning units to disturb nature's serenity. But you could hardly call it quiet. Insects have a volume button in direct inverse proportion to their size, and most of them only fall silent when you walk close by. Otherwise it's bedlam, which makes checking for voices or human movement harder than it should be.

I stopped with reluctance every few metres, aware that the clock was running. I not only had to keep moving through hostile territory, but had to avoid the villa by a pretty narrow margin if I was to use it as a landmark and find the boats.

I came across the first guard near the track. He was humming to himself, which was lucky for me. I sank down and watched him moving around. He was walking in a wide circle, covering the track and an area either side, then coming back the other way. I debated taking him out there and then, using the Ka-Bar. But as I didn't know how often the guards would be changed or if he might have been told to call in on a regular basis, I moved back a ways and skirted around his position by a good margin.

I came up to the villa not far from my previous hide. A faint light was glowing in the open doorway, enough to show a patrolling guard moving across the rear of the building. I gave it a few minutes to check his routine, then moved down the slope, giving the grounds a wide berth in case other guards had been posted further out.

I reached the dunes above the beach and stayed low for a couple of minutes, listening.

It looked quiet and peaceful, the insect noise now replaced by the hiss of the sea. It could have been any idyllic, exotic vacation setting had it not been for the rifle in my hand and the still lingering smell of explosives in the air.

I counted three boats, vague slug-like shapes against the sand and frothy tideline. I took off my boots and socks, then tied the laces together and slung them round my neck. If any eagle-eyed guards came this way and saw the shape of western-style footwear where there should be none, the game would be up. Then I stepped off the dunes and walked across the beach.

Just like that.

I felt the hairs on my neck prickling all the way. I felt vulnerable like never before, as if stepping across a minefield. I was counting on being mistaken in the poor light for a patrolling guard. Not that I looked anything like a Somali pirate, but the rifle held loosely over my shoulder might throw off any suspicion.

I reached the boats unchallenged and checked them out. They looked and felt ready for sea, and held the same kind of water and fuel containers I'd found in the boats I'd destroyed what felt like a lifetime ago. There were floats, nets, extra clothing, and even coils of rope with grappling hooks and rope ladders. Everything a pirate could wish for. Even the shelters were rigged with the canvas coverings in place, which I took to mean they were ready to move come morning.

It made me even more determined; if I was right, come morning the boats would be gone and we would have no way out.

I checked each of the engines by feel. One had a stripped-down feel, with sharp edges and recesses covered in thick grease and oil and layered in dirt, and was fitted with an extra-long propeller shaft. Tober had warned me to avoid these, as without silencers they were very noisy, slow and difficult to use in a strong sea. The other two were very different beasts; they were fitted with twin outboards, which felt like newer models, but I couldn't tell if they had been disabled or not as the casings were in place and impossible to shift.

Now was not the time to debate the issue. I ripped the power leads from the stripped-down engine and tossed them into the water. If we couldn't use it, there was no point in allowing anybody else to do so. I couldn't tell if either of the other two was in working order, so I'd have to get Tober to advise on them when we got back.

Then I walked back up the beach and replaced my shoes, before making my way back past the villa and back into the bush.

I reached the pickup and watched it for a few moments in case the searchers had come out this far and discovered it. Then I gave a brief whistle and walked across to the far side, where I'd left Tober.

He was gone.

Sixty-Five

I checked inside and underneath the cab in case he'd heard a noise and ducked under the only cover available. No dice.

I began searching the area around the truck, gradually widening the circle and hoping to pick up a trail. I kept telling myself that he couldn't have gone far. Even if he was confused by shock and pain, he'd looked too done in to go anywhere without falling over.

Ten paces out from the truck, I found the Vektor.

It was nose down in the dirt, showing a glimpse of starlight off the barrel. I brushed it off and stowed it away. A little further on I found a scrape in the dirt where Tober must have stumbled and dragged his injured leg. At least I was on the right track.

Another fifty paces out and I heard a low snuffling sound in the night somewhere ahead. Instinct told me it wasn't human, but I couldn't identify it for certain. I should have paid more attention to the National Geographic channel.

It came again, this time followed by a bunch of squeaks and squeals, and my neck bristled. I knew what it was now, and it wasn't good news. If Tober had stumbled on them, he was in grave danger.

It was a warthog with young. Warthogs tend to avoid contact with humans, but when they have young with them, which this one did, and felt threatened, they'd attack anything that moved without hesitation.

I stood very still and waited for the noises to be repeated so I could pinpoint their position. Neither the Vektor nor the AK were any defence against a charging adult warthog, especially in the dark. They could move with devastating speed and a hog's tusks were a formidable weapon against soft human skin.

Eventually I heard a crackling noise and a series of low grunts, gradually moving away.

Then silence.

It took me another ten minutes to locate Tober. He'd fallen into a small hollow, and lay almost hidden in shadow. I reached down and checked his pulse. It was there but weak.

He was a lot worse than I thought.

I risked using the flashlight. The side of his shirt was dark with fresh blood. He was leaking again. I shook him gently and he eventually lifted his head and looked up at me. He moved as if he were drunk. I couldn't tell if that was because of the pain or exhaustion, but I was guessing falling into the hollow hadn't helped.

I eased him on to his feet and got him back to the pickup, where I propped him against the cab. If he went down again, I wasn't sure I could lift him another time.

'Stay with me, Doug. We've got to go.' I gave his cheek a gentle slap. It was rough on him in his condition, but I needed him mobile and focussed for at least the next twenty minutes, otherwise we were done for.

'OK, OK,' he mumbled and swatted my hand away. It was a good sign.

I collected the trauma kit and put it in my backpack and slung Tober's AK over my shoulder, then pointed him towards the coast. I intended taking the most direct route I could find. It would place us uncomfortably close to the villa, but with Tober getting noticeably weaker and in no condition for a lengthy route march, I had no choice.

We approached well away from the area where I'd seen the guard, but he'd changed his patrol route. The first indication I had was hearing a faint cough and a spit right where I thought would be clear space. Then I saw him. He was walking along the track, still looking fully alert, a rifle slung over his shoulder and head turning to listen over the noises of the night bugs. I froze and held on to Tober. Fortunately he got the message and went still.

Getting us both across the track without being seen was going to be tough. It was wide here and Tober couldn't move fast or stealthy any longer. And we didn't have the time or energy to circle round.

There was nothing for it. I let Tober sink slowly to the ground and put the AK down beside him.

I didn't want to have to do this, but it was the guard or us. I took out the Ka-Bar and moved forward, then waited for the guard to come back along the track.

It didn't take long. I heard the soft slap of his sandals on the hard earth. He was probably walking briskly to keep himself awake.

I waited until he was almost past me, then stepped out behind him. He sensed my presence and began to turn, but too late. I slapped my free hand over his mouth from behind and thrust the knife into his ribs.

He struggled momentarily, then stiffened and went still. I eased him down and dragged him off the track for some twenty paces, dumping the body into a dip in the earth. I took his spare AK magazine and stuffed it in my pocket, then hauled Tober back to his feet and we scuttled across the track into the bush.

After that it was a relentless shuffling of one foot in front of the other until we hit the slope above the beach. I paused for a moment, out of breath and feeling nauseous. I hadn't eaten enough to keep up my energy levels, and my arm around Tober was aching with the strain of holding him up. I checked our surroundings. I couldn't see the villa guard from here due to the lay of the land, even though there was way more light than on my earlier trip.

Great timing; just as we were going to have to walk right across the open beach to the water.

Still, we had what we had. It was time to move.

The trip across the sands seemed never-ending, and I was expecting to be challenged every step of the way. With the cloud cover shifting and exposing us, we would have looked an odd shape if anybody had been keeping an eye on the boats. I kept up a whispered commentary all the way to keep Tober in touch, letting him know how close we were. He didn't respond but his legs kept moving, so I figured he was still in there somewhere, doing his bit.

We passed the first boat with the stripped-down engine, the water slapping gently off the hull. I steered Tober towards the middle vessel. Maybe it was the familiar noise or the smell of the sea, but suddenly his feeling for boats seemed to kick in. He lifted his head and looked around at the long dark shapes and gave a nod of approval.

'You picked a good one?' he asked, his words slurred. At least he remembered what he'd said to me earlier. Another good sign. His mental faculties were still in working order.

'Two,' I said. 'Neither of them are dogs but you'll have to check the engines and get one started. Can you do that?'

He grunted and shoved me away. 'Do it with my eyes closed, pal. Just watch. Don't reckon I'll be able to push, though.'

He was looking down as he said this, and my gut went cold. I hadn't noticed that the hull of the nearest boat was further up the sand than it had been earlier. It meant we'd have to move it by muscle-power alone.

Tober wasn't waiting; he clambered into the other boat which wasn't as far aground, and I heard him humming slightly as he traced the engine casing with his fingers, patting it like you would a pet dog and mumbling in approval.

'S'right to go, baby,' he said, and waved at me. 'C'mon, Portman, y'fuckin' Yank landlubber. Time to go sailing.'

I placed the backpack and rifles on board, then put my shoulder behind the boat and heaved. Nothing happened. It was firmly grounded.

'Shit.' Tober swore and almost fell out of the boat. He crouched down alongside me and put his shoulder against the stern, alongside the twin engines. 'Nice,' he muttered dreamily, patting the nearest casing, and I realized he was on automatic pilot, his mind taking over as a fever gradually took hold of him. 'Go like shit off a shovel, these things.'

'Push,' I said, 'or we're going nowhere.'

Then we heard a shout from near the top of the beach, followed by a shot being fired.

We had outstayed our welcome; it was time to run.

Sixty-Six

Whatever energy Tober had left inside him resurfaced just in time. Or maybe it was the shot and pure survival instinct. With a grunt he leaned hard against the boat and I felt it shift smoothly into the water. It probably had something to do with him being out of the boat, or his feel for the weight and balance. Who knows?

I threw my weight at it, digging in my heels as hard as I could. The boat was afloat. Tober gave a wild laugh and scrambled aboard, and did something to the twin engines, dropping them into position. Moments later, as I jumped in, they started up with a deafening roar and the boat seemed to leap forward like a startled gazelle, throwing me off my feet.

I rolled across the bottom to where I'd dumped the rifles and came up facing the beach, AK in hand. And swore.

In the rush to get moving I'd forgotten to disable the other craft.

I fired several shots at the twin engine casings and a few more into the hull at water level, hoping I could do enough damage to make it unseaworthy. No float, no boat. I gave it another burst just to be sure, but by then we were bouncing through the waves and too far off to be certain of hitting anything.

Several figures were now visible racing across the sand, weapons glinting in the moonlight. A couple of the men started shooting, but mostly into the air. Then one of them must have wised up because there was a shouted order and they stopped running and brought their guns to bear. The muzzle flares came first, then the sound of the shots reached us over the noise of the twin engines. One or two rounds came close, but by then we were two hundred metres offshore and moving fast out to sea, bouncing smoothly over the gentle inshore swell.

A few minutes later, when the coastline had faded into the gloom, with only the white line of froth on the sand to mark its position, Tober turned south, cutting across the waves, which were now small to medium and not so smooth. Instinct and guts were driving him on, and I hoped he could stick at it for a while longer. I could handle the boat if I had to, but nothing makes up for the feel and experience of a seasoned boatman at the helm.

I took out the phone and called Vale. This might be the last chance I got.

'We're offshore and clear, heading south,' I told him, shouting over the engine noise. 'The rest is up to you.'

His voice was faint, but I was just able to pick out the words. 'Got that. Call me when you make land.' He cut the connection.

We had been running for about twenty minutes, with no visible signs of pursuit, when I noticed the bow beginning to drift. First to port, then starboard. And the shift was getting wider each time. I looked at Tober. He was slumped against the side of the boat, one arm hugging the woodwork, the other just about holding on to the tiller.

I scrambled across and helped him into the bottom of the boat where he'd be more comfortable. I couldn't do anything to help him right now, so I grabbed the tiller and corrected our course. If I could keep this thing going in the right direction and ahead of any pursuit, we might be able to stay out of trouble.

An hour later I stopped the boat to refuel. I had no idea of the range of these things, but leaving it too long and finding we were running out of fuel while being chased was a no-brainer. Although stationary in the water, we were being thrown around uncomfortably with the choppy action of the sea, and it made getting the fuel container into position and filling the tanks hard work, without keeping an eye out for pursuit. Eventually, though, liberally soaked with splashed fuel, I replaced the caps and stowed the fuel container away, and we set off again.

At one point Tober seemed to rally. He lifted his hand and gave me a thumbs up sign, before falling asleep again. Whatever was keeping him going with two holes in him you simply couldn't bottle, and I hoped if I was ever in the same position,

I'd be able to do the same. I wanted to check on his condition, but didn't dare stop again for fear of being caught.

After another ninety minutes, with the first signs of light stretching across the horizon to the east, and shivering almost uncontrollably in the pre-dawn cold, I turned to check the coast, trying to figure out where we were from the map in my head. I guessed we might be somewhere near the island of Lamu, although I couldn't separate it from the mainland, which was roughly two clicks to our right. If I was correct, it meant we were roughly halfway to Malindi and well inside Kenyan territory.

A pity nobody bothered to tell the pirates.

As I glanced back towards Kamboni, I saw a flicker of movement. It was there, then gone, merging against the sea. I slowed and blinked to clear my eyes, studying the area and looking slightly off to one side, wondering if tiredness was taking its toll. But no, there it was again, barely visible, a flash of something low on the water. A submarine? Way too close to shore.

Then the swell of the sea shifted and the picture became clear. Three dots were heading out from the shoreline towards us. They were too indistinct to make out any detail but I knew what they were.

Pirate skiffs. Musa had called up replacements.

I increased speed, nearly losing control as the engines bit into the water and the boat sat back, the nose lifting like a startled racehorse. Too much. I throttled back, my heart pounding with the rush of adrenaline, increasing the speed slowly until I felt the boat settle into a smoother rhythm.

When I next checked the position of the following boats, one was in the lead and kicking up a spray of white foam from powerful twin engines, with the other two not far enough behind. They were still a way off, running parallel to the coast but gradually moving out towards us, and I knew instinctively what they were doing: they were going to nudge us gradually out to sea and away from land, like cattle dogs controlling the herd. Then they would be able to finish us off at their leisure.

Musa must have been feeling royally pissed at us with all this attention, and I guessed he wasn't going to let this go, not now.

I increased speed. It had an immediate effect. The nose lifted, but sheets of cold spray began coming inboard and stinging my face, and the impact of the hull on the water was instantly heavier, threatening to shake the planks apart. I had no idea what speed we were doing, but sensed that it would take just one wrong move of my arm on the tiller and the boat would turn and we'd become momentarily airborne before going terminal.

End of game.

Another twenty minutes later and the lead boat was quickly gaining ground. It was coming up on a course further out to sea, while the others were holding station closer inshore. I recognized the tactics: the slower boats were ready to intercept us if we tried to make a break for land. It was another reminder that these men were old hands at this game. They had played it with much bigger vessels with huge engines and much further out at sea. They could dog us like this for as long as it took.

Running us down was just a matter of time.

I looked at Tober. He was still out of it. If he was as cold as me, it was probably a good thing to keep his body temperature down. Whatever I did now was going to have to be right. With no second chances, I had to carry on running, since staying to fight could only end one way. The men coming after us were also accustomed to spending long periods on the water and using weapons in an uneven and constantly shifting environment. All they had to do once they caught up was circle us like sharks and wait for an opening.

To add to our problems, the sea began to change temperament the further south we travelled. I didn't know if it was due to different currents or the shape of the ocean floor beneath us, but I could feel the tug and power of the water starting to take a greater hold on the boat, snatching at the nose and threatening to tip us over. I was forced to decrease speed to retain control as it threatened to swing away from me, and the boat began to bounce and dip, dropping with a crash into the troughs and ploughing through the waves head-on, showering us both with gallons of cold, salty water.

I looked back. The boats were edging closer, the lead one alarmingly so, but still holding station slightly out from our position. With the increased light I could just make out figures standing almost casually upright, rifles held over the shoulders as if they were out on a day cruise. By now they would have entered the same area of rough water as us, but it wasn't slowing them down one bit.

I estimated we had maybe another thirty minutes of this before they got close enough to start shooting.

It wasn't going to be enough.

Moments later, something made me turn and look back again. I didn't want to see how close the skiffs were; they were coming up faster than we could move away. But something had tugged at my senses; something different. A sound, maybe? An instinct?

The boats hadn't changed their position much, so I checked the sea behind them. Nothing but the same expanse of open water, grey in the thin light and seemingly flat. A sheet of nothingness. I looked up at the sky, but that, too, was empty.

Then I saw a flicker of movement in the distance, back where we had come from. The flicker turned into something dark, and I realized I was looking at a column of smoke, lifting gently away from the land and rolling into the air like a sinister mushroom. A split second later I thought I heard a faint pulse of sound, but it might have been my imagination.

I smiled, feeling the crack of salt on my face. Columns of smoke didn't just occur in the middle of nowhere for no reason. Smoke needs fire and fire needs something to feed on.

Vale. He'd kept his word.

Sixty-Seven

The senses become overworked in times of stress, leading to confusion and misunderstandings when normally the brain would be able to filter each piece of information received and sort it into a logical sequence. Tiredness plays its part, too.

Spurred on by the realization that Musa's position had been

hit by a drone strike, I concentrated on the course ahead. Being stopped now would be too cruel. It couldn't happen.

But the euphoria didn't last long.

It seemed like only moments later that I heard the heavy beat of approaching engines bearing down on us, and realized we had run out of time.

I ignored the itch between my shoulder blades, imagining the guns of the pirates coming to bear on my back, but didn't look round. Instead I moved the tiller as much as I dared to get a snake-dance going and put them off their aim. It would undoubtedly use more fuel, but it was the only way I had left to fight back unless I elected to stop and use the AKs.

As a last resort I made sure the Vektor was ready.

Time seemed to drift as we pounded through the swell, and I kept my gaze firmly fixed on an out-jutting piece of land in the distance. I had no idea where it was; it was probably just a deserted piece of rock and scrub miles from anywhere. But it represented a haven of sorts if we could reach it, and easier to hold off an attack for a while. I heard an occasional shot coming from behind us, but nothing came close. They were trying to intimidate and show how near they were.

Then something about the engine noise demanded attention. It had changed in volume and depth. Exhaustion made me slow to respond, and I made do with thinking that the pirates had tired of the game and had put on a burst of power to finally run us down.

Seconds later there was a blast of sound and a dark shape swooped by overhead. The familiar thudding noise of helicopter rotors was beating down on us and ripping off the tops of the waves, and I felt the battering of the down-force across my shoulders and tugging at my shirt.

I looked up and saw a grey Lynx helicopter curving round on an intercept course to meet the oncoming boats. A figure in dull green was crouched in the doorway, giving me the nod, the early sun flashing off his visor. I could see other faces crowding behind him, peering out. Helmeted marines at a guess, ready to do their thing.

I nearly lost the tiller at that point, and remembered in time to hold on tight.

I checked the position of the Somali boats. The two slower

craft had already peeled away and were heading north, unwilling to take on the helicopter's superior firepower. But the lead boat was on course and coming up fast, the men on board crouching down. As I watched, three of them aimed their rifles at the Lynx, one letting off three rapid shots. The sounds were lost in the rotor noise, but the puffs of smoke from his barrel made it look like tackling an elephant with a pea-shooter.

The Lynx didn't waver and the figure in the doorway stayed where he was, supremely confident. He shook his head, then gestured deliberately with a gloved hand at the missile pods slung beneath the aircraft. To emphasise the point, the pilot swung the nose round to focus menacingly on the pirates and show them what was about to come winging their way if they didn't back off.

For a few seconds there was no response. The Somali boat continued on its course, the men still waving their rifles, although the shooting had stopped. The Lynx held its position, edging backwards to follow the boat's course, the pilot doing a superb job of holding it steady. I imagined the count-down going on in his head and waited for the spurt of a missile leaving its pod. Would they, wouldn't they?

I found myself hoping they would. This shit had gone on long enough.

Finally the pirates saw sense. The helmsman waved his arm and the boat's nose dipped and turned, immediately losing way, the members of the crew grabbing the sides to hold their balance. As soon as it was pointing away, a heavy spray burst out from the stern and the twin engines powered them on a wide curving course to follow the other two craft to the north.

Seconds later, they were mere dots in the distance and the Lynx was hovering alongside us, the crew member in the doorway grinning and signalling for me to slow and stop.

I smiled back and cut the engine. I'd never been so pleased to obey an order in my life.

The pleasure was short-lived. As they sent down a crewman with a stretcher and winched Tober gently on board, eager hands pulling him inside the fuselage, I happened to glance back at the smoke rising near Kamboni. Something about it looked wrong. At first I couldn't figure out what it was. I'd seen lots of smoke from many war zones and scenes of destruction. And this didn't look right.

Then it hit me.

It had dispersed too quickly. It was now little more than a wisp of grey drifting lazily along the shoreline. Yet I was remembering all those rocket-propelled grenades Tober and I had seen stacked up inside and outside the villa. If a drone strike had hit that lot, the explosion would have been bigger, the smoke darker and longer-lasting as the fabric of the building continued to burn long after the initial bang.

But there was none of that.

It was a miss. Musa was made of Teflon.

I heard a whistle and looked up. The winch was coming down again, this time with a harness for me. The crewman guiding it was signalling for me to get it on fast so they could get out of the area.

I waved it away and signalled that I was going back to land.

This wasn't finished yet.

Sixty-Eight

Tom Vale walked up the steps into the US Embassy in Grosvenor Square, and was met as usual by a Marine guard, immaculately ironed and polished. He'd been in this building several times before, but still felt as if he were stepping into a magic kingdom.

He blamed Hollywood.

'Mr Vale, sir,' the man said briskly, handing him a visitor's badge. 'Mr Scheider said you were coming and to take you right up. If you would follow me, sir.' He swivelled sharply on his heels and stiff-legged away, leading Vale without delay through the internal security screens and up to the second floor.

They stopped at a doorway at the end of a long corridor, and the marine knocked and asked Vale to go inside. He found himself in a long room with a conference table complete with two communications consoles, a tray of juices and a line of empty chairs. A huge flat-screen monitor bracketed by two US flags dominated the end wall.

'Tom.' Scheider greeted him and indicated a younger man. 'You know Dale Wishaw, I believe?'

Vale shook hands and murmured a greeting. Why he was here was a mystery. A surprise invitation had been waiting for him on arrival at the office, and intrigued by the air of urgency, he had immediately called for a car to bring him here. The car was one of the tangible signs of his new, albeit temporary role in MI6 following Colin Moresby's resignation. He had felt little sympathy for the man's abrupt departure, and no hesitation in assuming the position of special operations director while the department was being reformed.

Coffee was served and Scheider complimented him on his new role. 'Sorry to be so guarded about the reason for this invitation, Tom. I wanted to keep the spread of information strictly limited. You'll soon see why.' He put down his cup and nodded to Wishaw.

The younger man picked up a remote, indicated the monitor on the wall and said, 'Private showing, Tom, just for you. If news of this got out we'd have them queuing down the hallway three deep and that guy Portman would be a Hollywood legend.'

'Who?' Vale stared over his coffee cup and the American flushed.

'Quite.' Scheider threw Wishaw an unhappy look. 'Run the footage.'

The image on the screen was hazy at first, a jumble of shadows and shades of grey, reminding Vale of the first unflattering pictures of the moon so many years before. This looked like water but he couldn't be certain.

His chest went tight as he realized what he was seeing.

Sensing Vale's thoughts, Scheider signalled for Wishaw to pause the film. 'What you're about to see,' he said, 'is camera footage of a Hellfire strike fired from a Reaper MQ-9 drone over the coast of Somalia.' He smiled grimly. 'I think you know the coordinates so I won't bore you with the details. The missiles are totally self-destruct, so nobody gets to send any coded parts to a technical lab and find out where it was made.' He nodded at Wishaw to continue.

The film showed the ground racing by as if being pulled on a rail. Then the camera steadied and locked on a central point, the focus becoming sharper, more real. The image now showed solid terrain, with recognizable trees and shrubs around the faint line of a road or track. Moments later the man-made lines of a building appeared, trembling momentarily before growing, almost filling the screen. A vehicle – Vale guessed a pickup truck – stood nearby. Men, too, some standing still, others moving around slowly, unhurried.

Totally unaware, he reflected, of what was coming their way.

'Knock, knock,' Scheider said softly as the target area was magnified, trembling again as the camera lens picked up the image and fed in more detail. Then a flickering, lightning-fast movement showed to one side of the screen and a vast dust cloud rose upwards and outwards, obliterating the square shape, the truck and the men. A delayed flash spread out from north of centre as the Hellfire found its target.

'Nice shot.' Scheider tapped his desk. 'Let's hope Musa was home to enjoy the visit.'

'Amen to that,' Vale murmured, and asked for a copy of the footage, to which Scheider agreed. He wanted to check the results for himself. Not that he distrusted the Americans; they had done what he had been unable to achieve, which was to place a missile right down Yusuf Musa's scheming throat. But he'd known deadly enemies escape certain death before, in spite of incontrovertible evidence, and this was one man he was determined not to allow off the hook.

He put down his cup and wondered if this was a dry office. As early as it was, he was suddenly in need of something stronger.

When he returned to his office, he learned that Portman had not boarded the Lynx with Tober, but had instead returned to land, for reasons unknown.

Sixty-Nine

Waiting for a target to present itself is the hardest part of making a kill. It requires patience and stamina in equal measure, and a fair degree of luck.

At least the conditions were ideal – at least, as ideal as I could wish. A friendly breeze was coming off the ocean, light but not excessive, bringing with it the smell of salt and a promise of warm air. The few clouds in evidence were tufts of cotton wool, high in the sky and inoffensive, strung out across the Indian Ocean in silent decoration.

Down on the beach area to my front, the sand was dotted with small birds, burrowing for breakfast and snatching at bits of debris brought in by the tide, tossing them aside in disgust before going on to the next piece of flotsam.

I checked once more that the ghillie net was securely in place and that nothing had slipped from the overhead covering of camouflage I'd put in place during the night when I'd arrived and dug in. Then I took a sip of water. Dehydration can be a killer.

A movement caught my eye, and I felt a flutter of tension in my gut. Tension is OK. As long as it doesn't take over the motor senses and induce the shakes – or the opposite and just as bad – paralysis. I relaxed as a white pelican cruised by, effortlessly elegant as it followed the waterline and used the air currents to keep it aloft, a gentle giant among the smaller birds in the region.

It reminded me of Piet and his beloved Daisy, now waiting several clicks inland, checking fences while waiting for my call. Not quite so elegant as the pelican, but just as confident when off the ground.

More movement, this time land-based. I checked the scope on the AK and watched as a group of figures appeared. They were about three hundred metres away and walking down the beach from the villa, moving over the damaged area of sand and debris thrown up by the Hellfires. Vectoring in too low and taking out a large area of dunes right in front of the building, they had thrown up, according to Vale, a misleading image which had convinced analysts that the building and everyone in it was toast.

Vale, though, like me, had found otherwise. The villa had survived and the pirates were still in place, now reinforced with extra men and boats and no doubt counting on the strike's failure as an omen for the future.

Down at the water's edge, two of Musa's skiffs were anchored in the shallows, long black slugs against the blue sea and white sand. Their on-board shelters were up and ready to go, and I figured they would soon be heading out to the Gulf in search of prey.

Nothing had changed. It's what pirates do.

The two men in the lead were easy enough to identify. Musa, tall and arrogant, clan chieftain, al-Shabaab member and a man with a deep hatred of the west. And with him, Xasan, chubby fixer, go-between and suck-up with an abiding love of money and the ability to talk a good talk while managing to avoid risking his own skin.

The two men walking behind them carried AK-47s, but looking bored by the regular morning walk Musa made them take just so he could have them watch his back. According to drone footage they followed the same route out along the beach and back twice a day, invariably at the same times. It showed the amazing arrogance of the man, assuming himself to be beyond the reach of any punishment just because his enemies had tried once and failed.

I zeroed in on Xasan. He was lagging a half-step behind Musa, walking with the great man but obviously not his equal. He didn't look any happier than the guards and appeared to be finding it difficult to walk on the sand, which I put down to his soft build and lack of exercise. I hoped he was suffering as much as he looked. He wore a loose robe with a simple belt around his large gut, and looked more like a comic figure from a Disney film than the extremist he really was. But soft as he appeared, he was no less dangerous in his way than the man he was following.

Musa, on the other hand, looked ready for the day. He was

dressed as I'd seen him the very first time on this same stretch of beach, climbing out of his boat and striding up to the villa: in a traditional *kameez* under a waistcoat, with a small skullcap on his head. The belt of shells across his chest and a cell phone in a pouch completed his attire. As always, he walked like a man on a mission, head high and chest out, and I wondered how much of it was for his own benefit rather than for his followers.

I stretched out in the shallow trench I'd dug myself, bracing my toes against the dried roots of an ancient palm tree that had seen better days. It had lost its crown, but cast enough of a shadow to give me ample cover against the sun. The ghillie net and a layer of crackly palm fronds did the rest, making me invisible from all but the closest observation.

I checked the beach to the south, beyond the villa and the fishermen's huts of Dhalib, and further, the town of Kamboni, which was just out of my line of sight. A distant clutch of boats lay moored at the water's edge, the building heat haze already making them shimmer and bob about. There was no sign of other movement, though, which was good.

I bent back to the scope and the targets leapt into view. The two guards had veered off towards the water, and I guessed they had been told to go check out the boats. After what I'd done to the previous three, I was surprised they didn't have a twenty-four-hour armed lookout posted. But maybe Musa was as guilty as anyone would be in this remote and deserted spot of that simple belief: that lightning couldn't possibly strike more than once.

Don't believe it, pal.

In spite of the guards walking away, Musa hadn't relaxed his pace, and was clearly intent on covering some ground before getting down to the business of the day. Maybe it was some kind of zen thing; preparing himself by focussing on exercise and isolation, and clearing his mind ready for making plans. Although with the fat man slopping along behind him and puffing like an old horse, I doubted it could have been very peaceful.

I checked the suppressor was good, and flicked off a stray fragment of leaf that had fallen on to the barrel. I could take my time; get it right.

I'd spoken to Vale twice since coming back. He hadn't been happy with my plan, but wasn't in a position to argue. What he had done was provide me with the latest intel from camera drones, courtesy of his friends in the CIA, and get Piet on stand-by for a pickup.

'If you clicked your fingers,' he'd told me, sounding faintly envious, 'you'd have most of the Basement joining you on this job – and they'd do it for free. Tober's got a lot of friends who all figure they owe you for pulling him out.'

'Nice of them. I left a man once before; I won't do it again. How is Tober?'

'He's fine. Restless, but fine. Pryce says hi, too.' I knew he was desperate to ask questions but it would have to wait. I said I'd be in touch and signed off.

The two guards were coming back from inspecting the boats. But they weren't watching Musa, as they should have been doing; they were staring up at the top of the beach and the area beyond.

Right where I was lying in wait.

I wondered if something had given me away. One of the men stopped walking and plucked at his shirt, producing a small pair of binoculars. He held them to his eyes and began scanning the area.

I knew I'd run out of time. Work on guard duty long enough and you get a feel for when something isn't right. It doesn't have to be obvious, like a person standing out of place or a strange vehicle parked where it shouldn't be, or even the absence of birds, which I was guessing was the case right now. It could be something in the air, a feeling that made the hairs move on the back of the neck.

Some call it instinct.

I stayed absolutely still, aware in my peripheral vision of Musa and the fat man moving along the beach. I mentally crossed my fingers. If Musa picked up on his guards' concerns, he'd have the phone out and the rest of his men heading on down here in an instant, armed and looking for bear.

Which would leave me no way out.

Seventy

'd gone over this several times since coming back ashore and hiding out, waiting for that blinding flash that tells you when a plan is a going to end badly and should be aborted.

So far, though, other than deciding I should have stuck with a less dangerous line of work, no flash had occurred. Instead the plan seemed to sit looking back at me as if daring me to duck out. During that time I'd been talking to Vale and learned that Musa and his men were far from done, and had been very active since the drone strike. One craft had already picked up a Dutch-registered yacht that had sailed too close to the coast, taking three family members hostage and killing the captain; another had attempted getting alongside a tanker, only to find a group of armed sub-contractors out of London waiting for them; while a third had raided a small coastal trader, killing five of the crew before scuttling the ship as not worthy of their time. This same crew was believed to have then got close enough to a passing tanker that had slowed down to discharge waste and attached a bomb to the hull before pulling away and using a remote to detonate the device. The device had worked, but resulted in minimal damage.

As Vale had concluded, it had probably been a first attempt. Next time they might get lucky.

So far, there had been no attempts at curbing their actions by the Kenyans, who already had their hands full to the north of here. Incursions by al-Shabaab into Mogadishu, where several bombs had been set off, had pulled in their resources, and chasing after pirates was a very much secondary task. But it was only a matter of time before they did what Musa had been planning, and the results would be catastrophic.

That, and knowing Musa was still alive had been enough to convince me to go ahead.

I eased off the safety and took a deep breath, letting it out slowly. I felt calm, my heartbeat steady, and the conditions were ideal, with minimal breeze and no obstacles in front of me. I had done this before and knew the drill.

The man with the binoculars was now staring right at me, and had probably seen the tip of the suppressor move, even fractionally, against the background of dried foliage. His mouth dropped open and he started to speak.

I squeezed the trigger, dropping him with my first shot.

The second man had been standing slightly ahead of him, eying an area to my left, his rifle held by his side, beginning to relax when he saw no obvious threat. Against the soft hiss of the sea, all he would have heard to tell him something was wrong was the slap of the bullet hitting his colleague in the chest. But the sound would have been sufficiently out of place to put him on the alert.

Sure enough, the moment his colleague fell backwards, he began to move, bringing up his rifle ready to start spraying the scenery, Somali-style.

It took two shots this time, but he went down without a sound, without touching the trigger.

I swivelled to my left, picking up Xasan in the scope. The sun flashed off his spectacles as he turned his head inland, his lower lip open in horror when he saw the two men down. There was also a flash of gold on his hand, a reminder that he was simply here for the money and nothing else. I had earlier reminded myself that it was Xasan who had coolly lured Angela Pryce and Doug Tober here with a non-existent plan to talk. While some of the blame lay with Moresby and his colleagues for giving it the go-ahead, it was Xasan who had stood to make money out of the deaths of the two SIS people, by way of his initial fee and by arranging sales of the execution DVD on the side. He was that kind of operator.

I aimed for the main body mass. In these conditions and the size of the target, it was hard to miss. My shot knocked off his spectacles and he flopped over like a big wet fish. He tried to get up, flapping his arms and honking, and made it on to his side. He was made of tougher stuff than I'd thought, or maybe his fat helped absorb the shock of the bullet. Not for long.

I gave him another shot and he lay down and died.

Musa turned and looked at where Xasan lay. When he saw his two guards were down, too, he looked up the beach, his mouth working while scrabbling for his phone. He must have been freaking out. Having someone drop right close to you, but hearing no shot, is a weird thing to witness. You might hear the impact of the shell, depending on ambient sounds; you might hear a cry or a sudden exhalation of breath as it leaves the body. Without further information, your brain tells you somebody has fallen down for no good reason.

I centred on Musa. He seemed to be having trouble processing the thoughts rushing into his head while trying to focus on hitting the right buttons on his phone. Perhaps multi-tasking wasn't his strong point.

I helped him rationalize.

My first bullet slammed into the leather cartridge belt across his chest. He staggered under the impact and dropped the phone, but managed to stay on his feet. He lowered his chin and I thought he was looking for the phone; then I realised he was staring down at his chest where the bullet had struck.

Moments later something unearthly happened. His body shook and he threw his arms out wide, and there was a bright flash of light as his chest seemed to catch fire. A split-second later a puff of smoke formed an almost perfect halo around him as one of the shells went off.

It didn't end there. There was a crack as a second shell exploded, the bullet tearing upwards and taking away the lower part of Musa's face and lifting off his skullcap along with part of his head.

I watched as his body remained upright for a second. Then his knees got the message and his lifeless shell collapsed. This time, not so elegant.

I listened for signs of alarm from the villa. The bullets going off on Musa's chest had made a sharp crackling noise, but nothing like the full sound you'd get from a normal gunshot.

Job over. It was time to go.

I shrugged aside the covering of dried palm leaves and slung the ghillie net and rifle over my shoulder. Then I walked out of Somalia and back across the border.